THEY

THEY

a biblical tale of secret genders

A Novel By

JANET MASON

BOOKS

Adelaide Books
New York / Lisbon
2018

THEY
A Biblical Tale of Secret Genders
A Novel
By Janet Mason

Published by Adelaide Books, New York / Lisbon
An imprint of the Istina Group DBA
adelaidebooks.org

Editor-in-Chief
Stevan V. Nikolic

For any information, please address Adelaide Books
at info@adelaidebooks.org

ISBN13: 978-0-9995164-3-0
ISBN10: 0-9995164-3-4

Printed in the United States of America

BOOK ONE

Chapter One

"Whoever heard of a divine conception?"

Tamar rolled her eyes. She looked skeptically at her twin.

Tabitha wrinkled her brow and looked thoughtful.

Outside, the wind blew. The black goat skin walls shook. In the middle of the tent, the pole quivered. Stacked in a pile, clay pots rattled. One of the Patriarchs might have said that the gust of wind was a sign from God. But Tamar knew better. It was spring. The winds were on them. Anyone who even thought of venturing forth knew that sandstorms would drive needles into their eyes. She didn't fear God, but she did fear the wrath of the villagers. All the signs were there. No bleeding for almost three months. Sickness in the mornings and afternoons. Tabitha had been asking for fresh springs of dill sprinkled on her terracotta bowl of pomegranate seeds. Tamar told herself she should have known.

Tabitha stared into the bowl of water that she cupped in her hands. She turned the bowl counter clockwise once, twice, a third time. She stared longer, deeper. It looked like she was staring at her reflection. But Tamar could tell that she was staring past it. *God knows I have seen her stare at her reflection often enough,* thought Tamar.

"I am going to give birth to twins. I will be the mother of nations. From my line, a messiah will be born," proclaimed Tabitha.

There was a snort from the other side of the tent.

Tabitha looked over to the shadows. Aziz sat on his haunches. The outline of his shaggy fur led up to his hump. He shook his head and snorted. He pulled his thick dromedary lips back into a smile. He looked over at Tamar as if to read her mind. *Messiah indeed,* thought Tamar. Was her sister nuts?

Aziz was more than the desert transportation that Tamar shared with her sister. Aziz was Tamar's companion, her familiar. He could angle his dong out of the tent flap to make rivers of pee in the sand -- even during the high winds. He pooped in the same bucket she did. She always emptied it in between and buried the waste in a deep hole at the edge of the tent.

"I've heard of lots of divine births," responded Tabitha. "Remember the old stories that Great Grandmother used to tell us? In the beginning there was Eve. Great Grandmother told us that after Adam and Eve were cast out of the Garden of Eden, Eve gave birth to two sons: Cain and Abel. They argued in a field, and Cain slew Abel. Generations passed -- at least four. This was before God saw evil everywhere and caused the great flood and recreated the world with Noah and all the animals on his ark. This was generations before Abraham and Sarah came along. Years after Abel was slain, the Lord saw that his parents still missed him sorely. So he sent them a replacement for Abel -- a son who would be named Seth. Eve must have been over a hundred. There was no way she could have given birth -- unless it was a divine conception.

"That's true," mused Tamar. "Adam would have been too old to get it up."

Tabitha narrowed her eyes and looked at her sister. "That's not what I meant," she said and continued. "Then there was Abraham and Sarah. Sarah was barren all of her life. Her bleeding time had passed. So Sarah told Abraham to lie with her Egyptian maid servant and then the servant conceived a son, Ishmael. Sarah became jealous -- naturally. So, the maid servant and her son, Ishmael, went off into the desert. Then God came to Sarah and told her that she would bear a son and that he would be named Isaac. Sarah laughed at first. She was in her nineties. She had been barren all of her life. How could God change that? But he did. I remember Great Grandmother telling us that 'the Lord visited Sarah' and 'the Lord did unto Sarah as he had spoken.' And then Sarah conceived and gave birth to Isaac."

"Abraham would have been too old to get it up, too. There is a theme with these old stories," commented Tamar.

"It's not only the men. The women were way past their bleeding time -- and would have been too old to conceive," replied Tabitha. "We've talked about this before. You're always blaming things on men. It's not always their fault. Besides, older men can still father a child. It's women who can't conceive after their bleeding time."

Tamar shrugged her shoulders. She looked at the flame

burning on the low table. The wick had burnt down so that it was level with the narrow mouth of the lamp. She and her sister had talked about this before. Tabitha just didn't get it. Tamar sighed. It was going to be a long night.

"I never believed the stories that Great Grandmother told us," said Tamar. "She liked to make things up. Her mind wandered. She told us that she was as old as Methuselah. Methuselah was nine hundred and sixty nine years old. Besides, she just told us that Sarah was past her bleeding time. I don't remember her saying that Sarah was in her nineties. You must have imagined that. Plenty of women give birth when they are past their bleeding time. She was probably still having relations with her husband Abraham. Although, I don't why she would. He was always saying that she was his sister to pawn her off on kings so that they would give him oxen and asses."

"I bet Abraham got plenty of ass," retorted Tabitha. "Supposedly, it was his wife's idea that he sleep with Hagar, the maid servant, who bore him his first son, Ishmael. But who knows, maybe he planted the idea into her mind. Sarah died when she was a hundred and twenty seven. Abraham remarried. God sent him a woman named Keturah who bore him six children. He also had concubines, not to mention the she-goats and the she-asses." Tabitha covered her mouth with her hand and snickered.

Tamar laughed along with her sister. Who was the one poking fun of men now? But she didn't say anything. She was trying not to want to be right all of the time. At least she could control what she said -- even if she still had the thoughts. And she was right.

Tamar sat cross legged on the floor of the tent. Her favorite camel-hair blanket was folded under her. She stood and went to the back of the tent to where she kept the jugs of olive oil. Her sister always could make her laugh -- even if she was crazy.

Tamar walked to the back of the tent while there was still light to see and picked up a jug. It was dim in the tent. Shadows lurked everywhere. Still, she knew exactly where she was going. She stepped lightly around a pile of blankets to the center of the tent. Then she bent over the small blue flame so that she could pour more oil into the lamp. She felt for the spout of the lamp and aligned the jug of oil to the lip. She knew the movements by heart. Still, she was cautious. She didn't want to become another story about a tent going up in flames. The light in the tent brightened as the wick fed fresh oil to the flame. Tamar put the half filled clay jug in its place at the back of the tent.

Tamar turned around, walked back toward her sister, and spoke: "As it turned out, Sarah was his sister -- his half sister. Auntie Namaah told me that. She said that you couldn't trust men. They mess everything up and then blame it on women." She paused and considered telling Tabitha that's where she got her tendency to blame men. Auntie Namaah had taught her well. Tamar was usually right in her judgment of men. But she decided not to share her thoughts. Tabitha should be able to make the connection on her own.

"The old stories were created to put women in their place," continued Tamar. "It started with Eve when she listened to the crafty serpent and ate from the Tree of

Knowledge," continued Tamar. "The serpent is from the ancient times. The serpent represents the feminine. Circling from tail to toe, it represents the universe. It symbolizes wisdom and rejuvenation through shedding its skin..."

"Maybe Eve was just hungry." Tabitha batted her eyelids at Tamar.

"You're in a fine condition to make jokes!" Tamar exercised her older sister prerogative. "Everyone knows that women are stronger and came first. There is no way that Eve was born from Adam's rib," exclaimed Tamar. She was stating the obvious. But her sister needed to hear this.

Tabitha studied her reflection. The surface of the bowl of water shimmered. The light in the tent was too dim to reflect from the bowl of water. The oracle must be providing her own light so that she could speak to Tabitha. Tamar was impressed, but she didn't say anything. Her sister's tendency toward grandiose notions didn't need any encouragement.

Tamar stared into her sister's face. Looking at Tabitha was like looking at herself. They were born the same day to the same mother. They had never known her. But she had carried them in her belly. They both had long hair, dark and shiny as onyx. They had creamy skin. They had light complexions for Arab girls. Their wide spaced dark brown eyes, deep set in their oval faces, flashed when they were angry. Whenever they had something to hide, they both lowered their long lashes and looked completely innocent. Tamar hid her beauty behind a widow's veil. She wasn't sure she believed in God. But her late husband Er, who liked to slap her around, may have made a believer out of her. Afterwards he was always remorseful and said that he only did it because it was expected. But she could tell from the gleam in his eye that he enjoyed it. She was desperate. So she started praying to God to protect her. She prayed and prayed. Finally, God smote down Er. She was left childless. Later, her father-in-law, Judah, promised her that he would give her to one of his other two sons so that she could bear a son. When she was a young woman, a virgin, she had seen Judah in the village market staring at her while he fondled melons. His wife Shuah pretended to be interested in the fruit, but Tamar could tell that she was just really keeping an eye on him. In the old days -- just a few generations ago -- it was unheard of for a man just to have one wife. He usually had two or three. Sometimes he had several hundred wives along with entire harems and concubines too. It wasn't yet written in stone that a man should just have one wife. A wife as beautiful and regal as Shuah would never stand for her husband to have other women. But he was still a man. Tamar suspected that since Judah couldn't have her for himself, he picked her for his first born.

Desert life was harsh. A woman around these parts was nothing without a husband and sons. Tamar knew that she could have done worse than to be chosen to be a mother in Judah's line. So she said yes. Not that she had a choice. If she had turned Judah down, she would have been burned at the stake or exiled. Judah was well off. It was rumored that he had a connection to the one God. That's why God smote down Er. Another man could have been behaving badly, but God wouldn't have noticed. Er was meant to continue

Judah's line. God didn't want him polluting the gene pool.

Her women friends saved her. After Er was smote down, they came and comforted her. They baked cakes and burnt incense for the Queen of Heaven. Iscah -- Tamar's closest friend since childhood -- prophesized that women would come seeking Tamar's knowledge of herbs and healing. Tamar had thought Iscah was just talking. The priests said only men could be physicians, and most of them came from Egypt. The priests also said that praying to God was the only way to become healed.

But the women needed help, and Tamar could help them. Soon they brought silver coins to her, as well as food. It wasn't forbidden for a woman to be a healer. Yet. Tamar suspected that soon it would be. The priests pretended that they could solve everyone's problems. Tamar kept a low profile. She only treated women who were friends of friends, and she never gave advice at the market where someone could overhear.

Many of the women who came to her were terrified of dying in childbirth. If it were early enough, Tamar could give them a mixture of herbs that made a bitter drink that would end their travails. Tamar had never felt any maternal stirrings -- despite the fact that a son was still promised to her by her father-in-law. A son would take care of her -- at least during the years when he was old enough to fetch water and do chores around the tents. Then he would grow to be a man and leave to start a family of his own.

Tamar wasn't gullible enough to think that Judah was promising a son from his line because he cared about her well-being. He wanted his line to continue. And this was a fate Tamar wanted to avoid. God had smote down Onan, Judah's second son, for spilling his seed. It was possible that Tamar had something to do with God's intervention. She had prayed to remain childless. After God struck down Onan, Tamar said another prayer to thank Him. Who could say? Maybe there was a God.

"Everyone does not know that women are stronger," said Tabitha. She looked at her sister levelly. "The only ones who know are the women in your goddess cult who come to your tent in secret. And they are afraid to talk about what they know. You are too. Look at you hiding in this tent because you are afraid of Judah's promise to give you to his third son -- since Er died and left you childless and since Onan died too."

When she mentioned Onan, Tabitha started to snicker.

Tamar looked at her sister sternly.

"I am NOT hiding in this tent. I prefer it in here. It's dark and cool. Aziz likes it too. And as for Onan being struck down by God for spilling his seed, I don't for a minute believe it. How people can believe in a God they can't see, is beyond me. Onan most likely died from pulling on his dong so much. I don't know when he had time to eat and drink. I've never seen anyone so obsessed with himself. When Er was living and Onan came to visit, he would go behind the tent. He said he had to relieve himself. But we could hear him jerking and moaning. He didn't even take a tablet with him. He didn't need any etchings to get him going."

Aziz groaned in the corner. Tamar heard him shiftinghis weight and moving to his left side. It was his favorite sleeping position.

"I have a feeling that the villagers don't really believe in a God they can't see. They'll never buy divine conception. They'll stone you to death or burn you at the stake," said Tamar righteously. She was going to hold back, but there she said it.

Tabitha's eyes widened. Tamar was sorry she had scared her. But she was only trying to protect her. Tabitha was younger -- even if it was by five minutes. Their mother died while giving birth to them. Tabitha had to be cut out of her lifeless body. Their father had left when they were babies. Auntie and Great Grandmother took turns caring for them.

"It'll be okay," said Tamar softly. "It's too late for the herbs, but I know a midwife who I can send you to."

"To end the pregnancy?"

"Yes. And to save your life."

"But I want to have this baby -- I mean these twins. I have wanted children as far back as I can remember. I didn't have a mother. I want to be one. I planned this. Soon I will be past my bleeding time, and I don't want to wait until I'm ninety for God to come along and help me conceive."

"So it wasn't a divine conception," concluded Tamar. She narrowed her eyes.

"No, of course not. I was out walking one day -- along the rise of desert that is not far from here the rise that leads to the mountainside -- and I saw a shepherd boy that I liked. He had curly golden hair. I found out later it was brown, the color of mud. When I first saw him the sun was setting behind his head. The rays blazed behind him."

"I think I know who you are talking about. His mother has been coming to me for a long time, since her son was born. He must be all of fifteen years. His name is Abib."

Tabitha shrugged. She wrinkled her nose and then scratched it. "I never asked him his name. If it is the shepherd you speak of, he is younger than I thought. But I wasn't thinking of those things. I was watching the way his tunic draped over the lines of his hard-muscular body. His rod stiffened when he saw me. It didn't take much convincing to get him to lie down with me. When we were done, he went back to his flock and I went on my way down the mountainside picking the purple wildflowers that grow in the shadows of the boulders."

"But he is too young to marry. If the villagers find out, they will blame you. They might decide that he has to marry you. Or they might stone him to death. It depends on what day it is. His mother will be devastated."

Tamar calmed herself by standing and going over to check Aziz's clay food bowl. There were still a few cactus stems in it. Dromedaries could store food as fat in their humps for six months, but Tamar liked to make sure that he had food and water. His leathery lips always looked parched.

"You and that camel," said Tabitha. "You should get married."

"Aziz is not a camel," said Tamar. She stroked his long fuzzy nose from top to bottom, just the way he liked it. His fur bristled against her hand. He sighed in contentment. She could feel warm breath coming from his large nostrils. "He is a dromedary. Dromedaries have one hump not two. They have a different ancestry than camels," said Tamar as she stroked Aziz's long nose.

Tabitha gave her a blank look.

"And I do love him -- more than I ever loved Er. He's better than a husband. He's my companion. I'd do anything for him. He takes me wherever I want to go. He's more loyal than most humans. He'd never betray me by placing my friend's child in danger."

Tamar glared at her sister.

"Don't worry," replied Tabitha. "You're the only one who knows that the shepherd boy is the father. You're the only one who knows about me being with child."

Tabitha was quiet.

"If you don't think that the villagers will believe that it is a divine birth, then I have to come up with a different plan," she said softly.

"You could have your baby in secret and then build him a small boat and cast him off in the rushes by the river. It's been done before," said Tamar thinking about the stories Auntie had told them about the ancients in Mesopotamia. "Maybe a water drawer will find him and he'll live in a palace and become a God."

Tabitha glared and said, "The time isn't right for that. We're getting ahead of ourselves. Besides, I told you that I want these twins. They are my line. I just told you that the oracle prophesized that I will be the mother of nations and from my line a messiah will be born."

Tabitha sounded self-righteous and irritated.

"Unless you're burned at the stake before you give birth," retorted Tamar.

Tamar sucked in her breath. Maybe she shouldn't have been so direct, but she had to break through her sister's stubbornness.

Tabitha folded her hands in her lap, and looked down at them.

"I need your help," she said.

They both sat in silence. Tamar picked up one of the clay figures given to her by one of the old women from the province of Arzawa. The figurine fit into the palm of her hand. The nose and hands were worn off. But the figurine's arms reached up toward her breasts. The breasts were flat. But the circles around them gave the impression that they were protruding. The figurine's hips were wide and inviting. Her sister had probably looked like this when she cast her gaze on the shepherd boy. Tamar stifled a sarcastic comment. She let the feeling pass. She took a deep breath and felt the weight of the figurine in her hand. A tingling overtook her. She felt swept clean. It was as if the winds that ruffled the walls of the tent had entered her. She took another deep breath.

Finally, she spoke.

"I have a plan."

Tabitha looked at her.

"You will wear a harlot's veil and meet my father-in-law, Judah, on the side of the road. I know that he is taking a trip soon and I know his route. He will be away from home, and should be susceptible to your charms. But he must not see your face uncovered. We look too much alike. He will think that you are me and that I set a trap for him because his first son died and left me childless. The opposite is true. I am happy that his son died and left me childless. In fact, I may have encouraged God decide to strike down Er. But now I am talking nonsense."

Tabitha looked at her shrewdly.

"His wife has died recently and he will be happy to be comforted," continued Tamar.

"Shuah died?" Tabitha's dark eyes widened.

"Yes. I may have forgotten to tell you. She was a good woman and I was sorry to hear of her death," answered Tamar. She paused before she spoke again.

"Judah is travelling to Timnath to shear his sheep. If you sit by the road in a harlot's veil, he is sure to see you. It will be easy to seduce him. But you will need proof that he lay with you. Then you can claim that he is the father of your child. Afterwards, we'll pretend that you were me. He owes me progeny because he never sent his third son, Shelah."

"I don't know if I want to lay with Judah. Besides, I am nearly three moons gone already," said Tabitha.

"It doesn't matter. You're hardly showing," said Tamar. "You don't have a choice."

Tabitha nodded.

Tamar smiled at her twin and spoke: "I know a midwife who owes me a favor."

Chapter Two

"It's too low. Pull the veil up to your eyes. If Judah sees your face, he might think you are me and turn away."

"Oh? Is there a law that fathers-in-laws shouldn't impregnate their daughter-in-laws? I've never heard of it," said Tabitha. "Auntie Namaah told us that Abraham's nephew Lot impregnated both his daughters and that God didn't stop it from happening."

"I remember that, too," replied Tamar. "It made me doubt the existence of God. If He really did exist, then why didn't He intervene — even if giving birth to their own sisters and brothers was what Lot's daughters wanted to do? Why didn't God intervene when Lot offered his virgin daughters, in lieu of the two male angels who were his guests, to the villagers who came to his door in Sodom? The villagers wanted to 'know' the two angels who were disguised as men. Why would Lot offer his daughters? Why had God bothered to burn down the villages of Sodom and Gomorrah, if He was just going the let Lot lie with his daughters? And why did God turn Lot's wife, Edith, into a pillar of salt just because she looked back at the burning cities on the plains when she was fleeing with her husband and daughters?"

When Tamar finished talking, Tabitha looked at her and shrugged indifferently.

"Beats me," she said. "It's just an old story. I thought we were talking about me. How does my veil look now?"

Tamar ignored her. But she had to admit that Tabitha was right. Tamar was digressing, and time was of the essence. But she didn't want to encourage her sister to always be focusing on herself. One day, Tabitha would thank her.

Besides, Tamar's concerns were important too. Ever since she had first heard the stories, Tamar had questions. At first she had questioned her aunt who had no answers. But when Tamar was old enough almost to be a bride, she told her aunt that she had figured out the answer. It was because Lot's daughters were his property, and that was the only thing that mattered. Her aunt turned away when Tamar had told her this, but not before Tamar could see the answer in her eyes. This was the main reason why Tamar didn't want children. She didn't want to give birth to some man's property.

Tabitha, on the other hand, was a believer. She took the old stories at face value, or thought what she wanted and had faith anyway. Tamar knew this about her, so most of the time she didn't bother to share her thoughts. Not that it mattered. Because Tabitha was her twin, she could usually read her mind. Besides, it was too late for Tabitha. She was going to give birth to some man's property. At least that's what Tamar and Tabitha wanted Judah to believe.

Tamar had a surge of compassion for her sister. This wasn't going to be easy for Tabitha.

"There isn't a law against a father-in-law laying with his daughter-in-law, but it is frowned upon," said Tamar. "You're right. Perhaps I spoke too soon. The stories that Auntie Namaah told us when we were children were from the olden days. People lived so long then that the stories were probably legends and not truths. Besides, it was the beginning of time. People had different morals then."

Tamar adjusted Tabitha's veil.

"There, you look just like the village harlot. Judah will never suspect a thing."

"Won't he wonder why I'm sitting along the roadside waiting for him?"

"Believe me, he won't wonder. Men like Judah think that the world revolves around them," stated Tamar. "Besides, he is still grieving for Shuah, his late wife, and he will be in need of some comfort. She was buried in her native land of Canaan, a two day's journey from here. I would have gone to her burial, but I didn't want to see Shelah. He is Judah's youngest son, and he would be grown by now. Judah promised him to me, but he hasn't sent him. He probably forgot."

Tamar looked down. There was a good chance that Judah was superstitious enough to think about the fact that his first two sons were struck down by God when they were with her. He wouldn't want to risk losing his youngest.

"I could have gone to the burial with you," said Tabitha. She adjusted her veil.

"We've talked about this," said Tamar sternly. "That's why we are hardly ever seen together in the village. If the townspeople learn of your existence, someone would insist that we need two husbands, one for each of us. It is better to stick to Grandmother's story that you died with our mother in childbirth. This way we have a little bit of freedom.

Tabitha nodded. Then she flashed a smile and spoke: "I didn't wear your widow's veil when I lured the shepherd boy to come into me."

"That's good," said Tamar. She was curious to hear the details -- when they had more time. How was it that her twin sister was so different from her that she could just go out and pick up a shepherd?

Tamar decided to change the topic. "Since I always wear the veil, people that you know -- including the shepherd boy -- do not know what I look like and wouldn't mistake us for each other. That's why I put on my widow's veil when I go out -- so people won't know me. Let's get back to the task at hand. I was told that Judah is travelling to Timnath to visit his flocks and his sheep shearers. Timnath is on the outskirts of the land of Canaan not far from where Shuah is buried. It's a two day journey. We'll take Aziz and I'll drop you in Judah's path. We'll have to take care not to tangle with any Philistines. And we'll need a story, just in case anyone stops us."

"A story?"

"You know, a story of why two women are travelling together," replied Tamar. "I'll be wearing my widow's veil, and I'll say that you are the niece of my late husband and that I am taking you to his family so that they can find you a husband."

"Why do I have to be the niece? We are the same age, even if I was born second."

Tamar started to roll her eyes, but stopped. She would have to remember that Tabitha was sensitive about being the younger one. "It's just a story."

"But you always --"

Tamar cut Tabitha off in mid sentence. "It's better than being burned at the stake."

"Okay." Tabitha stuck out her lower lip.

"Now listen -- we'll need proof that you lay with Judah."

They waited until the winds died down and the moon was new. Then they embarked on their journey. In the time of about half a day, Tamar spotted a place that was perfect. She dropped Tabitha off at the roadside. She quickly looked up at the sun. By her calculations, she had enough time to find a well for Aziz and to walk back and hide herself before Judah came by.

She hitched Aziz to a short palm tree near a well. She trudged through the white hot sands. The sun moved to the highest part of the sky. She saw her sister sitting on the boulder by the roadside where she had left her. Tabitha's head was bent. She looked as though she was praying. Even in her harlot's veil, she looked devout. Tamar found a boulder about fifty feet away and hid behind it. It was tall enough to throw shade – even at mid-day. Tamar adjusted her veil. She peered down the road. The black veil was almost suffocating. But she was determined to see this through. Soon she saw a camel approaching with a man riding on it. The camel came closer. It had been a long time since Tamar had seen Judah. He rode tall on the camel's high saddle. His long white robe with its vertical black stripes rippled in the breeze. He looked different that the last time Tamar had seen him. It wasn't just that he was thinner. He was gaunt. As he came closer, she saw that his face was wizened. She couldn't tell if it was age, or if he looked this way because he was still in mourning. Maybe Tamar had been wrong about Judah. Was it possible that he wasn't like most men? Perhaps he wouldn't stop for Tabitha.

Tabitha must have been thinking the same thing. As he approached, she pulled up the side of her tunic and put her bare leg toward the road. She wasn't taking any chances.

The camel came to a standstill.

Tamar could see her sister talking to Judah. She must have listened to what Tamar had told her. Tamar saw the sun glinting off his bronze bracelets as he took them off and handed them to her. Then he took off his signet ring and handed it to her along with his long, skinny staff.

Hmmm, thought Tamar. *He must really be in need of some comforting.*

He took her by the roadside behind the boulder that Tabitha had been sitting on. Tamar tried not to look. It was her father-in-law and her sister, after all -- but she couldn't stop herself. Judah hitched up his robe and fell on Tabitha. He pumped up and down. His ass looked like a pale moon under the harsh sun. He must be pretty sure that no Philistines would happen by, either that or he didn't care. He was going to see his flocks and his sheepshearers. Men with money could do anything.

He was rutting on top of her sister like a tentyard animal -- maybe a donkey or a goat. At first, Tamar thought that it was his long journey or that he was still mourning Shuah and just going through the motions with a woman he thought was a harlot. Tabitha was pretty convincing. But his first born, Er, had been the same the few times that Tamar had lay with him. He preferred berating her to humping her. The few times that he had humped on her, Tamar was sure afterwards to take the mixture of herbs that she had heard would stop a child from growing. She couldn't be sure they would work, so she prayed to God that she would not conceive. She wasn't sure that she believed. But what was the harm in a little prayer? Everyone, it seemed, was doing it. In the old stories that their Great Grandmother and Auntie had told them, the women were always praying to God that they would have sons, even though they stood a good chance of dying in childbirth.

Like father like son, thought Tamar as she watched Judah pump up and down on top of her sister. She wondered how Shuah had put up with him. But she only had three sons -- so maybe she had just lain under him every now and then. Either that or she had known the way of the herbs, too. Tamar watched her sister laying under Judah. The veil was pulled up to just under her eyes. Tabitha stared up at the blue desert sky as if there was something up there -- angels perhaps, messengers from God.

Her sister could believe what she wanted. Their plan was working.

Judah stood and shook down his robe. It didn't look like he said anything to Tabitha. He just went over to his camel, sitting by the roadside, mounted the saddle, adjusted his headscarf and went on his way.

Tamar ducked behind her boulder. When she stuck her head back out, a few minutes later, her sister was sitting back on the boulder by the road. Her face was tilted down. Her hands were folded in front of her, palm to palm, in prayer.

Tamar adjusted her veil and hurried back across the desert. Hot, sharp grains of sand slipped into her sandals and lodged between her toes. The strap of her left sandal slid down to the bottom of her heel. She thought about slipping her sandals off, but the sand was too hot. She stood on her right foot, lifted her left leg, and bent it, shaking the sand from her sandal. She reached around and adjusted the leather strap.

Suddenly, she became anxious about Aziz. At first she thought that she shouldn't have left him for that long. But then she looked up in the sky. The sun had barely moved. Watching Judah pump on top of her sister had been interminable. It may have seemed like an eternity, but actually hardly any time had passed.

When she arrived at the grotto where she had left Aziz tied up next to the well, she found him rolled on his side. His head was stretched behind him at an odd angle. For a long terrifying moment, she thought that someone had broken his neck. What would happen to her and Tabitha without him? They would be two women stranded in the desert. Then she heard him snoring softly. His large nostrils quivered. Tamar had never been happier. She lifted her veil and bent down to kiss his velvety ears.

Chapter Three

"This is beautiful." Judith held a clay figure in her hand. "Where did you find it?"

Tamar looked at the black and white terracotta figure. It had a triangular head atop the curves of a woman's body. Her waist narrowed the middle. White lines zigzagged across the black background. It was the only figurine of its kind that Tamar had ever seen. Leave it to Judith to pick it up. She liked expensive baubles.

I'll have to keep an eye on it, thought Tamar. As soon as she had the thought, she was sorry. She shouldn't harbor bad feelings against one of her cult sisters.

"One of the old women from Arzawa gave it to me. She told me that it is a bird goddess and has the powers of creation and regeneration. That's why you were drawn to it. You should keep it with you for a time. Wear it in a bag around your neck. Be sure to put in some of the herbs that I give you."

"I'll do anything to give birth to a daughter," said Judith. She sighed. Her six silver necklaces rose and fell on her heaving bosom. Her husband had given her a necklace each time she bore a son.

"Whenever I pray to God for a daughter, He gives me another son. I am thankful to Him that they all are healthy and strong. And I am thankful to you for the herbs and exercises that you showed me to keep me strong so that I can bear again. But I really want a daughter -- someone who I can mold in my own likeness, someone I can rely on for the rest of my life."

Until she becomes a woman and must leave you for her husband's family, thought Tamar. It was no wonder that Judith had a problem conceiving a girl. The mind was everything. Judith's intention of wanting a daughter had to be pure and true. Tamar rummaged around in a tall pile until she found a pouch. Then she pinched some herbs out of a bowl. The herbs were only dried hyssop from the plants that grew everywhere in the desert. The hyssop had cleansing powers. Combined with the powers of the bird goddess, the hyssop might help. Tamar put a large pinch in the bag. She tied the brown pouch to a long white string. Then she handed it to Judith.

Judith slipped the terracotta figure into the bag.

Tamar nodded. "Wear it well," she said.

"Thank you," said Judith. She put the string around her neck and tucked the bag under the folds of her robe.

A blazing light fell into the tent. It illuminated Aziz's empty blanket in the far corner. Tamar relaxed when she remembered that Tabitha had taken him to the well to get water.

Serah stood in silhouette against the opened tent flap. She entered, carrying a basket. She set it on the table in the center of the tent. Tamar eyed the basket. The lid seemed to be on tight.

The flap closed behind her momentarily and then opened again in a flash of light. Leah came in. Her scarf was wrapped loosely around her head like a turban. She took the scarf off and draped it on a chair. The flap opened again and someone was in silhouette against the harsh desert sun. Tamar saw -- by the shape of her long flat forehead and because she carried herself more erect than the other women -- that it was her sister, Tabitha.

"I tied up Aziz in the shade behind the tent. He is comfortable," said Tabitha, "and will be fine for the afternoon. Don't worry," said Tabitha, before Tamar could say anything, "his water bowl is within reaching distance -- though that's why camels have humps -- they have their own store of water."

"I've told you a thousand times. Aziz is a dromedary."

"Like that matters."

"Dromedaries don't store water in their hump. That's a myth. They store fat that they can use if food is scarce. One time when we were riding in the desert for a few days, Aziz's hump got smaller and smaller because he didn't have food. Then we got home and I fed him, and his hump went back to normal."

"Whatever." Tabitha inspected her fingernails.

Tamar was going to go outside and bring Aziz inside. But then she eyed the basket sitting on the table and thought better of it. The basket was a mottled dark brown, the color of the rushes that grew along the Nile. The weave of the basket was tight. It was fatter at the bottom and curved toward a narrow top. The tight-fitting lid was flat with a straw knob on the top.

"Where's Iscah?" asked Serah. "She's always here."

"She sent word that she couldn't be here because her father is dying," said Tamar.

The others were silent.

"We can pray for him and his family," said Judith. "We have a minyan. There are five of us. And if we count as half men -- better off seen and not heard -- then we only need five of us to pray, not ten."

"According to those calculations, we would need twenty women," said Tamar. She had taught herself numbers and letters too, using Er's books after God smote him down.

"But it does not matter. We represent all of the women who want to be here with us today but cannot leave their families."

"We are thankful that the men tell us that we cannot pray with them. They have set us free to pray in our own way," said Serah.

Tamar smiled serenely.

"As long as we do not tell them," she said. Her smile faded. "Not that they ask. And no one ever bothers us here. We are far away enough from the village that the towns-people forget about us. Besides we are only women. What we do is of little consequence."

"It is time," said Serah.

The women sat in a circle around the table. Tamar sat next to Tabitha.

"I call on the spirit of the East," said Tamar. "Each morning, the sun rises over the edge of the desert, bringing the day to us. We thank the Sun God Ra for all that grows, for the cycle of life and death."

Tamar honored a different deity every time she called

on a direction. This was the first time she had invoked Ra, but she had long admired him -- the disk of fire above his birdlike head, the ankh sign in his hand.

"Spirit of the South," said Judith. She stood to the left of the circle, "I call on Isis to answer our prayers, the goddess of children and the mother of her son, Horus, who suckled at her breast."

It was all that Tamar could do to not roll her eyes. She liked Isis, too -- especially her independence and craftiness in tricking Ra to give her power. But most women insisted on worshipping her as the ideal wife and mother. Tamar was tired of hearing that the sole purpose of women's lives was to bear the next generation. It was true that human evolution could not go on without women giving birth. For this reason, Tamar respected a woman's choice to have a child. But she also valued a woman's choice to remain childless. Tamar knew women had minds of their own and could do great things. She also knew that as long as Judith worshipped Isis and Horus, she would not bear a daughter. Judith had to know the power of woman before she could give birth to a daughter. She had to know her own strength.

Leah called on the North, ushering it in. The North was embodied by Ishtar, the Babylonian goddess of fertility, love and war. On the other side of the circle, Serah called on the West. She invoked the spirit of Renenūtet, the Egyptian goddess with the head of a cobra. As she invoked her direction, facing the outside of the circle, her back to Tamar, her neck elongated. The back of her head seemed to flatten.

Tamar liked these goddesses too. In particular, she had

always loved the story of Ishtar's descent into the underworld through the seven gates where she had to give up all her worldly possessions. She too admired Renenūtet. It was necessary to know how to regenerate yourself. Shedding your skin was one way.

The problem with the ancient religions was that there were so many gods and goddesses to worship -- too many altars to build. Forget about remembering all their names. Tamar was forever coming across new god and goddesses that the women from faraway lands told her about when they stopped at her tent. The new religion, worshipping the Lord God of Abraham was easier. There was one God. But Tamar suspected that the purpose of religion was to control people as well as to unite them. You couldn't pick and choose with the one God. You couldn't believe in some gods and not the others. You had to have faith. You couldn't be a believer on one day, a non-believer the next. You had to swear your allegiance to God, our Lord. If you were found worshipping other gods and goddesses, you were stoned to death or burnt at the stake. But sometimes, Tamar needed the old gods and goddesses, just as the women who came to her needed special remedies. Other times, she heard the one God speaking to her. The voice wasn't deep and booming or high and melodious. It wasn't male or female. But it was loud and clear. But Tamar didn't know if the voice was from the one God or from her own intuition.

"All of the directions are with us," said Serah.

Serah approached the basket, leaned over, and whispered into it. Then she pulled the lid off the basket. A serpentine head popped out. This was not Renee -- the pet serpent that Sarah usually brought to the rituals. Renee was wider, with golden triangles against a tan background, and more friendly looking. She liked to scuttle sideways across the floor. This serpent was sleek and black as pitch. Its jaws opened. A long and red forked tongue stuck out.

HISS. The women stepped back.

"Don't be afraid," said Serah. She draped the serpent -- a good three feet long -- across her outstretched arms. "This is a new friend who I found in the desert."

THE SNAKE MIGHT BE POISIONOUS. Was it the voice of the one God or her own intuition that Tamar heard in her mind?

"You just picked it up?! I hope you used a stick. It could be poisonous," whispered Tamar. She spoke in a hushed tone so that she wouldn't upset the serpent.

"But most snakes are harmless. And this one seems to like me. I haven't named her yet. Maybe you can help me."

Tamar kept walking backwards. She was glad that she let Tabitha keep Aziz outside. He was spooked by snakes crawling across the desert. She didn't know what would happen if he was in the tent with a strange one. She thought of Tabitha and panicked.

Her sister was standing in front of her, closer to Serah and her serpent.

"Tabitha, get behind me," warned Tamar.

"I'm not afraid of the snake," said Tabitha. "Look, he's cute!" Slowly, she reached her hand toward his head. Tamar reached forward and yanked her sister by the arm. She pulled her toward her, away from the snake.

"You're with child -- you have to be careful!"

Tabitha glared at her.

"Thanks," she said dryly.

The other women stared at Tabitha. Serah turned and put the snake back in its basket. Tamar thought quickly. She walked behind her sister Tabitha so it might seem like they had traded places.

"You know that Tamar's father-in-law, Judah, owed her a child," Tamar said. She never spoke of herself in the third person. She hoped that the others would think she was Tabitha.

"So finally he sent Shelah to father a child. Did you marry in secret?" Judith was the first to speak. The six silver necklaces on her bosom rose and fell. Her eyes gleamed. She was naturally curious. But there was something else there too -- in the arch of her right eyebrow, the tight line of her bottom lip. Jealousy? Judith had always gotten her power through bearing sons. Now, another woman had what she wanted. Conception. The possibility of bearing a daughter -- someone in her own likeness.

"No," answered Tamar firmly. She didn't want anyone to think that she had married Shelah, even if she was pretending to be Tabitha. Shelah was too young, for one thing. Rumor had it that he had never lost his baby fat -- or maybe he had acquired adult habits like drinking mead. He looked like he himself was with child.

Tamar quickly stepped behind Tabitha. She didn't think anyone knew that they were trading places.

"No. Judah gave me a child himself," said Tabitha.

Tamar looked at her sister approvingly. Tabitha had caught on. The threat of being burnt at the stake was a powerful motivator.

"Your father-in-law lay with you?" Judith's eyebrows formed two arches.

"Wait a minute." Leah stepped forward. She was the quietest of the group, and she was very observant. "You're not Tamar. You're Tabitha. You changed places. When I first came in, Tamar was wearing a brown striped robe -- and Tabitha was wearing a white robe. You are trying to trick us. But there is no need. You are safe here."

Tamar and Tabitha were both silent.

Tamar looked around the circle of women and said, "Is that true? Can I trust you with my life and my sister's life?"

She knew that she should be able to trust the women in the sisterhood of her cult, but she needed them to tell her.

"You can trust me," said Leah, looking at her directly in the eye.

"And me," echoed Serah, who turned to Tamar after she put the snake back in the basket.

"Of course, you can trust us," said Judith, looking down at her necklaces. "We come to you and tell you our secrets. So why can't you tell us yours?"

Judith looked up and gave Tamar a calculating glance. She arched her right eyebrow. "Don't you trust us?"

"Yes," said Leah."I thought we were sisters. You can tell us anything."

Tamar was still thinking about Judith's calculating glance. The loud and clear voice in her head told her that she couldn't trust Judith. But she had to tell them something. She spoke quickly before Tabitha spoke up and told the women the juicy news about the shepherd.

"Tabitha wanted to bear a child while she still could,

and Judah owed me a child, so we devised a plan," said Tamar.

"So Judah didn't lay with his daughter-in-law," said Judith. She looked relieved.

Tamar wondered if she had misjudged Judith. She hated doubting her, but the voice in her mind told her not to trust Judith. She wondered if there was a place for doubt in faith. Even if there wasn't, it was only natural for her to be cautious. There were, after all, at least two lives at stake -- Tabitha and Abib, the shepherd. And Tamar was involved in the trickery, too.

So Tamar and Tabitha told the circle of women a version of the story. They told them that Tabitha had conceived from Judah -- and that God had told Tabitha that it was her fate to carry Judah's line. Tabitha had told them this last part. She was making it up as she went along. Tamar didn't comment.

The women nodded. They were happy for Tabitha but concerned for her also.

"What did he say when he found out?" Leah sat down on a camel hair blanket.

"At first he thought that I should be burned at the stake, because he believed that I was Tamar and that she was a harlot," said Tabitha, settling down on the floor across from Leah.

"That's when we knew that our plan had worked," said Tamar. "Judah believed it was me who was with child. I went to the village well and told several of the villagers that I was with child."

"Who did you tell?" Judith's eyes gleamed.

"Jacob and Samuel," said Tamar. "They are always at the village well, catching up on the latest news. They can't keep anything to themselves. I asked Samuel for his help drawing the water because I was with child. Then I asked him not to tell anyone. I expected the news to be all around the tents by sundown.

"So when Judah and his men came to my tent the next day demanding that I be brought to the pyre for the heresy of whoredom, I was ready," continued Tamar. "I told him that he was the father -- and that he had brought it on himself by promising me seed from his line. Then I brought out his staff, his bracelets, and his signet ring. He couldn't deny me."

"Didn't he know that it was Tabitha that he lay with? You do look different. You are a little taller and more serious looking around the eyes," said Serah. "Sorry about the snake, by the way. It seemed like a good idea at the time..."

"Don't worry about it," said Tabitha. "Tamar was the one who was alarmed. And believe me, it wasn't my eyes that Judah was concerned with. He barely looked at me. He saw my harlot's veil and my outstretched bare leg and that was it -- he got off his camel and hump, hump, hump. It didn't take very long."

The women laughed.

"What did he say, Tamar, after you showed him his possessions?" Leah shifted her weight on the cushion and took some red grapes that Tabitha had brought with her from the village. She held the cluster up above her mouth, letting the grapes hang down. She nibbled on the end.

"He said that I was more righteous than him and that it

was true that he did owe me a son. So I told him that since I was with child, I would need a place in the village to stay so I would be near my midwife and the well. And then he said that I could stay in the tent left vacant by one of his maidservants who had gone away to marry a shepherd. Then he said that he would lay with me no more."

Chapter Four

"Bring me the pitcher of water and the sea sponge," said Orpah without turning.

She had her back to Tamar and stood in front of Tabitha.

Tamar saw Tabitha's knees jutting to each side of Orpah. Tabitha was crouching on the birth stool. Orpah was the midwife friend of Tamar's. The woman standing behind Tabitha, her arms circling Tabitha's upper arms and breasts, was a friend of Orpah's. Judah's maidservant had the afternoon off.

Tamar stood in the back of the tent. Even though she was inside, Tamar kept her everyday brown veil wrapped around her hair and the lower part of her face. She didn't want Orpah's friend to suspect that she was Tabitha's twin.

"I didn't know it was going to be this painful," cried Tabitha.

A bead of sweat the size of a small olive slipped down her forehead.

Tamar shook her head as she went and got the sponge and the pitcher of warm water so that Orpah could bathe her sister.

Of course, Tabitha hadn't thought about how painful it was to have a child, thought Tamar. She had no doubt that Tabitha hadn't thought about anything -- other than the fact that she wanted a baby. Perhaps she had just thought she wanted a baby when she laid eyes on the shepherd boy and his fine physique. And then, when Tabitha found that she was with child, she wanted to keep the baby. As usual Tamar had been there to make things okay. Tamar immediately regretted the thought. She took a deep breath. It was important for Tabitha to have this child.

Even so, Tamar feared for her twin's life. Women died in childbirth all the time.

If Tabitha came through the birth okay then Tamar would be grateful -- not only to Orpah, but to Isis, to Ishtar, to the goddess Asherah. She even prayed to the one God for help. Tabitha was the only family that she had left.

Tamar set the pitcher of warm water on the dirt floor next to Orpah and handed her the sea sponge. Oprah picked up the sponge, dipped it in the water and bathed Tabitha's forehead. Droplets slid down the sides of Tabitha's face. Orpah dipped the sponge in the water again. She began bathing Tabitha between her legs.

Thunder boomed in the distance. The sky was red when Tamar had come in. Soon the storm would be on them.

"Oooh. Oooh," moaned Tabitha. She was making sounds as if she were a child going to the bathroom.

Tamar rolled her eyes. It sounded like Tabitha was pretending. It was her nature to be dramatic. She was probably just doing what she thought women did in childbirth.

But then Tabitha began to wail. It sounded like the

wind roiling across the desert in the worst sandstorm -- shooting daggers into the eyes of all who dared to watch. It was all the voices of the women before them -- those who had survived childbirth and those who had not -- slicing through Tabitha in one blood curdling scream. Orpah's seat was lower than the birthing stool. She took a scarlet thread and knotted it into a tiny bracelet. She took it in her right hand and reached up between Tabitha's bare legs. Tamar knew that she was doing this in case Tabitha might be having twins. The custom was to put the thread on the arms of one of the babies so they would know later who was the first born. Tabitha had grown so large that she had been bedridden for the last three moons.

"OH GOD OH GOD OH GOD." Tabitha broke off into a scream.

The short hairs on the nape of Tamar's neck began to rise.

"Remember to breathe," coached Orpah. "Push as hard as you can. Push again. PUSH LIKE YOUR LIFE DEPENDS ON IT."

"I am pushing," wailed Tabitha. "IT'S TOO HARD."

"PUSH," commanded Orpah.

"I AM."

"AGAIN," said Orpah.

Thunder cracked the sky. Rain pelted against the tent -- or was it hail? It wasn't unheard of for hail to fall in the desert. But Tamar wondered if the storm was a sign from God. Maybe He was angry that they had tricked Judah. What was next? A plague of locusts?

BOOM. It sounded like the sky was cracking in half right above the tent.

"OH GOD AAWWWGH." Tabitha bent forward and pushed.

Tamar shut her eyes.

Then she heard a wail.

She opened her eyes. Orpah started washing the infant with warm water, olive oil and salt.

Tabitha groaned and said, "It feels like there is still a baby inside of me."

She began to groan louder.

"OOOOOH. LET IT BE OVER," she wailed.

"PUSH. PUSH AGAIN," commanded Orpah as she turned and handed the infant to Tamar.

"You have a nephew," she told Tamar. "Judah will be happy to hear that he bore a son."

Tamar took the infant. She noticed that there was no string around his wrist. Either Orpah had left the string inside of Tabitha or...

There was another scream. Tamar wasn't sure if it came from Tabitha or from the second baby whose head was between her legs.

Could it be? wondered Tamar. She wasn't sure if she had spoken aloud or not. But it was true. Tabitha had birthed twins. The oracle was right. Tamar wondered if this was a sign from God. Suddenly, it became clear. She and Tabitha were twins. It made sense that her sister would give birth to twins, too. But this time she had lived -- instead of dying like their mother.

Tamar held the baby and looked down at his little penis. He would be different from other men. He would grow to be a man who knew how to love himself and how to love women.

Tabitha looked at his face -- his tiny eyes, his snub nose, his open mouth, wailing for his mother, for the food that was her body, as he looked around at this new place where he was: the world. She marveled at his tiny fingers and then looked at his sex. It was smaller than she imagined it would be. She picked up his tiny penis. Underneath was a vagina -- as much of a female sex organ as her own, only much smaller. The infant in her arms seemed perfect. It was as if people were meant to be born with two set of genitals -- one male and one female -- a complete set.

"It seems that I don't only have a nephew," Tamar said as Orpah turned toward her with the other infant. "I have a niece, too."

"What are you talking about?" asked Orpah.

"Look." Tamar held the infant in her arms and picked up the sex to show Orpah what she had found.

"Oh... well that is not that unusual," said Orpah.

She took the first twin and handed Tamar the baby with the string around hir wrist.

"This is his brother, born second, but with the scarlet thread that I placed on his wrist. They must have traded places in the womb," said Orpah.

"This one looks like a boy, too," replied Tamar, "but let's see." She picked up the tiny sex. Underneath a opening, just like the twin.

"A perfect set of genitals -- male and female -- on each child. It's a miracle," said Tamar.

A gentle rain played on the tent. The storm had passed.

"I have seen this before," said Orpah. "Usually, the opening is stitched up and the child is raised as a boy."

Both infants wailed.

"I want to wait," said Tabitha from her bed.

It was the day after Tabatha had given birth. Tamar was staying with her for a few days. It was just she and her sister and the twins. Orpah had stayed through the night after the day of the birth, and left the next morning. Tamar had stayed and was careful to wear her veil when she went outside to make sure that Aziz had enough food and water. The infants were sleeping on a low bed on the other side of the tent.

"Pharez and Zerah will make up their own minds."

"But you have given them male names -- and you know it will be easier for them to live as men." Tamar stood and folded the camel hair blanket that she had brought with her. She found another camel-hair blanket on a pile near the side of the tent. She also folded this blanket. She put the first folded blanket on the floor and the second folded blanket on top of that. Then she sat down on top of the blankets, cross legged.

"God came to me and told me their names. But He did not tell me that they will live as men."

Tamar narrowed her eyes and stared at her sister. She doubted that God had spoken to Tabitha. If she had heard a voice in her head, it was her own overactive imagination. Tamar wondered where Tabitha had heard the names. Pharez was the elder. Zerah, the younger -- by several minutes. Their names sounded oddly familiar. But she could not recall where she had heard them. Tabitha had probably heard the names somewhere too, and stored them away for future use.

"Is that true?" Tamar reached toward her cup of water.

"Is what true?" Tabitha reclined on a high pile of blankets. "Could you get me a cup of water?"

"Oh, for God's sake," said Tamar as she rose and walked over to the pitcher.

"You don't have to be like that," whined Tabitha. "I just gave birth -- to twins!"

Tabitha sounded smug as if she were gloating.

Tamar ignored this.

"I was referring to the fact that you forgot to tell me earlier that God spoke to you." Tamar paused. "If God did speak to you, it seems like you would've told me sooner."

"It just slipped my mind. But He did speak to me. I can't help it if I'm the chosen one."

Tamar handed her sister the cup of water.

"Now that you have children, maybe you'll come to understand that not everything is about you," she said. "You have to admit, they'll have an easier time as boys. Besides, Judah will never stand for you raising his sons as daughters."

Tabitha took a sip of water.

"He doesn't have to know," replied Tabitha. "He told you himself that he's never going to lay with me again. He sends a servant when he wants Milcah. She goes to his tent. Like I don't know what they're up to. Believe me, it's no big deal. He is still ashamed that I tricked him into giving me these twins. We sent word that he has fathered two sons. That's enough to keep him happy. He'll let me stay here and use Milcah as my maid servant. He'll stay away and leave the child rearing to me. I know this to be true. God told me. Besides even if he does come around, there's no danger that he'll find out. He won't touch the infants' swaddling. God forbid that a father might be expected to change his child's diaper -- even a son."

Tamar nodded. Her sister had a point.

"Besides," said Tabitha. "The twins are perfect. They're just as they should be -- created in the image of God."

Tamar looked at her sister. She was taking this God thing a little too far. "What do you mean?"

"In the beginning, God did a good job with creating heaven and earth, but He missed the mark with Adam and Eve."

Tamar took the last sip of water from her cup and put it down beside her right knee. She gazed on her sister's face.

"I've been thinking about this for a while," said Tabitha. She pulled a thin blanket up to her chin. Great Grandmother told us that God created Adam and Eve in his image. That meant that God must have been male and female, not just male like we thought."

"Then why does everyone refer to God as a He?" Tamar had to admit that she was sucked into her sister's version of how the world was created.

"It's just more convenient to say He. Besides, everyone knows that 'he' means 'she' and 'they' too," said Tabitha.

"They?" asked Tamar.

"Yes, they. It can be used to mean a single person who identifies with both sexes or neither," replied Tabitha.

Tamar looked at her sister. The herbs that she took for the child bearing must have been strong. Tamar wondered what Orpah had given her.

"I'm not sure that Great Grandmother had the story right," said Tamar, shaking her head. Auntie Namaah told me the same story from the serpent's point of view. In her story God was female and remembered the old ways. God was just pretending to be male, because the men wanted Him to be male like them."

"You're always changing the subject and showing off about being older than me -- and knowing more." Tabitha put the blanket down further. She crossed her arms on top of it. "What's the point anyway? That everyone should be female? That I should raise Pharez and Zerah as girls?"

Tamar shrugged. "They won't have the freedoms of men. But they have to be one or the other. Being both male and female will be too hard on them."

"There have been plenty of boys who have become girls after the slip of a priest's knife during the circumcision. I won't have that happen to either of the twins." Tabitha stuck out her chin.

"Circumcision! What are you going to do? Surely Judah will want his sons circumcised." Tamar hadn't thought of this before, but it was inevitable.

"Relax," said Tabitha. "I have everything under control. This afternoon when you were out of the tent checking on your camel, I talked to Orpah about circumcision. She told me that it is perfectly acceptable to do it in a few years, when the children are still small. She knows a priest who is really a woman, as well as a man, who will be glad to help me."

Tabitha looked triumphant -- as if she was *finally* happy that she had thought of something before her sister had.

Tamar took a deep breath and then spoke. "I'm glad you talked to Orpah about it and that she knows a priest who can help you. Orpah really is a good midwife. The birth looked like it was hard, but you came through it. And the twins are beautiful." Tamar was thankful that her sister survived the birth. She closed her eyes and said a little prayer.

"They're perfect and they are created in God's image," said Tabitha, looking over at the babies. "They will give birth to the line that will bring forth the messiah -- just like the oracle told me."

Tamar shook her head. Her sister could have ended with "perfect." But she had to go further. She looked across the tent to the other side where the twins were sleeping peacefully. Pharez -- or was it Zerah? -- made a tiny fist and stretched it overhead. The twins were perfect. Tamar couldn't argue with her sister -- although she didn't think it had anything to do with God.

Chapter Five

"Close your eyes and imagine the long ago city of Babylon, in a land called Mesopotamia, near the mighty Tigris. A gentle wind blew. There was a beautiful Goddess named Ishtar. She was also known as the Queen of the Night," said Tamar.

"Which night, Auntie?" asked Pharez, sitting on the floor of Tamar's tent, playing with one of the figurines. Zerah crawled toward Aziz.

"Zerah, look at Pharez's doll. See how pretty? Here's another one just like it." Tamar grabbed a clay figurine from the woven basket. Zerah came crawling back.

"Ishtar was called the Queen of the Night because she was known as the goddess of love and ... well of love," said Tamar.

Ishtar was the goddess of love, war, fertility, and sexuality. And she may have been a sacred prostitute. Tamar felt protective of the twins. They were too young to hear about war and sex.

"What did the goddess look like, Auntie?" Zerah looked up at her with big brown eyes under long thick lashes. The child was sitting cross legged.

"She was tall and beautiful and she had wings," answered Tamar. "She had a face like... well a goddess ... with wide set eyes shaped like almonds and a high forehead under a crown that was piled very high with ridges like a fancy temple. She held her arms up. Her hands grasped two loops of rope that also may have been hand mirrors. Her two pet owls were usually by her side."

"Ooooh owls! Do you have an etching?" Pharez dropped the figurine.

"I have one that we can look at later, but first I want to tell you the story of someone called Asushunamir who was both male and female, like you. Asushunamir was a spirit guide and a trickster who rescued the Queen of Heaven from eternal death..."

"What's a trickster?" asked Zerah.

"A trickster is someone who gets his or her way -- or his and her own way -- by playing tricks on someone."

"What's eternal death?" asked one of the twins. Their dark eyes shone like starlight in the desert night sky.

"That's what happens to us eventually. We cease to exist. But don't worry. It won't happen for a long, long time. And if you meet a spirit guide like Asushunamir it might not happen at all." Tamar told herself that lying was okay if it made people feel better -- especially children.

"How did the spirit guide save the goddess?"

Tamar could tell now that it was Pharez who was asking the questions. Pharez's nose was a little more snub than Zerah's. They had the same oval faces ending in pointy chins.

"I was just about to tell you that," continued Tamar.

"Ishtar wanted to go somewhere new and she had never gone to the underworld where her evil sister, Ereshkigal, ruled."

"Ha. Ha." Zerah covered hir mouth with a small hand.

"'Evil sister,'" repeated Pharez. "It sounds like you and mama."

Zerah shot Pharez a look.

The twins were silent. Both looked down. The fringe of their long lashes covered their secrets.

Tamar wondered what Tabitha had told them. Her sister had left the twins while she went shopping at the market. She said she would be back this afternoon. They had agreed not to tell the twins that they were sisters, so that they wouldn't have to worry about one of them blurting it out around Judah. They told them that Tamar was a good friend of their mother's. The twins called her "Auntie."

Unless she was busy, Tamar always watched the twins. Sometimes it felt like they were her children. She loved them that much.

"Ishtar wanted to go to the underworld. But first she had to ask the other gods if she could go. They ignored her so she asked again and then again. Finally, they said she could go."

Tamar paused.

"The underworld had many gates," she continued. "There were seven in total. Ishtar came to the first gate and rang the bell. Claaanggg. There was one ring for the first gate and two for the second gate and so on. Ishtar rang the bell and waited. She tapped her foot. Finally, the gatekeeper came, but he did not open the gate. Like most goddesses,

Ishtar had a temper. She was used to getting what she wanted. She told the gatekeeper that if he didn't open the gate, she would smash it down."

"Oh goody," exclaimed Pharez. "I love smashing things."

Uh oh, thought Tamar. She gave the child an odd look before she went back to the story.

"So the gatekeeper went to Ishtar's evil sister Ereshkigal and told her --"

"The evil sister!" Zerah was rapt.

"That's right," said Tamar. "Ishtar's sister was moody and prone to fits of fury. Ereshkigal was already mad at her sister for being a beautiful goddess. Then she heard that Ishtar had decided to come to her kingdom. Ereshkigal was not pleased. The gatekeeper was old and walked with a cane. He was used to dealing with demanding people. He decided that Ishtar was not so bad. He liked looking at her. Ereshkigal told the gatekeeper that Ishtar could only enter if she agreed to obey the laws of the underworld. In death all are equal. So the dead who came to the underworld had to leave their possessions behind, including clothing and jewels. Plus there was no light in the underworld. The souls had to feel their way along the corridors. Since there was no food, they had to eat clay and dust."

"Eww," said Pharez. "I could never eat clay and dust. My favorite meal is figs and almonds. Sometimes locusts and honey."

Tamar smiled at the child. "Yes, I know. But let me go back to the story of Ishtar and her journey to the underworld. Since Ishtar agreed to obey the laws, she could visit the underworld even though she wasn't dead. To pass through the first gate, Ishtar had to take off her glittering gold crown. She took off her earrings at the second gate and her breast ornaments and her necklace at the fourth and fifth. At the sixth gate, she removed her shining silver bracelets from her arms and her legs. They sounded like musical chimes. Then at the seventh gate, when the bell clanged seven times, she removed her white tunic, so she was..."

"Naked!" shrieked Pharez.

"We're not supposed to be naked," said Zerah. "Mama told us so."

"Did not," retorted Pharez. "She said that everyone is naked sometimes, but she also said that we can't be naked in front of anyone -- especially father."

"We never know when he's coming," said Zerah. "So we're not supposed to be naked. I was right." Zerah looked at Pharez triumphantly.

"Father thinks we're boys," said Zerah. "He likes boys better since he is one."

Tamar hesitated. She had been trying to avoid saying the word "naked" in front of the twins but, evidently, they had heard it before.

"You're both right," said Tamar. "Ishtar was naked. And after she had passed through the sixth gate, her sister confronted her and asked her why she came. 'If you want to know what it is like to be dead, I can show you,' said the evil sister." Tamar raised her eyebrows and her voice and unleashed a cackle. "Ereshkigal was in an especially bad mood so she was very wicked. She told her soldiers to torture her sister by afflicting every part of her body. But Ishtar was favored by the gods. They were watching over her from their thrones in the sky."

"Just like our God," interjected Zerah. "He lives in the sky."

Hmmm, thought Tamar. She wondered what her sister was telling the twins. Or maybe it was Judah filling their heads -- the few times he saw them -- with the notion of the new God.

"Kind of... but in this story there are many gods and goddesses. Some of the gods decided that as long as Ishtar was in the underworld, the world would come to a standstill. Trees and plants would stop bearing fruit. No children or animals would be born. All of creation would die if Ishtar stayed in the underworld much longer. The god of all things that grow and the moon god got together and made a plan."

"And then what happened?" Zerah and Pharez looked up, eyes gleaming.

Tamar wasn't sure which one had spoken.

"Ishtar's and Ereshkigal's brother was the god of water. From the dirt under his fingernails, he created Asushunamir, the spirit guide who was both male and female. "

"I keep my fingernails clean," said Zerah.

"Not me," said Pharez. "I have enough dirt under my fingernails to make a spirit guide. See?"

Tamar looked at the child's hands and smiled.

"So you do. Asushunamir was more beautiful than any man or woman because ze was both male and female. The plan was to send Asushunamir to the underworld so that Ereshkigal would forget about her sister and everyone else.

When Asushunamir knocked on the first gate, the gatekeeper told Ereshkigal that the most beautiful man he ever saw was coming -- just for her. Now, Ereshkigal was not nearly as beautiful as her sister. In fact, her moodiness had etched itself into her face. Her right eye drooped. Her cheeks were sunken. And because she was Queen of the underworld, she wore a drab dress with a large belt buckle that was a skull."

"Ooooh," said Pharez and Zerah in unison. They shrank back. Tamar suspected that they had seen the skulls set on posts in the village square.

"Ereshkigal rarely met anyone in the underworld who wasn't already dead. She became very excited when the gatekeeper told her that the most beautiful man in the world was coming down to see her. So the gatekeeper hobbled back up to the first gate. Just as the gods planned, Ereshkigal forgot all about Ishtar."

Tamar paused as she heard Aziz in his corner of the tent sigh and roll over. *He must be having a dream*, she thought and went back to the story.

"Ishtar started coming back up. She left the underworld and returned through the seventh gate first. Her clothes were given back to her and she put them on so she was no longer naked. Her bracelets chimed again as she put them back on. At the same time, Asushunamir entered the first gate and kept going down. Just as Ishtar left the first gate and was given back her crown and was free, Asushunamir passed through the seventh gate and was forced to give up all clothing.

Ereshkigal saw that Asushunamir was a man and a woman, not just a man as she was expecting. She was furious.

The gods had tricked her! Ishtar came back from the dead, and the land flourished.

Because of Asushunamir, Ishtar was resurrected and lived forever.

"Why was Ereshkigal upset that the trickster was a man and woman instead of just a man, Auntie?" asked Pharez.

Tamar thought quickly. "Because...Ereshkigal liked men better and she wanted one as a... playmate."

They seemed to accept her answer. But then Zerah spoke up.

"And what happened to Asushunamir?"

Tamar actually didn't know. The myth that she knew ended with Ishtar coming back from the underworld. But these two children wanted to know what happened to the spirit guide who was two sexes, like them.

She decided to make up a new ending.

"Ishtar had her powers restored. She was a goddess again. She blessed Asushunamir and freed hir from the underworld."

"Did they live together forever and ever?" Zerah always wanted a happy ending.

"Yes," said Tamar. "They lived together forever and ever, and ... Asushunamir was grateful not to have to stay in the underworld with the evil Ereshkigal."

"I don't believe that story," said Pharez, standing up and stomping hir foot. "Whoever heard of someone coming back from the dead and living forever -- even if she is a goddess!"

Just then a swath of light fell into the tent. Aziz snorted and sat up on his haunches.

Tabitha entered. The tent flap fell closed behind her.

"Uggh. It smells like camel in here. Why didn't you put Aziz outside?" asked Tabitha.

Tamar sniffed and said, "It smells fine in here."

"That's because you almost never leave the tent. It smells normal to you. But when I came in, I smelled camel pee. I think Aziz has been going too near the tent -- maybe on it, said Tabitha, curling her nostrils in disdain.

Tamar scoffed. "Aziz knows better than to pee on the tent. Besides, I don't care if he does. And you know I don't like to go out when you're out. What if someone sees us in two different places?"

"Who's going to see you in this Godforsaken place?"

Tamar put down her basket and turned to the children.

"You look like you've been cooped up too long. Why don't you go to the well and get a pitcher of water?"

"Check on Ezzie while you're outside. Make sure she's safe in her pen and that she has enough water," said Tamar. Ezzie was her pet goat who gave her milk to make cheese. Ezzie was the she-goat offspring of the goat that Judah had promised when he lay with Tabitha. That day under the hot desert sun, when Tabitha dressed as a harlot, she had made Judah promise to send her a kid as payment for her laying with him. Tabitha had convinced him that she needed proof that he would send the kid and that's when he gave her his bracelets, staff, and signet ring. True to his word, Judah had the kid delivered to Tamar -- since he thought that she was the harlot that he had laid with. Two years later, the kid was full grown. Tabitha mated her with a male goat. Five months later, she gave birth to Ezzie.

The twins were headed toward the tent flap. Zerah turned back.

"Auntie promised that we could see a drawing of the Goddess Ishtar."

""I'll show you when you get back," said Tamar.

Zerah ran after Pharez.

"The Goddess Ishtar? What kinds of things are you putting into their heads?" Tabitha undid her widow's veil and sat down on a folded blanket.

"The old stories are part of their world, too. I'm just telling them the tales that Auntie and Great Grandmother told us." Tamar went over to Aziz's clay food bowl and saw that there were a few pieces of cacti left in the bottom.

"Tales are right. Those old stories are completely unbelievable," said Tabitha.

"The twins thought so too. They asked so many questions that I had to make up a new ending," answered Tamar.

Tamar came back to where Tabitha was sitting, bent over and picked the terracotta figurines off of the tent floor. She put them back in the basket with the other figurines. Then she reached behind the basket. She pulled out the twenty-inch high bas-relief of Ishtar standing naked with her wings behind her, flanked by two owls. She was standing on the sturdy back of an animal that looked like a two-headed lion.

"Here," she said, handing the bas-relief to Tabitha. "Maybe you should show it to them. I'm sure they'll have lots of questions about Ishtar's nakedness. You're the mother."

The words came out differently than Tamar had intended. It sounded like she was questioning Tabitha's parenting skills -- but she wasn't. Tabitha was a good mother.

"What I meant was that you're the one who should be talking to them about such things, not me."

"I don't have a problem with nakedness," said Tabitha. "And I don't want them to be ashamed of their bodies."

"But, if Judah finds out..."

"Oh, Judah, smudah. I'm so sick of him. He thinks he can just walk in anytime and take his sons out for camel rides. He doesn't treat me any differently than Milcah. In fact, he pays a little more attention to her. He invites her to his tent and she comes back all flushed and flustered and acts secretive. I feel like telling her that I know it's no big deal. If I wasn't concerned that Judah might do something to the children, I'd tell him where they really came from."

"But you have status as the mother of Judah's children," said Tamar. "You'd be wise not to do anything to anger him." She chose her words carefully. Tabitha was at the mercy of Judah. Both of them were. If he found out that they had deceived him, he'd have them burnt at the stake. And there was no telling what Judah would do to the twins if he found out they were from another man's seed.

"I've never understood the story about nakedness," said Tabatha, changing the subject. "Adam and Eve didn't know that they were naked until Eve listened to the serpent and ate from the tree of knowledge. Then when God came down for a chat, Adam and Eve knew they were naked and hid themselves. "

"I remember Great Grandmother telling us those stories

like it was yesterday." Tamar's eyes misted. "We were children and would sit at her knee and she would tell us about Adam and Eve and their son Cain who slew his brother Abel in a field. Generations passed. God saw that the people he had made were corrupt. He destroyed everything in the great flood and started anew with Noah and his family and the animals, two of every kind, on his ark. When they reached land, they formed settlements. Noah lived until he was nine hundred and fifty years old. Noah's line descended to Abraham who God sent forth from Ur to the land of Canaan so that he could make a great nation. God had recreated humankind but nudity was still forbidden.

It seems like everyone was ashamed of their nakedness. Are we supposed to believe that this is still Eve's fault?"

"Don't forget the serpent," answered Tabitha.

"I remember that we had lots of questions when we were little." Tamar walked over to a basket and pulled out the bas-relief of Ishtar.

"And Great Grandmother didn't have the answers," said Tabitha as she reached up and took the bas-relief.

"Maybe she should have made up a different ending," replied Tamar.

Chapter Six

"So this is what the Goddess Ishtar looks like." Tabitha held the bas-relief on her lap so that it faced the children.

"She's NAKED!" exclaimed Zerah. "Just like in the story. And she's really pretty. She looks just like you Mama -- when you wash -- except her breasts are bigger."

"And you don't have wings," chimed in Pharez. "Wait a minute. Where's her penis?"

"Silly, goddesses don't have penises!" Zerah smiled triumphantly.

"But WE do. We have boy parts and girl parts," pointed out Pharez.

"Are we going to grow breasts?" asked Zerah. "Will they be as beautiful as Ishtar's?"

"What about wings?" Pharez hopped up and down.

"Do you have to go to the bathroom?" asked Tabitha.

"No. I'm just excited about the beautiful naked goddess!" Pharez kept hopping.

Tabitha glared at Tamar like this was all her fault.

"Auntie told you the story," she said to the twins. "Why don't you ask her?"

Pharez turned toward Tamar. "Where's the goddess's penis?"

"Are we going to grow breasts?" asked Zerah.

The two children stared at Tamar. She had no answers.

"I don't know," she said honestly. "When you get older, you'll find out. But remember Asushunamir in the story? Asushunamir was the spirit guide who helped the goddess come back to life. Asushunamir was both male and female -- just like you. Without Asushunamir there would be no story!"

"I want to be a goddess!"

"Me too! Me too!"

"But I want to have a penis, too," insisted Pharez. "Maybe her penis broke off."

"I'm sure she had one once," said Tamar. "Maybe we just can't see it in the picture."

Tamar hated telling lies. She was starting to regret telling the story.

Tabitha held her lips in a smug "I told you so" smile as she stared at Tamara.

Then she turned toward the twins.

"The important thing to remember," Tabitha said, "is that you should never be ashamed of your body. Just remember, though, that not everyone feels the same way. They don't understand and they might hurt you."

"Understand what?" asked Pharez.

"That some people are both male and female," explained their mother.

"Why would they hurt us?" Zerah looked up at Tabitha.

"Because they have been taught to believe that everybody should be a man or a woman, not both," explained Tabitha.

"But it's not true," said Pharez. "You told us that lots of children are born both girls AND boys. And Auntie told us the story about the spirit guide who was both male and female and the most beautiful person in the land."

"Asushunamir saved the goddess," chimed in Zerah.

Tamar smiled. *So the story had been worth telling*, she thought. The children remembered that the spirit guide was both male and female, like them.

"Did the spirit guide have to pretend to be a boy?" asked Zerah.

Tabitha cocked an eyebrow at Tamar.

Tamar looked down and spoke to the twins. "In those times, people were more understanding. Asushunamir was a hero. Now, people are more afraid. They are afraid of their own bodies, and they are afraid of anyone who is different."

"But why are they afraid?" asked Pharez.

Zerah looked up, too.

"The priests teach them to be afraid," said Tamar. "They teach that it is better to have a son than a daughter, even though it's not true. The priests control who the property goes to when someone dies. This way they amass more wealth for themselves. If a man dies, his property goes to the priests and not to his wife. The woman is the man's property. If her husband dies, she is expected to remarry or to become a family member's servant. None of this is right, of course. Women are just as smart as men. This is just how the priests keep their power."

The twins stared up at her with vacant looks.

"What's 'a - mass' mean?" asked Zamar.

Pharez was looking across the tent at the blocks that Tamar kept for the children.

Tamar realized that neither child understood what she was explaining. It was as if she were speaking Greek.

"This way, the priests only have to teach the boys to learn to read and write and to do their numbers. They're lazy and this is less work for them." When Tamar finished speaking, she looked at Tabitha and shrugged.

How could she explain this to these children when she could barely comprehend it herself. Why were men thought to be superior to women? Why did people have to be one sex or the other?

She prayed to the one God for understanding and patience. She was a skeptic, but she wanted to believe. When praying to the one God didn't work, she prayed to Isis, to Ishtar, and to her old standby the goddess Asherah. Some said that Asherah was the consort of the one God. Others said she was the Queen of Heaven. When she prayed to the one God, Tamar just became angry. Why was Asherah said to be His consort? Why wasn't She the one God? Through her anger, Tamar kept on praying.

Tabitha jumped into the conversation.

"People are more afraid than they used to be. Sometimes they don't understand," she explained. That's why your father can't see you naked or know that you are more than the sons he thinks you are. If anything happened to you, we would be sad. That's why it's important that you don't tell anyone. We love you too much to let anything happen to you. You have to promise not to tell, okay?"

"Okay." Pharez and Zerah answered in unison.

Tamar and Tabitha smiled at the children. Tamar loved the twins more than anything, even more than she loved Aziz. She hoped that they understood and kept their promise. She also hoped that they would not be damaged by keeping secrets. Could she ask for both?

Tabitha went over to the pitcher of water. She poured it into clay cups.

Pharez held out her arms and started running in circles around the tent. "Look at me. I have WINGS and I'm going to fly high in the sky so that I can see God."

Pharez circled around a few more times and then collapsed from dizziness.

"I'm the goddess," said Pharez. "Except -- I'm better. I have a penis AND a vagina."

"I want to be the goddess," said Zerah, pouting.

"I want to be a goddess with a penis and breasts," said Pharez. "And when I grow up I want to marry a goddess."

"Of course you can marry a goddess when you grow up," said Tamar. She felt like what she said should be the answer, even though it most likely wasn't the truth. "When you grow up, you can marry anyone you like."

As long as you choose to be a man, she thought to herself. *And even then...*

"Here." Tabitha came over with two cups of water in her hands. She handed a cup to each child. "Don't drink the water. Stare into it. Ask yourself -- quietly in your head -- any questions that you have about the future. Then stare into the water until the oracle gives you an answer.

"I just see my reflection," said Pharez.

"You have to be quiet," said Tabitha as she sat down on a folded blanket on the floor. "Or the oracle won't come."

There was a long stretch of welcomed silence.

"I want to be the mama. You can be the father," said Zerah.

"Yippee! I get to be God the Father," exclaimed Pharez.

"Yes. God the Father who is rarely there -- just like our father," said Zerah.

Tabitha smiled serenely at the twins playing on the other side of the tent.

Tamar wondered what Tabitha had told the twins about Judah, but she didn't ask. It wasn't her business. She unrolled the cheese cloth from the block of cheese that she made from Ezzie's milk. She marveled that the goat milk curds clumped together so well.

Last night, she had hung the block inside the flap of the tent so it would be near the cool air of the desert night. Now, she poured olive oil from the spout of a small clay pitcher. The white cheese turned golden under the oil. She picked up a red clay jar with holes in the top and shook it.

"I'm glad that we didn't eat Ezzie when you wanted to. Now that she is old enough to calve and we have mated her, she has given us milk nearly every day," said Tamar.

"I didn't really want to eat the goat that came from Judah. I do like goat's meat, but the price that I paid for that kid -- posing as a harlot and having sex with Judah -- was too high. Having that old goat around was just a reminder of Judah. However, goat meat is succulent. But I knew you feel guilty about eating the Lord's creatures -- and wouldn't want to kill the goat. But now that I think about it, I could have overlooked that the goat came from Judah. I wouldn't have minded eating Ezzie when she was young and tender." Tabitha unwound a piece of white cloth from the hard brown nose of a loaf of bread.

Tamar glowered at Tabitha. She had come to think of Ezzie as family, second to Aziz. But she let the feeling pass. She realized that Tabitha was probably just being flippant about Ezzie. It was obvious that she was trying to get Tamar's goat. Tamar hadn't told Tabitha that she had watched Judah hump on her under the hot desert sun. She thought about mentioning this -- to get at Tabitha for saying she wouldn't have minded eating Ezzie. But Tamar decided that two wrongs didn't make a right. She didn't know why she hadn't turned her eyes away when Judah got on top of her sister. At first she had just wanted to make sure that Judah arrived. Then she wanted to make sure that her sister was okay. But she had to admit that curiosity must have gotten the best of her.

"At least you and the children are safe," Tamar said. She felt like she had the wisdom of an older sister, even if she was older only by minutes.

Tamar looked past the tent pole to where the twins were playing on the other side of the tent next to Aziz. He looked irritated -- as if the children were keeping him from sleeping.

"Wait a minute. Why can't I be both mother and father?" asked Pharez.

"You heard Mama and Auntie. We have to pick one, because people want us to be one or the other. I already said that I'm the mama."

"But I want to be both." Pharez plopped down on the hay next to Aziz and started to cry.

Aziz sat up on his haunches.

"It's almost time to eat," said Tamar.

"Wait," said Tabitha. "Let them play. They are trying to figure things out for themselves. That's what I want them to do."

"They're bothering Aziz," whispered Tamar.

"Stop worrying about your camel. He's fine. In fact, I think he likes the children playing near him. It's good for their game too. Aziz can be part of the scenery. They can pretend that he's the family camel who lives OUTSIDE the tent."

"Oh, okay," said Tamar. "I still have to slice the bread and get the rest of the meal ready."

"You're acting like a baby, and we already have a baby," said Zerah, holding up one of the larger figurines."Now it's time to wrap the REAL baby in swaddling so that we can go to the market."

"Why do we have to wrap the baby in swaddling?" Pharez was still in the straw but was sitting up straight and leaning forward to stroke Aziz's soft fur. Aziz closed his eyes.

"Because silly, our baby has a penis AND a vagina, and we have to wrap it in swaddling so no one in the village will know," said Zerah.

"But, I'm the FATHER. I don't have to touch the swaddling."

"Fine, I'll do it myself. It's not like you do anything around the tent anyway. You don't even live here. You just breeze in and out of here like you own the place." Zerah began furiously circling hir arms around the figurine, wrapping it with imaginary strips of swaddling.

Tamar looked up from putting a bowl of almonds on the table. Tabitha shrugged and turned away. Tamar suppressed a smile. It sounded like Zerah might be repeating what her mother said.

"Fathers do own everything!" said Pharez. "That's why I'm the father."

"No, you're the father, because I said you are," said Zerah triumphantly.

"But I get to ride on the camel when we go to the marketplace. Maybe I should start putting the saddle on him," said Pharez.

"But I'm not done wrapping the swaddling. And then I have to make a list of everything that we need from the market. You just sit there and do what you do best -- nothing. I'll tell you when to get ready to go."

Tamar slowly broke off the sections of a pomegranate. One by one, she broke off the juicy red seeds from the white flesh. She put them into a clay bowl. She took her time. She was enjoying listening to the children.

"First you have to write the list for me. We need locusts, honey, a cluster of grapes, three hundred fig cakes --

"Three hundred!" said Pharez.

"We're having a party. Our baby is going to be circumcised soon," said Zerah.

"Cir-cir... What's that mean?" asked Pharez.

"It doesn't matter," said Zerah. "It's what everyone does. Just write down what I say. I can't read or write because I'm the mother and females aren't taught anything

-- because they already know everything. They have the babies and tell the men what to do."

"But I can't read or write yet, either. Father said he will teach me," said Pharez.

"He said he will teach his SONS. That's why we can't tell him that we have girl-parts, too," said Zerah. "For now, just pretend that you're writing down what I say. We're just playing."

"I'm sick of this game," said Pharez. "I want to take Aziz out for a ride."

Just in time, thought Tamar. The table was set.

"Time to eat," she said to the children.

Chapter Seven

"I heard a rumor that Joseph was freed from the pit by Judah. Judah convinced his other brothers that it would be more profitable to sell Joseph as a slave to the Egyptians than to let him die."

"What pit?" asked Tamar. She lit an oil lamp and set it on the table. She had just cleaned her tent. The women of her cult were coming.

"You don't get out much, do you?" Judith set down her bag. The brown woven pouch swung out from the folds of her robe as she bent over. Tamar was glad to see that Judith was still wearing the amulet that she had given her. As far as Tamar knew, Judith was not yet with child.

"Actually, I don't. Before Tabitha had the twins, I used to go out more. But now, I don't want to risk being seen. We could be found out. Life is more complicated now that I have switched places with my sister."

"You could wear a veil," said Judith.

"Tabitha wears the widow's veil to identify herself as part of Judah's tribe," answered Tamar.

"You could wear a different veil," said Judith. "No one would know who you are."

"That's true," replied Tamar. "I could wear my brown veil. It covers my face, and no one would know me."

"See. I'm right. You can go out anytime." Judith looked at Tamar.

Tamar stared back at her with a level gaze.

"But why should I go out? I'm perfectly happy here. I have Aziz to keep me company, the women of the cult come here, and Tabitha brings the twins over to visit. She brings me all the supplies that I need."

Judith rolled her eyes. "I like being part of public life. What I don't find out from my husband, I find out from Jacob and Samuel at the village well. In fact, I learn more from Samuel and Jacob than I do from Bram. Joseph was the late in life son of Israel and Judith. His line descends from Abraham. His father had a fancy coat made for Joseph. It was a very expensive coat -- beautiful, too, with many colors woven into the fabric. When his brothers saw the coat and found out it was from his father, they were jealous."

Tamar was skeptical. She had heard this story -- or at least part of it. Who hadn't? But even when it was first news, she hadn't really paid much attention. It didn't have anything to do with her.

"Joseph was clueless. His brothers already envied him. Then Joseph told them that he had a dream in which they were all sheaves of wheat in a field. He told them that they were bowing down to him. So they put him in a pit. I don't blame them, really. What else could they have done?"

Tamar shook her head. She could think of any number of things they could have done -- for starters, the brothers could just have ignored Joseph's comment about the dream.

It sounded like he was delusional. When Tabitha sounded this way, Tamar just ignored her. She would have commented on this, but something stopped her. Maybe it was that Judith thought that it was okay to put someone in a pit. Tamar never even entertained the thought of putting her sister in a pit. By taking the side of the brothers who put Joseph in a pit, Judith was telling Tamar something about her personality. Tamar thought that maybe she was right not to trust her.

"At first, his brothers wanted to slay him," continued Judith. "But then his brother Reuben spoke up and wanted to leave Joseph to die -- to starve to death or to be eaten by wild animals in the land of Dothan. This way when Joseph's carcass was delivered to their father, he wouldn't suspect that his sons had slain Joseph. So they dug a pit and put him in it. First they took his precious coat of many colors. Then Reuben went away. The rest of the brothers were sitting near the pit when clever Judah had an idea. He saw a caravan of Ishmaelites in the distance. He could tell who they were by their gold ponchos with the blue trim. This gave him an idea. If the brothers sold Joseph into slavery, they could pocket the money. The Ishmaelites approached, slowed down and stopped."

Judith paused.

"I wish I could have seen them. I've always wondered if the Ishmaelites still resemble Abraham and Hagar after all these generations. Anyway, they came to an agreement, and the brothers sold Joseph for twenty pieces of silver. Not a bad price," said Judith, with a glint in her eye. "Tabitha was smart to pick Judah to be the father of her sons. Don't you agree?"

Judith looked at Tamar.

Tamar ignored Judith and looked down at the table. She cut the fresh goat cheese into six even pieces. She had never told Judith that the real father was the young shepherd. She and Tabitha agreed not to tell anyone -- not even the women in their circle. All the women from her cult were coming tonight -- Iscah, Serah, Leah, and Tabitha -- to celebrate the full moon. Judith had gotten there early. She always did. She had a husband and six sons. Tamar suspected that no one listened to Judith aside from the women in the cult.

Tabitha was leaving the twins with her maid servant. Five years had passed since Tamar had told them the story of Ishtar and Ereshkigal. She couldn't believe how fast they were growing. They were old enough now to stay with Milcah without fear that she would try to help them bathe and find out that they were female as well as male. True to his word, Judah was educating them. He sent a tutor for their studies. Tabitha and Tamar had also agreed not to tell the women of the cult that the twins had two sets of genitals each. Chances were that the women would keep the secret. But they couldn't take the chance of word spreading around. Besides, Tamar didn't trust Judith. It was a gut instinct, but she had her reasons.

Judith loved to gossip. Ordinarily, Tamar didn't gossip. But, as it turned out, she had told Iscah about the twins. She wasn't going to. But she and Iscah were like sisters. They told each other everything. Tamar slipped. One night, when it was just the two of them and they were sharing a goatskin of wine, Tamar told her everything, including that the seed had come from the shepherd. She also told her that the twins were not sons but sons and daughters and that Tabitha wanted to let them decide for themselves how to live. Iscah said that she wouldn't tell anyone, but the next morning Tamar was sorry she had confided in her. She shouldn't have taken that chance.

"Reuben came back to the pit and found that Joseph was gone. The other brothers didn't want to share their money with Reuben so they didn't tell him that they sold Joseph into slavery. So the brothers killed a kid and dipped the coat in its blood and brought the coat to their father," continued Judith.

Just then the tent flap opened and Leah came in. "I have been scouring the desert for hyssop to make these brooms," she said breathlessly.

Judith nodded at Leah and kept talking. "Naturally, Israel had recognized the coat he had given to his favorite, the son of his old age. He said that it was Joseph's coat and that an evil beast must have devoured him. Then Israel rent his clothes, put a sackcloth around his loins, and mourned his son for many days. He was so grief stricken that he said he would mourn for the rest of his days. No one could console him."

"Israel? Don't you mean Jacob?" asked Tamar.

"He goes by two names. Those of us in the know call him Israel now," replied Judith.

Tamar thought Judith sounded a bit snide. Deciding to ignore Judith's tone, she replied:

"Didn't his sons feel bad that they made their elderly father sad? They might have had a change of heart and told him that Joseph was alive -- that they had sold him into slavery?"

Judith looked at her for a second and said, "Of course, not. When they saw that their father was so grief stricken over his precious favorite son, it just made them more angry and confirmed that they had done the right thing."

"You must be talking about Joseph and his coat of many colors," said Leah. She leaned over to sweep out the corners of the tent with bunches of hyssop that were bound together at the stalks.

"The tent is already clean," said Tamar.

"But after I cleanse it with hyssop branches, it will be sacred space," answered Leah. "That's why I do this before every ritual."

I know, thought Tamar, *and after every ritual, I have to sweep up the long skinny green leaves and the purplish blue petals that are strewn everywhere.* But she said nothing.

Just then the flap opened. Tabitha entered.

"I found everything you wanted at the market," said Tabitha. She handed Tamar a sack. "I tied Aziz outside." She gave Tamar a look. "He's fine."

"Does he have water to drink?"

"Of course." Tabitha answered her sister with a frown. "He's near the well and I put his bowl next to him."

"He's getting older in camel years," said Tamar. "I worry about him."

"Camel years!?" exclaimed Tabitha. "Those beasts live longer than we do. I've heard stories about camels being passed down from one generation to another."

"That's only when the older generation raises camel cubs and then they keep them in their families by giving them to their adult children," countered Tamar. "Aziz is getting older. The knobs around his knees are getting larger. It takes him longer to stand."

"Enough already about the camel," said Judith. She jerked her neck, and her silver necklaces tinkled. "I was talking about Joseph being sold into slavery. What have you heard?" she asked, turning to Tabitha.

"Aziz is NOT a camel. He's a drom--"

Tabitha interrupted Tamar in mid-sentence.

"Milcah told me that she heard that the Ishmaelites sold Joseph to the Egyptian Potiphar, the Pharaoh's officer and the captain of the guard."

"I heard that the Lord was with Joseph and that the master treated Joseph well and made him the overseer," said Leah. She finished whisking the far corner next to Aziz's empty straw bed.

"Good luck getting rid of that camel smell," said Tabitha.

"I TOLD you that Aziz is NOT a camel -- he's a dromedary." Tamar glared at Tabitha.

"One hump, two humps. The smell is the same." Tabitha took off her robe and carefully put it over the back of a chair.

The front flap opened again. Serah entered. She wasn't carrying her basket. Tamar breathed a sigh of relief. She respected the serpent as an ancient sign of wisdom. Still, she liked to keep her distance. Serah was followed by Iscah.

The women caught them up on the latest news about Joseph.

"I heard more at the market," said Serah.

"Camel cheese," -- she said, handing a small sack to Tamar -- "fresh from the maker."

"What did you hear?" asked Judith.

"You know that Joseph is a good looking lad -- tall, handsome and well endowed, too, according to the women who saw him being led naked from the pit," said Serah.

"I would've liked to have seen that!" exclaimed Judith.

Leah, Serah, and Tabitha snickered.

Tamar suppressed a grin.

"I heard that Potiphar's wife took a liking to him and asked him to lie with her. Joseph refused her. He said that this would be a great sin against God. But he probably just didn't want to. The woman who sold me the camel cheese said that she heard that Potiphar's wife is from a wealthy family and that he married for money. His wife is ... no great beauty to say the least, " said Serah.

Tamar nodded. The others were silent. One of the rules of the cult was to honor women and not talk badly about themselves or others. Honoring themselves meant that they had to honor others. Tamar tried to do this even when she wasn't with the members of her cult.

"Joseph probably just made up the part about the sin against God. Maybe he was telling the truth -- who knows?" Serah looked at each woman's face carefully.

She doesn't want to be caught offending the one God -- even here, thought Tamar.

But the other women either didn't care or they were more interested in hearing the news from the marketplace.

"And?" asked Judith. "What happened?"

"Potiphar's wife wasn't buying it. When Joseph turned

her down, she began chasing him until she caught him. Then she snatched off his garment."

Serah paused. A titter went around the circle.

"Potiphar's wife went to her brothers, who lived in the house, and said that the Hebrew servant was mocking them and wanted her to lie with him. The woman at the market didn't know if her brothers believed her or not. But she did hear that when the master came home, his wife told him the same thing. Potiphar must have been confused since he was close to Joseph. The camel cheese maker heard they were very close. Potiphar wouldn't be the first master to favor his man servant over his wife. And I don't remember hearing that Potiphar and his wife had any children."

A knowing glance spread from Iscah to Judith, to Leah, to Serah to Tabitha.

"But what could Potiphar do? His wife said that Joseph dishonored his master. Even if no one believed her, she ruled the purse strings. She could always go back to live with her father and he would cut Potiphar off. So Potiphar had Joseph put into prison," said Serah.

"That must be the Egyptian prison that I've heard about -- the place where the King's prisoners are sent. Life there isn't so bad. There's no hard labor," interjected Leah.

"It's just outside of Memphis -- on the Nile," said Serah with great authority as if she had been there. "It's not far from the Land of Goshen where Pharaoh lives. The great Arabian Desert is across the river."

Maybe she has been there, in her quest for the perfect serpent, thought Tamar. She stifled her sarcasm.

"The maker of the camel cheese told me that before long the prison keeper put Joseph in charge of all the other prisoners. But the woman at the market told me that prison keeper was just lazy -- and he was looking for someone to do his job. But the followers of the one God were saying that the Lord was with Joseph," said Serah. She looked around the circle, and searched the women's faces.

Tamar looked around the circle, too. Was there anyone here who couldn't be trusted? It wasn't yet against the law to worship in the old ways, but people had been stoned to death for less. Tamar's eyes rested on Judith.

Judith exclaimed, "No doubt, the Lord was with Joseph. He endured his brother's jealousies, being thrown in the pit, and sold into slavery."

Just a short while ago, she was defending Joseph's brothers, thought Tamar. Judith seemed to defend the ones who had power -- even when it was the prison keeper and his favorite, Joseph. That fast, Tamar regretted her thoughts. Maybe Judith had a change of heart. Perhaps that was why she was taking Joseph's side over his brothers.

"That is right," said Serah contritely. "I was just telling the story the camel cheese maker told me. I'm sure the Lord was with Joseph."

"Is Joseph still in jail?" asked Judith.

Judith is too interested in what Joseph is doing, thought Tamar. She doesn't even know him.

Tamar knew she would have to step in the get the ritual started. Catching up on the village news was okay, but it was not the reason that the women came to her tent. No one knew Joseph personally, and he had nothing to do with their full moon celebration.

But before Tamar could say anything, Serah answered Judith.

"Yes, he is still there. It came to pass that the butler and the baker of the king of Egypt had offended the king. They were put in the prison and Joseph was their keeper. One morning, Joseph looked at them and said, 'Why do you look so sad today?' So they told Joseph that they had dreams and they were sad that there was no dream interpreter. So Joseph told them that he could interpret their dreams -- even though dream interpretations 'belong to God.'"

"Can you imagine a jail where the inmates have their dreams interpreted?" asked Leah, looking up from a scroll that she had brought with her. Aside from Tamar, Leah was the only one who could read. Like Tamar, Leah had learned in secret.

"This is what the camel cheese maker told me," said Serah. She sounded more than a little defensive.

"What did he mean, dreams can only be interpreted by God? I interpret dreams all the time -- usually, my own." Tabitha was waving hyssop ties in the air above Aziz's bed as if she were making a statement about how she thought the air smelled. Tamar glared at her.

"The king's butler told Joseph that in his dream there was a vine and, lo and behold, there were three branches in the vine. Right before his eyes, the plants started blooming. It flowered. Clusters of grapes ripened. The butler said that in his dream he saw that he held Pharaoh's cup so he took the grapes and pressed them into the cup, and then he gave the cup to him. Joseph told him that the tree branches represented three days and within that time, Pharaoh would have a change of heart and take him back as his butler," said Serah.

"And what about the baker?" asked Leah.

Tamar sighed. The rest of the women were intrigued with the story. Tamar had to admit to herself that she was interested. She resigned herself to listening until the end. Then they would have their ritual.

"The baker told Joseph that in his dream there were three white baskets stacked on his head. In the top basket were meats for Pharaoh and the birds flew down from the sky and ate them. Joseph told the baker that in three days, Pharaoh will have his head, 'it will hang on a tree, the birds will eat his dead flesh.'" Serah looked around the circle.

Everyone was silent.

"Eeww," said Leah finally. She shuddered. "What a thing to say. Couldn't Joseph have made up a different story?"

"As it turned out his interpretations were true," said Serah. "That is exactly what happened to each of them. Before the butler was freed from the prison to return to his post with Pharaoh, Joseph asked him to put in a good word for him with Pharaoh. He emphasized that he was sold from the land of the Hebrews through no fault of his own and imprisoned although he was innocent. Then the baker was executed and the butler was freed. The butler promptly forgot about Joseph's request."

"The butler forgot about him? What kind of ending is that?" retorted Leah.

"I'm sure the butler was so relieved at his own good luck that he didn't want to burden Pharaoh with Joseph's request."

"Hmmm..." said Tabitha. She sat cross legged on the floor and fiddled with the folded blanket that she sat on. "If

I were the dream interpreter, I would've made up a different ending for the baker. Sometimes if you imagine a different ending, it will happen."

"Maybe someone had to lose his head that day, and when the executioner saw the terrified look on the baker's face, he decided to take him," said Tamar, shrugging. "That makes sense. I do believe in the power of suggestion."

That's ridiculous," snapped Judith. "The whole point of the story is that Joseph believes in his innocence and that someday soon he will be freed from the prison. I predict that he will become an important man in Egypt and that he will want to see his nephews, Judah's sons, Pharez and Zerah."

Tamar looked at Judith. "That hadn't occurred to me. But I guess you are right. Joseph will want to meet his family. Judah was the one who spared his life."

"IF the twins want to meet Joseph -- and IF he is freed from prison, they will go. Right now, they're too young to travel that far," stated Tamar.

"They're almost men," said Judith. "Soon they will have to be circumcised."

Tamar saw a Judith look at Iscah gloatingly. Iscah lowered her head looked at the tent floor. A chill suddenly went down the Tamar's spine. Iscah and Judith were becoming friendly. Iscah had mentioned she had shared a goatskin of wine with Judith.

A voice boomed in Tamar's mind: *WHY DID YOU TELL ISCAH EVERYTHING?*

Tabitha must have seen the fear on Tamar's face.

She glared at Tamar.

"The twins have already been circumcised," said Tabitha. "Not that I believe in it. It can be dangerous, and it seems like it would harm the man's pleasure when he is grown."

"There is absolutely a reason for it," contended Judith. "It means that the boys have entered the covenant of Abraham and his one God. I have six sons and they all have been circumcised."

Tabitha blanched. "Of course, my sons have been circumcised, too, and have entered into the covenant."

"When was the ceremony?" asked Judith accusingly. "Your friends were not invited?"

Judith exchanged a look with Iscah.

Tamar took a deep breath and tried to cleared her mind of anger and anxiety. *I must not lash out,* she thought. *It will only make matters worse.* As betrayed as she felt, she also felt compassion for Judith. As long as she was bragging about having six sons and jangling her six silver necklaces that her husband gave her as a reward, she would not conceive a daughter. Tamar took another deep breath. No matter what Iscah had told her and no matter how Judith could benefit from the information, she could still have a change of heart.

"Orpah recommended a priest. He did the procedure on the Sabbath and said it was okay for me not to have a ceremony or a reception since I find the procedure distasteful. I sent word to Judah that his sons were circumcised. That was enough."

Tamar nodded and said, "It is true."

Tabitha had not told her anything about circumcision and Tamar hadn't asked. But Tabitha was saying what she had to. Tamar, also, was fiercely protective of the twins. She would protect them with her life. If only she hadn't shared the goatskin of wine with Iscah.

"It is time to start the ritual," Tamar said. "Leah is leading us tonight and she has something new for us to try."

"Yes," said Leah. "Let us sit down in our circle before casting the directions. I have been reading a new scroll that was passed along to me and have learned some new prayers that I can teach you. First let us thank the gods and goddesses who brought us this far. Let us thank the men for excluding us from their prayers and their learning. For by doing so, they have set us on our own path. We can more deeply know ourselves and, by doing so, know the God inside of us.

"Thank you Mother God and Father God," she said, folding her hands in front of her heart.

"Breathe in and out. Follow your breath in and out ten times each."

The tent was filled with the sound of deep breathing and after a time, a simple sound started by Leah: "OM."

Tamar had not read this scroll yet. But somewhere deep within her, she knew without a doubt that this was the first sound of creation.

Chapter Eight

It came to pass that Judith was right about Joseph. He had been freed from prison and became an important man in Egypt.

"It all started when Pharaoh couldn't find a decent dream interpreter," said Judith. She was sitting at a chair next to the small wooden table in the middle of Tamar's tent. Many moons had passed.

"He called for all the wise men and all the magicians of his land. Not one of them could interpret his dreams." As Judith spoke, she fingered the faded pouch hanging from a string around her neck.

Seven years had passed since Judah and his brothers had taken Joseph from the pit and sold him into slavery. Tamar noticed that Judith's stomach was still flat. There was a glow about her face. Tamar suspected that the glow came from gossiping. Judith had still not given birth even though she said she longed to conceive and prayed for a daughter.

"Then the chief butler to Pharaoh remembered that Joseph, the overseer at the prison, had interpreted his dream correctly and that Joseph also predicted that the baker would be beheaded which came to pass," continued Judith. "The chief butler described the man -- 'a young man, a Hebrew, a servant to the jail keeper.' Pharaoh had Joseph brought to him. He told Joseph the dreams that had left him troubled. In his dream, Pharaoh was standing by the Nile when seven well-fed cattle arose from the waters and went to feed in a meadow on the banks of the Nile. Seven lean, underfed, almost skeletal cattle arose from the water and stood on the river bank next to the well-fed cattle. And then the skeletal cattle ate the well-fed cattle."

"Such a waste," said Tamar.

She picked up three of the folded camel-hair blankets from the floor. It looked like it would just be she and Judith tonight for the full-moon ritual. Judith loved to talk. For many years, if someone would've asked Tamar, and if she had answered honestly, she would have said that Judith's talking was too much for her. But now she realized that there was something mesmerizing about it. The other women in the cult had become absorbed in their own lives and only came to the rituals intermittently. Judith, who otherwise was stuck at home with her husband and six sons, came religiously. Tamar rarely went out. She relied on Tabitha to take her goat's milk to the market to sell. The news of the outside world was welcome.

"Waste? What do you mean?" asked Judith.

"I mean it was a waste for all those cattle to eat each other. They could have produced milk and cheese. Not to mention the fact that they would have had calves. Those calves would have grown up and kept their owners in milk and cheese for generations," replied Tamar earnestly.

"I was talking about a dream -- Pharaoh's dream that

Joseph was called to interpret." Judith gave her an irritated look. "Pharaoh awoke. Then he fell back asleep and had another dream. In this dream he was in the field looking at a stalk of corn. Magically seven good ears grew on the stalk. Springing up directly after them on the same stalk, came seven sickly ears of corn. The seven sickly ears devour-ed the seven good ears."

"Whoever heard of vegetables eating vegetables? It doesn't sound right to me," said Tamar. *Pharaoh must be having delusions,* she thought.

"It was a DREAM," said Judith. "But it was disturbing. That's why Pharaoh called on Joseph. Joseph's interpretation was Pharaoh's only chance at understanding."

"So what did Joseph say?" Tamar had to admit that she was curious.

"I was just getting to that," said Judith. "The first thing that Joseph said to Pharaoh was that God was giving him the answer."

"So Joseph said that God was speaking through him?" asked Judith.

"Yes," answered Judith.

"Hmmm," said Tamar. She bit her tongue and said nothing more.

"Joseph told Pharaoh that the seven well-fed cattle represented seven years and that there would be seven years of plenty throughout the land. Seven years of famine would follow the period of seven years of plenty," continued Judith.

"That sounds right," said Tamar. She shrugged and sat down on her blanket.

"What do you mean?" asked Judith. She moved her chair back and stood up next to the wooden table. She reached over and picked up a piece of crumbling goat cheese.

"It's just common sense that seven years of plenty would be followed by seven years of famine and that each of the cattle that rose from the river and each ear of corn that grew from the stalk would represent a year. It doesn't take a genius to figure that out," said Tamar.

"This was Pharaoh's dream. It was interpreted by Joseph and GOD." Judith folded her arms across her chest. "Do you want to hear the rest or not?"

"Go ahead," said Tamar.

"Joseph told Pharaoh that he had two dreams because God was showing him that the dreams were serious and that He would bring the years of plenty and the years of famine to pass. Joseph, being diplomatic, said to Pharaoh that God had given him this dream because He knew that Pharaoh was a wise man. Pharaoh took off his ring and put it on Joseph's finger. He dressed him in the best garments and gave him a gold necklace. Then he gave him the second best chariot in all of Egypt. Pharaoh told the people to bow down to Joseph, for he was the new ruler of Egypt, second only to Pharaoh."

"A Hebrew ruling in Egypt? How long do you think that will last?" Tamar was surprised at her own vehemence.

Judith looked at Tamar sternly.

"Joseph is a great man. He is favored by God and by Pharaoh. He can do no wrong. Mark my words, he will want to be reunited with his brothers and their children. It is a shame that his nephews won't be making the journey with Judah."

Tamar felt a chill in the room though it was a warm evening. She sat cross-legged on the folded blanket. She breathed in and out. Taking another breath, she willed herself to be calm. This helped but she still felt the blood drain from her face. She stood and faced Judith.

"What do you mean, they won't be going? Pharez and Zerah are nearly grown. If Judah wants them to go with him, they will," said Tamar.

"But they are not his sons -- in fact, they are daughters, too, but not his," said Judith. She had a sly smile on her face. "Iscah told me after I plied her with wine. There was something off about the story you told us that day in the tent when the cult first found out that Tabitha was with child. Tabitha is too much of a free spirit to pick someone like Judah to father her sons. I rightly suspected that she picked him as a cover so that she wouldn't be stoned to death."

Tamar looked at Judith and said nothing. Her intuition had been right. Judith couldn't be trusted. But neither could Iscah, and she had been a close friend. This explained why lately Iscah was always busy when Tamar wanted to see her. When Tamar had been with Iscah, there had been no warning message in her mind. God must not speak to those who have had too much wine. Tamar thought through her options. She could plead with Judith not to go to Judah, to spare her life and her family. But pleading never worked. Besides, it wasn't Tamar's style. She could point out that Judith was only a woman, and Judah probably wouldn't listen to her. But this might anger Judith and she would want to prove that Tamar was wrong. Judith so identified with men that she thought she was one. But she wasn't. She was a woman who was praying for a daughter. She was a member of Tamar's Goddess cult. She practiced the old ways. If Judah knew this he would have Judith burned at the stake. Tamar could threaten to tell Judah, but what good would come of making Judith angry? Most likely she would go to Judah to prove a point, and then she and Tamar and most likely Tabitha and the twins would all be burned at the stake together.

Tamar needed more time to think. She walked over to the oil lamp. The wick had burnt down to the end. She picked up the jar of oil and set it down next to the table where the lamp sat. She bent over, picked up the jug of oil, put her finger on the wide opening of the clay lamp and poured. She rubbed her fingertips together. They were slippery with oil. The light scent of olives reached her nose. She imagined a flowering olive tree -- like the small one that she had planted in her garden. After olives had replaced the blossoms, she saw herself beating fruit from the tree with a long stick. Then she saw the olives put into sacks and then poured into a vat where they were tread on by a barefoot oil presser. She remembered that Judith had given her the olive tree last spring -- three moons ago. Tamar had almost forgotten that she suspected Iscah of revealing Tabitha's secret to Judith. But now she realized that Judith must have felt guilty for what she was planning on doing when she gave Tamar the olive tree. Tamar was genuinely sorry for the thought. When the tiny white blossoms had begun blooming, Tamar had been excited to tell Judith. She was thankful for the tree. She was thankful for Judith. She lit the wick of the oil lamp.

YOU CAN HELP JUDITH HAVE A CHANGE OF HEART. JUST LISTEN TO HER. ASK HER WHAT SHE WANTS.

Tamar was startled at the loud, clear voice in her head. It was so loud that it erased all other thoughts. She had no choice but to listen.

"What do you want?" asked Tamar.

Judith was speechless for a moment. She seemed shocked at the question. But then she regained her composure.

"When I tell Judah that you and Tabitha tricked him and the sons that he thinks are his are actually from another man's seed, he will be more likely to want my two oldest sons to go to Egypt with him to meet Joseph, his long lost brother," said Judith calmly. "He can say that my sons are his sons. Long will they prosper by their association with Judah. They will take care of me." Judith's sea green eyes were normally murky. But now they glittered like a serpent's eyes. She was speaking with forked tongue. She had been Tamar's friend -- even if Tamar had never fully trusted her. Rightfully.

A wave of anger washed over Tamar. So this was all about Judith wanting to give her sons power. She should have known. It was obvious that Judith had thought the plan through. If only there was some way to stop her. Tamar wished she could smite down anyone whose behavior she didn't care for. But she wasn't God. The anger was like a cloud of sand that blew through her, with stinging particles. Tamar closed her eyes tightly. A thought came to her.

"Have you told Bram -- or anyone else?"

"No, I haven't told my husband -- or anyone. I want to use this information to get what I want from Judah." Judith looked triumphant.

Tamar stared at Judith. She felt emotion forming on her face as her eyes narrowed in disappointment.

Judith's face crumpled.

"I'm sorry," she said, between sobs. "You have been a friend to me. It's just that... I'm scared. I'm scared and lonely. I didn't even think about going to Judah until I heard my oldest say that he'd give anything to be part of the tribe of Judah so that he could journey with them to Egypt to meet Joseph. I thought that if I could help him, he would love me for it."

Judith sobbed until her eyes were red. Her voice came out in gasps.

"I don't know what is going to become of me in my old age. Bram has an eye for each new servant that we have -- and not just the maid servants."

As Tamar listened to Judith, the anger in her heart passed. She wasn't God. She couldn't smite down Judith even if she wanted to. And she didn't want to. The voice in her head had said that she could help Judith have a change of heart. Tamar knew that meant she would have to have a change of heart, first.

Something inside of her shifted.

"You've been part of the goddess cult for a long time -- close to two decades now," said Tamar. She was still standing across from Judith. "You've come to me for help to conceive a daughter."

"I wore your amulet, but it didn't work. My child bearing years have almost passed. But at least there is still time to help my sons," stated Judith.

"The amulet didn't work," said Tamar carefully, "because in your mind you still think sons are more important than daughters. You have to realize that you are a worthwhile person -- as a woman -- without your husband and sons."

"But I am almost past my bleeding time," lamented Judith. "Why didn't you tell me earlier?"

"I didn't tell you earlier, because I didn't want to offend you," said Tamar. "And I was afraid because I didn't fully trust you. But now that you have revealed your plans to betray me, I can trust you. Finally, you have been honest. You are ready to hear what I have to say."

"But now it is too late." Judith's eyes were wet.

"It is not too late." Tamar reached up and took Judith's hand. "You can still conceive a daughter."

"How?" said Judith. "I will do anything."

"First, you have to examine your mind. You must also look closely at your actions. You have to stop talking about your husband and sons. You have to take off the silver necklaces." Tamar saw the look of horror on Judith's face.

"But who am I without my husbands and sons? They are everything to me -- even though my husband barely looks at me, and my sons never listen to me."

Tamar nodded. Judith didn't have to tell her this. She already knew. A feeling of deep calm settled into her. She opened her mouth and uttered words she had never heard: *"You are yourself; you are the first and the last; you are the honored one and the scorned one; you are the whore and the holy one; you are the wife and the virgin; you are the mother and the daughter; you are the barren one; and many are your sons; you are the silence that is incomprehensible; you are the utterance of your name."*

Deep within her, she knew these words to be true. Tamar didn't know where she had heard these words before or where they had come from. Still, they echoed through her as truth. Judith was all of these things and more. Tamar liked the sound of these words. She would have to remember to write them down later.

Judith looked at Tamar and nodded. Tamar looked at the light in Judith's eyes -- and saw her beauty. There was not much light in the tent -- only from the one oil lamp and the desert sunset that filtered through the opening above the pole in the center. But Judith's eyes caught all the light and cast it back. Her long dark hair shone. Her oval face held the luster of dark olives. Tamar knew that the things that were undefined were larger than Judith's existence as a wife and mother. Judith was ready to know her own greatness.

All Judith had to do to fly was to let go of the past and to let Tamar's words enter her. But she wasn't ready -- yet.

"The necklaces are all I have to show my accomplishments."

"Just put them away for a while. You can always put them back on later," answered Tamar. "Each day, in the morning, sit and breathe until the sun is higher in the sky. Let go of the outside voices that say you are less than. These voices might come from your husband or from your sons. They might be the voices of the women in the marketplace. They might be everything that was told to you since you were a girl. They might seem to be all that it is in your mind. But you have your own inner voice deeper inside of you. And that voice will free you."

"Okay," said Judith. "How do I start?"

Tamar smiled serenely.

"Sit down with me," she said. Tamar sat down cross legged on one of the folded camel hair blankets.

"Remember several years ago, when Leah brought the scroll that had been passed onto her and we sat and watched our breath and listened to the sound of 'OM?'"

Judith nodded. "Yes I do remember. We started every ritual after that with watching our breath and making the sound," said Judith.

"Yes," answered Tamar. "And remember Leah and I said that it was good to start every day with a practice of quietness -- of watching our breath go in and out until the thoughts in our own minds go away and we are emptied. This way we are making a space for your own voice."

"I remember that you and Leah suggested that we do this at home in our own tents. But I had too much to do to practice. Besides, my husband and sons would wonder what I am doing."

"We can do it right now," said Tamar.

"Wait a minute. Tell me about the scroll that we learned 'Om' from. Where did it come from?"

Tamar looked at Judith. Tamar reminded herself that she could trust Judith now that she had revealed her plot and her motivations. The question seemed innocent enough.

"The teachings of the scroll are not outlawed," said Tamar. The voice in her head said, *Yet.*

This was true, but Tamar was wise enough to be protective of the scroll. "But no one knows of its existence. And because it does not acknowledge the one God, it will surely be destroyed if anyone finds out about it. You really want to have a daughter, right?"

"More than anything."

"First, you must promise not to tell anyone about the scroll -- not your husband and not Jacob and Samuel at the village well. Not anyone."

"I promise," replied Judith without hesitation.

"Leah had a friend of a friend who had gone to India and he brought back the scroll in a clay jar that her friend bought and gave to her. The man who had travelled to India was trading in scents and perfumes and creams. He sells his wares to the Nabataeans, the desert nomads in North Arabia."

"I've heard of the Nabataeans," said Judith. "They worship many gods, not the one God. My husbands and sons say that they are bad and to stay away from them when they sell their scents at the market."

"Do you always do what your husband and sons say?"

"I say that I do," admitted Judith. She sat down on a folded blanket and faced Tamar. "But I bought some jars of Egyptian water lily scented cream from the Nabataeans at the market. I use it on myself after I bathe. It really does soften my skin. The scent is delicate and fragrant. I keep the jar hidden. Bram doesn't notice the smell and neither do my sons."

"See. You know how to keep something to yourself when it suits you."

Judith nodded. "Yes, I can keep a secret."

"Then you must keep the secret of the scroll. It will be practice for keeping your own secrets. Do not tell anyone that you want to conceive a daughter," said Tamar.

"I know that," said Judith. "I learned when I was a girl not to say I wanted a daughter. Mother taught me that women only pray for sons, and those who pray for daughters never get what they want."

"That is what we are taught," said Tamar. "But all prayer doesn't have to be that way. This scroll talks about a religion that worships the feminine. By sitting quietly and noticing our breath, by feeling our oneness and saying the first sound of creation, 'OM,' we can remove all obstacles, because they begin in the mind."

"But is feeling our oneness the same as worshipping the one God?" asked Judith.

"I think it is the same, but others may not agree," said Tamar. She knew that if Judith felt bad about betraying the one God, she would have a hard time removing the obstacles that blocked the conception of a daughter. But Tamar was also telling Judith what she knew in her heart to be true.

Judith nodded.

"Remember," said Tamar, "to pray not only for yourself. Yes, you want a daughter more than anything, but you want to give birth to a daughter who will help others as well. You want a daughter who will make the land better when she walks upon it. You want a daughter because she will bring happiness, joy and peace to all who look upon her.

"I hadn't thought of that," said Judith. "But you are right. My daughter will bring contentment to others. She will make our land a better place."

"That's right," whispered Judith.

The two women faced each other and breathed deeply.

"We'll start with the first sound of creation, 'OM,' the first sound of creation that came out of the great void, that embraces all that exists and that has no beginning and no ending, the name of God."

"But is He our God?" asked Judith. "Our one God?"

Tamar shrugged. "Some would say so. Others would say not. Still others would say that this God is not a He or a She. This God is a vibration, the sound of the brightest stars as they shoot across the desert night sky, the shifting of the grains of sand that make up the endless expanse of the desert and the song of the wind as it sculpts sand.

"I see. This is the same as the one God, but different. *'Om'* is the sound of creation -- Yet the one God is said to have made everything. I remember the words that my mother passed down to me. They are the same words that I repeated to my sons: *In the beginning God created the heaven and the earth. And the earth was without form, and void; and darkness was upon the face of the deep. And the Spirit of God moved upon the face of the waters. And God said, Let there be light: and there was light. And God saw the light, that it was good: and God divided the light from the darkness. And God called the light Day, and the darkness he called Night. And the evening and the morning were the first day. And God said, Let there be a firmament in the midst of the waters, and let it divide the waters from the waters. And God made the firmament, and divided the waters which were under the firmament from the waters which were above the firmament: and it was so. And God called the firmament Heaven."*

Tamar blinked away wetness. "I remember Great Grandmother reciting these same words to Tabitha and I when we were children. The words lulled me to sleep then. Even now, I am moved. But many of the stories that Great Grandmother told us were disturbing -- like the story about God banishing Adam and Eve from the Garden of Eden because Eve listened to the serpent and ate the forbidden fruit and then convinced her husband to have some."

"As if serpents could talk!" Judith laughed abruptly.

Tamar looked perplexed. She had never questioned the talking serpent. But she let the thought go, nodded, and spoke: "Some of the stories are outlandish. And I hope they're not all true -- like the story about Lot after his wife was turned to a pillar of salt and he went to the desert with his two daughters. Since there were no other men, his daughters lay with him so that they could populate the new nations of Moab and Ammon."

"Yes. The story of God burning down the cities of Sodom and Gomorrah but then letting Lot lay with his daughters always troubled me," responded Judith.

"Perhaps I shouldn't have been surprised when I prayed to the one God for a daughter, and he gave me sons," said Judith. "Now that I have been praying for a daughter night and day, I have not conceived. Although I haven't laid with Bram in years. He says there is no reason since we already have six sons. To tell you the truth, I do not miss lying with him."

"Hmmm," replied Tamar. "It does not matter if you lie with Bram or not. If fact, it is better not to do the same old things. Conception starts in your mind -- and then your womb."

Judith nodded. "I am beginning to understand."

"You are right. The god of 'Om' and the one God are different but the same," said Tamar.

"But I prayed to the one God and only conceived sons," said Judith.

"Then it is okay to pray differently," replied Tamar, shifting on her blanket.

"That makes sense," said Judith. Her long dark lashes brushed her face as she closed her eyes.

"We will start with three 'Oms,'" said Tamar. "The first sound of creation."

"Om," said Judith.

"Om," echoed Tamar.

"Ommmm," they both said.

Together their incantation was larger than it would have been if they had been chanting by themselves. Tamar breathed in and out. She pictured a golden light around Judith. It pulsed.

"Just remember that you are made from light. The same light and water that makes the hyssop in the desert grow. Your daughter, too, will be created from light."

Judith nodded.

Both of them breathed in and out. Sometimes they chanted, and other times they were silent. After a time, Tamar felt her vision penetrate Judith's mind. Judith's mind was ablaze with white light. There was a child there.

The child was holy, and she was female. Wise men would bow down to her. Tamar wanted Judith to bear this child. She knew that now. She put her intention in Judith's mind and then lower, in Judith's womb. She saw the embryo of a daughter forming in a blaze of light.

Just then the flame from the oil lamp went out. There had been enough oil in the lamp for several hours. It didn't seem like that much time had passed.

Tamar sat in the darkness with Judith. She heard the sound of Judith's breath. She heard Aziz snoring in the corner. His snore was starting to sound like a wheeze. He was getting old and would die soon. Tamar was terrified of Aziz dying. But suddenly the answer came to her. She would get a baby dromedary -- a calf that was old enough to leave her mother. The calf would come and live with her and Aziz in the tent. Aziz would teach the calf his ways. Tamar smiled in the darkness. She welcomed the pitter patter of little feet.

Chapter Nine

"I'm looking for a baby dromedary." Tamar's veil muffled her voice. She was talking to the camel cheese maker at the open market, at the gates of the nearby village.

"FRESH GOAT TO SLAUGHTER FOR SUPPER OR FOR A SACRIFICE TO OUR LORD," shouted the man in the stall behind Tamar.

Tamar leaned forward so that she could hear the soft spoken camel cheese maker.

"A what?"

"A dromedary," said Tamar repeating herself. She moved her veil but the goat seller still drowned her out.

"I don't know what you're talking about." The cheese seller looked past Tamar at the people passing by. A woman in a brown and white striped robe stopped and exchanged several coins for a block of camel cheese.

The cheese maker put her cheese in a sack, smiled at the customer and said, "It's good to see you again."

When the woman left, the cheese maker turned to Tamar. "Did you lose something?"

"A camel. A baby camel. I need to buy a baby camel. Can you help me?"

"Oh. Now I understand. You are looking to buy a camel calf. That'll cost you. Camels are with calves for more than a year. Usually, they only have one calf when they give birth."

Tamar looked at the camel cheese maker expectantly.

"Fifty shekels," said the camel cheese maker.

"Fifty shekels!? That seems like too much. I'm not asking to buy a parcel of land. Just a baby camel -- to provide me with transportation and companionship in my old age. I've had my camel, Aziz, since he was a calf. Now he is getting old. His knees are knobby. They creak when he stands. I want to bring home a baby camel while he is still living so that he can pass on his gentle nature."

The cheese maker looked at Tamar and nodded. She was small and stooped. She wore a black and white striped robe. A sharp nose peeked out of her hood. She peered at Tamar with inquisitive brown eyes. Her skin was smooth but Tamar could foresee that it would someday be brown and crinkled like the skin of an almond.

"I know what you mean," she said. "I prefer life with the camels also. They're wonderful companions. Much better than most humans," she said, lowering her voice. She jerked her head toward the goat seller. "I'm a widow, too," she said.

"Me, too," answered Tamar. Then she realized that the camel cheese maker would know this by her black veil.

The camel cheese maker's husband must have died a few years ago, since she no longer wore the veil. She looked like she was about ten years or so younger than Tamar.

"The town meeting is starting in fifteen minutes," shouted a man several tables behind the cheese maker.

"Men and boys only. We are going to discuss important issues." His gloating voice faded away.

The cheese maker raised her eyebrows dismissively.

Then she looked at Tamar keenly. Her eyes radiated brown prisms of light.

"I have an idea," she said. "How much do you have?"

"I have twenty-five shekels," blurted out Tamar. She knew that by the laws of haggling, she should have started lower, but she was honest by nature. She had been saving for some time now. She brought almost everything that she had managed to put by in a clay jar that she kept behind the oil jars. She received some money from her cult members. It wasn't that much but Tabitha gave her what extra she managed to get from Judah. Then there was the sale of her goat cheese made from the milk of Ezzie's kids Yael and Yaffa.

"I can tell you don't get out much," said the cheese maker. "You have honest eyes -- even if the rest of your face is hidden by the veil. I believe you."

"I am honest," said Tamar. "It is true that I don't get out as often as I should."

"Yes," said the cheese maker. "You have that look about you. I like that your camel is your companion. I have a proposition for you. I need someone to make camel cheese for me. I can only make so much, and my business is growing. I could show you the ropes. This could make up for the fact that you only have twenty-five shekels."

"That sounds good," said Tamar, thoughtfully. "I already make cheese from the goat milk of Ezzie's kids, Yael and Yaffa -- so I will be a fast learner."

The cheese maker smiled. "I name my animals, too. We are destined to be friends. My name is Naomi."

"I'm Tamar," she said and bowed slightly.

Naomi smiled. "I will need you to make cheese for me for two years. I have a calf for you but she is only eight months old and will not be able to leave her mother for another three months. You and Aziz can come to visit."

Tamar extended her hand over the table between them that was covered with off-white squares of camel cheese.

"It's a deal," said Tamar.

They shook on it.

The next evening, Tamar's tent flap opened, revealing a triangle of soft light.

"Hello there," said Tamar.

"Hello," said a low voice.

Tamar was expecting Judith and the voice did sound like hers -- except that it was low and hesitant. Shy?

Judith entered the tent. She pushed back the hood of her dark robe. Shiny dark hair spilled out.

Tamar had set the table with her best pottery. Juicy red pomegranate seeds glistened in a small round bowl. In another, black orbs of oil cured olives shimmered. Chunks of white goat cheese sat on a small terracotta plate next to a bowl of fresh figs. Next to that was a small bowl of almonds. Purple spikes of hyssop extended from a clay vase.

Tamar had put Aziz outside for the evening, and she had swept the tent with brooms of hyssop. She had bathed earlier that day. Then she had oiled her skin. She even oiled the inside of her mouth. After she had spit out the mouthful of olive oil, she could feel her tongue slippery against her teeth. Shortly before Judith came, Tamar had lit the oil lamp but set it back further in the tent -- instead of on the table -- so the light was dimmed. A goatskin of wine peeked out from behind the vase.

Judith's eyes flickered toward the table. Her gaze returned to Tamar.

"How beautiful," she said.

Judith had been coming to her several times a week for two moons now -- since they started meditating together. She never wore her silver necklaces. Even tonight when they were meeting for pleasure, she didn't have them on. She rarely mentioned her husband and sons. Tamar had told her that even to complain about them was to give them power. Judith hadn't conceived yet, but she was ready. She had been coming to Tamar's tent several times a week. She had told Tamar that every morning she set aside time to sit quietly and watch her breath. Judith said the old voices were leaving her -- making room for the new.

Tamar had conquered the old Judith with love. She had assisted at the birth of the new Judith. This Judith was even more beautiful. Her long dark hair glistened like it was surrounded by shooting stars. Her sea green eyes looked like an oasis in the parched desert. They were deeper and darker than ever. Judith's eyes were shaped like almonds. They were wide in the middle and narrow on the ends. They slanted up slightly at the outside edges. Lines of smudged kohl rimmed Judith's eyes. The low light reflected from the single strand of gold around her neck. For a flickering moment, she looked like an Egyptian princess from ancient times, a dark eyed seductress painted onto a frieze. Tamar had never seen

Judith wearing kohl before. Gold powder dusted her cheeks. Tamar inhaled the dusty sweet musk of spikenard and saffron.

Tamar watched as Judith took off her outside brown robe and draped it over a chair. Underneath, her linen robe was as white as snow. It was diaphanous. Tamar could see the outline of Judith's breasts, ripe as pomegranates. Judith's erect nipples rose and fell. Tamar could tell that the daily meditation was working. Judith was breathing more deeply.

"It appears you are staring at my breasts." Judith's voice tinkled like the tiny cymbals attached to the sides of timbrels.

Tamar felt her face flushing. "I didn't mean to," she whispered. She was thankful for the oil that she had swished around her mouth. Her words came out smoothly.

"I don't mind, really," said Judith. "It's a compliment. Bram never -- " She stopped herself.

Tamar said nothing.

"Thank you." Judith lowered her thick lashes.

"Let's eat," said Tamar. "I prepared a small supper for us."

"Your table is beautiful," murmured Judith. "I brought some cakes of oiled bread and a goatskin of wine."

She leaned over to the chair where her robe was draped, pulled a satchel from the pocket and put it on the table.

It was Tamar's turn to laugh.

"I have a goatskin of wine for us, also," she admitted.

"Let's have a toast then," said Judith.

She pulled out another sack from the folds of her robe on the chair and produced two long-stemmed silver goblets.

They had identical wide mouths and indented gold lines circling the top. About an inch below the rim, thin gold lines looped in semi-circles like a ring of half moons.

"They are beautiful," exclaimed Tamar. "Where did they come from?"

"They were a wedding gift from Bram's father," said Judith. "We only used them once and then put them away. They will never be missed."

Tamar looked at Judith and nodded. For a moment, she felt the difference between the way that she and Judith lived. It was likely that Judith had many beautiful things. Tamar suspected that she and her husband never used or appreciated most of them. Tamar knew that she should feel envious. Women were taught to be competitive over which one had the richer husband or most valorous son. But Tamar never felt that way -- even when she was chosen by Judah to be married to his first son, Er. Judah was a rich man. Tamar knew that she should have been honored to be given to Er. But he treated her so badly that she was glad when the one God smote him down. In fact, she had prayed for it. But she wasn't sure that God had really smote him down -- or that her prayers had anything to do with it.

Er loved his meat -- freshly slaughtered goat, grisly venison, and fatted calf, even when it was supposed to be used for a sacrifice to the one God. Judith wondered if he died from overindulgence. Either way, she was glad that he was gone. And when Judah sent his second son, Onan, and he was struck down by the one God for spilling his seed, she was again glad. She knew that the townspeople considered her barren, so she never told anyone she was happy. When her scheme to trick Judah had succeeded, Tamar was relieved. She could live her anonymous life in the desert, content to share her tent with Aziz. Tabitha could pretend to be the mother of Judah's sons.

Tamar knew that the life of a wife to a wealthy man and a mother, even with many sons, looked better than it actually was. She didn't envy Judith's life. She had forgiven Judith for her plot to betray Tamar and Tabitha and the twins. Judith had just been doing what women did to get a little power through their husbands and sons. She thought she would gain power by being manipulative and conniving. But Judith had been honest and she had told Tamar her plans. To Tamar, this meant that Judith thought she could betray her, but her heart wouldn't let her do it. In forgiving Judith, Tamar came to understand that she loved her.

Again, Judith suggested that they have a toast.

"The goblets are beautiful," said Tamar. "And the wine is here to be drunk."

Then she filled their goblets. They held them aloft and clinked them against each other.

"To us."

"To us."

It didn't matter which one spoke. The feeling was the same. Their eyes met over the rims of the wedding goblets. They put the goblets down.

They sat on the floor next to the low table on the double camel hair blankets that Tamar had folded.

"Let me feed you," said Judith. She picked up an olive, held it between her fingers. Then she broke off a piece of the oiled bread. She reached out and fed it to Tamar.

Tamar felt Judith's cool fingers on her lips.

When she was done, Tamar fed Judith.

They saved the fresh figs for last.

"For my sweetness," said Tamar. She felt Judith's warm lips on her fingers.

Then Judith put some pomegranate seeds in Tamar's mouth.

Tamar began sucking on Judith's fingers. She was emboldened by the wine. They had been taking sips from their goblets and refilling them. They were on their second goatskin.

Judith pushed the bowl of figs away.

"I've had enough food," she said. She leaned in toward Tamar. "But I could never have enough of you."

Their lips met and it was good. This was the first time that Tamar had kissed someone -- with the exception of the kisses that she sometimes gave to Aziz on his furry forehead or the kisses that she had given to Pharez and Zerah when they were small. This kiss was born from passion and tenderness. Er had been incapable of both.

Tamar was consumed by moisture. They were both made of water and light -- like wild hyssop plants flowering in the arid desert. A brilliant sash of longing encircled them.

Tamar's lips parted. Judith's tongue slipped in. Tamar's nipples tingled. Her vulva opened.

"I've never felt this way," Judith whispered. She opened her robe. In the dim light, her nakedness gleamed.

Tamar's breath caught in her throat. She dropped her own robe and took Judith's hand, leading her to the softness of the bed that she had made for them.

She and Judith put their arms around each other. Tamar felt the silken smoothness that their bodies made together.

She was not ashamed of her nakedness.

Chapter Ten

Three moons had passed since Tamar had met Naomi in the marketplace. Tamar had learned quickly how to make the camel cheese. Naomi told Tamar that her son was planning on borrowing the calf's mother to make a journey. It was time to introduce Aziz to the calf.

Aziz was too old and frail to be ridden. Tamar walked beside him for the several miles to Naomi's. When they arrived, Aziz stood outside of Naomi's tent. He waited for his bucket of water that Tamar always gave him after a journey. After she set the bucket down, Aziz put his long nose into it and made loud lapping sounds. When he was done, Tamar patted his nose and told him that he was going to meet a new friend. Then she took his lead and walked him around the other side of the tent to where the calf was standing. Aziz bent down his long neck. He put his large face with his white beard hanging down next to her small beardless face. The short golden fur on her neck crinkled. Their long noses touched. Aziz pulled back his lips and smiled. He crouched on all fours and settled in the sand. The little camel sat next to him. She sat on her haunches just like Aziz and, in that moment, she looked like him. Tamar decided that she would name the calf Azizi.

After Tamar and Aziz returned home, she started every day by scratching Aziz's worn but still velvety ears and telling him that soon, very soon, his little friend Azizi was going to come and live with them. Tamar worried about Aziz. It took him a long time to stand. He wheezed and wobbled. But Tamar's heart warmed when she thought of Azizi coming to live with them.

Shortly after her trip to Naomi's, Tamar stood outside of her own tent. The white disc of the morning sun scorched sky. The desert shimmered. Tamar shook a coarse camel hair blanket. She was cleaning her tent in preparation for Azizi who would be arriving later that day. Nearly three moons had passed since she had lain with Judith. Judith never returned. Tamar missed her but had come to realize that she liked her own company best.

She shook out the blanket and hummed.

She finished shaking the blanket, folded it and placed it in the dark brown wooden basket sitting on the sand. Basket in hand, she ducked back into the tent. She put the folded blanket on the table. She rummaged in a pile of her belongings near the tent flap until she found a balled up blanket. Carefully, she pulled it out of the pile. Then she put it in the basket. The pile teetered. One of these days, she would sort through it.

She stepped outside. She held out her arms to shake the blanket when a small movement in the distance caught her eye. A stick figure was coming toward her. She wasn't expecting company. She held her hand up to shade her eyes.

A liquid mirage shimmered like a long pool of water in the distance. *Maybe the sun is playing tricks on me*, she thought. When she shook the blanket, it floated in front of her. Its dark weave fluttered against the white sand of the desert. She shook it again. Then she folded it and placed it into the basket.

She looked up. The mirage was gone. But someone riding a camel was headed in her direction. Tamar sometimes saw people passing through the desert. A few times she had seen long trains of camels crossing the desert. But the camels had never approached her directly. Her black goatskin tent was old and faded, but it was still visible against the white sand. Behind her main tent, Tamar had built a garden. The olive tree that Judith had given her seven years ago had been flowering and had just begun to bear fruit. Some of the olives had fallen into the soil that Tamar had brought in buckets from the patch of dirt near the well. Tamar had almost forgotten about them. But young olive trees had taken. Next to them, she had planted some artichoke plants that sprouted jagged leaves. One of the women in her circle said that the plants would spread. Tamar planted feathery dill at a six foot circumference around the baby artichoke plants.

The plants came back every growing season. She watered every other day with buckets of well water. Early in the growing season, she planted fava beans. Their wide flat leaves twined along strands of wool stretched between two poles. Tamar had put up a smaller tent behind her garden, and stretched a goatskin wall on both sides. The garden was hidden from sight to ward off robbers. But the goatskin that walled the garden and connected to the smaller tent behind her main tent, made her living quarters more visible.

The stick figure was coming closer. Tamar could see that it was a camel with a rider sitting up high. She couldn't tell if the rider was a man or a woman. The camel was coming straight toward her. Tamar stared into the distance. Then she bent over and picked up her basket. She moved slowly, not wanting to attract attention. Her legs trembled.

It could be anyone. She hoped it was one of the women who travelled to her for goddess lore. Maybe it was one of the old women from the province of Arzawa. Tamar remembered with a pang that most of the old women had died by now. Tamar didn't expect to see Judith again. Tamar missed Judith, but she realized that Judith must have felt guilty after their evening of pleasure and was trying to make things right with her husband. Tamar and Judith would be stoned to death if the villagers suspected what they did together. For years now, Tamar had counted on the fact that Judah was too much of an important man to come to the desert to see who lived in the black tent now that the woman he thought was Tamar (Tabitha) lived in a tent in his compound. If he discovered that Tamar and Tabitha had tricked him they could still be stoned or burned at the stake. Once, Tabitha had asked Tamar which she would prefer. Stoning or burning? Tabitha was joking, but Tamar had shuddered.

Tamar went back into her tent to get a veil. She hesitated for a moment. Should she wear her widow's veil? Or should she wear her brown veil? She decided on the brown one. If she was wearing her widow's veil, it would look like she was out here alone in the desert. The brown one would shield her face. If it was Judah who was approaching, he wouldn't be able to tell who she was. She put on the veil, brought a few clay pots with her, and went back outside. Maybe the passerby was just lost. There was no point in taking chances. Tamar brought a few clay pots outside with her. She started to rinse them out with a bucket of water from the well. They were just dusty so they didn't need to be scrubbed. She rinsed the pots and kept her eyes on the horizon. The figure was close enough that she could make out that the rider was wearing a black and white striped robe. First, Tamar saw the brown veil draped across the rider's face. Then she saw something bouncing up and down with the camel's steps. The rider had breasts – and over them, silver necklaces, glinting in the sun, rose and fell.

Tamar held a clay pot on its side and washed out the inside even though it was already clean. She placed it in the sun to dry.

The visitor came closer and stopped. The camel knelt down and the visitor disembarked and stood in front of Tamar.

"Tamar," said a husky, familiar voice. "It is me."

Tamar was silent.

The rider took off her veil and revealed herself.

"Are you glad to see me?"

"I thought I'd never see you again," said Tamar. She held her wet rag to the inside of a clay pot, swirled it around and set the pot in the sun.

"I needed some time to myself," said Judith. "And in that time I realized that things were different.I am different."

She reached down and put her hands on her stomach. There was a slight bulge. "For one thing, I am with child."

"Are you sure?"

"It has been more than three moons since I last bled," said Judith. "Plus I feel different. For one thing, I don't have the sickness that I suffered the last six times. A child is stirring in me, and I am sure it is a girl. And there has been no one else but you."

Tamar stared at Judith. *Rubbish, she must of laid with someone -- probably Bram,* she thought. She didn't believe her. But happiness bubbled up in her and spilled over. Tamar was happy for Judith. She had helped Judith create a daughter -- even if she had just paved the way by teaching Judith to silence the old voices in her mind and how to value herself as a woman.

"I see you are again wearing the silver necklaces that Bram gave you," said Tamar.

Judith nodded. "I figured that it didn't matter anymore -- since I am with child. I am certain that it must be a daughter. And since I always liked the necklaces..."

While Judith was busy making excuses, Tamar remembered the words of one of the old woman from the province of Arzawa who told her that in the ancient days women gave birth to daughters without the intervention of men. The old women told her that many of the goddesses were born this way. Suddenly, Tamar felt as proud as a father announcing the birth of a son.

So, it is true, thought Tamar. But outwardly, she bristled. She was proud but, at the same time, she could not believe it.

"Are you sure you did not lay with Bram?" she asked.

"I am sure," replied Judith. "I would've sent word, but if Bram finds out that I am with child, he will be angry. You know how men are. He will assume that I was unfaithful and lay with another man. And you know what happens to wives who commit adultery."

Tamar nodded gravely.

"I have decided that I love you and want to live with you. I brought some of my belongings, enough for a few nights, in these baskets behind me. I can send for the rest. Bram is off on a journey to settle new lands. He probably won't even notice that I am gone when he comes back."

Tamar looked at the baskets. They were wide and deep. They looked full. Judith needed this much stuff for a few nights? How many more baskets would she send for? Tamar considered the fact that Bram was a powerful man. He would come for his wife, or send someone. He would find out that she was with child. He would have them both burned at the stake.

"Wait a minute," said Tamar, holding up her hand. "You belong with Bram. You created six sons together. "

"But I want to be with you. Your people are my people. I will lodge with you, and be with you always."

Tamar was silent. It was true that she had missed Judith these past three moons. But she felt strongly that Judith had to make amends with Bram. Tamar had been heartbroken, but now she bristled. How could Judith say, "Your people are my people," when not that long ago, she had planned to betray Tamar, Tabitha and the twins? *I love her but do not trust her,* thought Tamar.

But she knew Judith well enough to know that it had to be Judith's idea to go back to Bram. Otherwise, she would come to resent Tamar for rejecting her.

"Okay," said Tamar. "But I have to leave soon to pick up Azizi, the baby camel who is coming to live with us," she said.

Judith raised her eyebrows.

"Okay?!" Judith stared at Tamar incredulously. "I tell you that I love you and want to stay with you always so that we can raise our daughter together and your response is 'okay'!!??"

"I love you too," said Tamar. "I've missed you these past three moons, but I thought I'd never hear from you again. It is natural for me to protect myself," she said.

And you could change your mind again, Tamar thought.

"Oh. I hadn't thought of that," said Judith, contritely. "I'm sorry."

Tamar nodded.

"Let me show you where you can put your things. I have the perfect place." Tamar turned around and walked toward the garden between the tents.

"The olive tree that I gave you really grew," exclaimed Judith. "And look at the little ones."

Tamar unhooked the goatskin wall so that she could enter the garden. She beckoned for Judith to follow.

Judith stepped into the garden, bent down and took the dark green leaves gently into her hand.

"Someday, we will live next to an olive grove. The olives will be so plentiful that they will make us rich."

"I have no need to be rich," said Tamar. "I have enough

-- between the goat cheese from Yael and Yaffa -- and what I grow in my garden."

Ezzie bleated from where she was penned on the other side of the garden.

Judith started. "I almost forgot about the goats," she said. She scrunched up her nose.

Tamar smiled serenely. "Ezzie and Yael and Yaffa are my family. They are my people," she said.

Judith gave her an odd look.

"I am making camel cheese for Naomi at the market," continued Tamar. "In a few growing seasons, little Azizi will be ready to calve and will be making milk. Then I can make my own camel cheese."

Judith laughed. "Camel cheese? You can't be serious. Maybe for a while until we become rich from the sale of the olives. Then we will eat fresh goat every night. And, of course, we will wash it down with the finest wine." Judith gave Tamar a loving look as if willing her to remember what happened the last time they shared wine.

Tamar saw the look, but did not return it.

"I prefer cheese to meat," she responded. "And I would NEVER eat Ezzie or Yael and Yaffa!!"

"I didn't say we would eat Ezzie. She would probably be too tough. She has outlived her years of making milk and should be put out to pasture. We will buy goats at the market -- goats who don't have names."

"YET." Tamar glared at Judith.

"Yet?"

"I name all of my animals," responded Tamar. "I have no intention of putting Ezzie out to pasture. She has helped me live by giving me her milk and her kids. When she becomes old and frail, I will care for her," said Tamar.

She leveled her gaze at Judith.

"I have never believed that old story about the one God giving man dominion over livestock and wild animals. Animals are just as intelligent as us, if not more," said Tamar adamantly. "Besides, we are not men, we are women. The one God gave man dominion over us as well. Therefore, we have many things in common with the animals."

"I didn't know you were so opposed to eating meat," replied Judith.

"Did you ever see meat on my table in all of the time that you have come to my tent?"

"No. But I thought that was because you were poor. I thought you couldn't afford fresh goat meat."

Tamar bristled, but she thought before she spoke. What Judith said was true. Tamar could not afford fresh goat meat. She had eaten it routinely the few years that she was with Er. Her late husband had never made much money, but he was Judah's son. Judah was a wealthy man. He made sure his sons would not go wanting. Tamar was so happy that God smote down Er that she was content to eat only vegetables and a little cheese. About six moons after she had stopped eating goat meat, she tried it again and found that she disliked it.

Tamar had an epiphany.

She liked her life the way it was. She loved the twins and never resented the fact that she had spent so much time taking care of them when they were small. She knew that Tabitha had her hands full with them, even though Judah had given her Milcah to help. But she was grateful when they had grown to the age when they were more concerned with their own interests. She had missed them a little at first, but found she did more gardening and spent more time with Aziz and Ezzie. Now Azizi was coming to live with her. She knew that she wasn't going to change -- not for Judith, not even for the baby they might have created together.

Tamar stared at Judith.

Judith stared back.

"Okay. We'll eat cheese," replied Judith finally.

Tamar smiled. "Let me show you where to store your baskets."

She walked past the garden, to the flap of the small tent behind them. She bent and opened the flap. "You go first," she said, holding the flap for Judith.

Judith poked her head in and then she pulled back. She faced Tamar and spoke:

"There's already too much stuff in there. Though I imagine we could sweep it out. It looks like debris. Besides, I'll need my belongings with me. We can put them in the main tent."

"Debris? You mean my clay pots? They may be cracked, but I've been saving them because I might need them someday. I've been wanting to make a walkway in the garden. Also, I might be able to fix some of them and use them again."

Tamar didn't know why she had started saving the clay pots. She had just started piling them up. At first she was comforted by the thought that anyone who came to rob her would never be able to sort through the cracked pots to find her true valuables. But recently she had started to worry that someone might come and steal the cracked pots. They were valuable, even if she couldn't fix them. They would make a nice terracotta path someday.

Judith looked at Tamar strangely.

"Besides, there won't be that much room in the main tent after Azizi comes," said Tamar.

"What does that have to do with anything?"

"Aziz sleeps in the tent with me. And so will Azizi. The point of bringing her here to live with us is so she can bond with Aziz and me. She will learn from him," said Tamar.

"But during the cult meetings, Aziz was always outside the tent. I assumed that's where the camel slept."

"I just put Aziz outside before everyone came, because I never knew when Serah was going to bring one of her serpents. Aziz was always spooked by snakes in the desert. But all the other nights, he slept in the tent with me. It is safer in there. There are all kinds of wild beasts in the desert. They could hurt Aziz and, now, Azizi." As Tamar spoke, she could hear passion trembling in her voice. She meant what she said. She would not have Aziz and Azizi sleeping outside the tent.

Judith's eyes narrowed as she stared at Tamar.

"I see," she said. "I was willing to eat cheese for you, but I will NOT sleep in the same tent with a camel. That goes double for two of them."

Tamar was about to explain that Aziz wasn't really a camel. He had one hump and he was a dromedary -- even if no one else knew what she was talking about. Azizi had two humps so she really was a baby camel. But Tamar had Judith where she wanted her. She didn't want to distract her. Tamar looked down at the sand and said nothing.

"That's my final offer," said Judith. "It's either me or the camels in your tent."

Tamar continued to look down. The leather thong of her sandal was wearing thin. She made a mental note to replace it before it broke.

"You give me no choice," said Judith. "I will return to my husband and sons."

"You are a rich woman," said Tamar, raising her face and looking at Judith. "You would tire of living here with me -- even without having the camels in the tent, which isn't going to happen. I have a plan to make Bram think that the child is his."

Tamar looked at Judith sadly. She really did love her.

"What is your plan?" Judith fingered her necklaces.

Tamar noticed that Judith didn't object to the fact that Tamar said she was a rich woman and wouldn't be happy living with her. She was disappointed for a moment. But she took comfort in the fact that she was right.

"You must cook Bram a good dinner -- something that he likes. Maybe, a roasted goat." Tamar suppressed a shudder. "Then give him wine, so much that he falls asleep. But do not drink any yourself. You need to keep your wits about you. The next morning when he wakes, act loving. Tell him that he was a wonderful lover, kind and giving."

"Flattery is a good idea. He is a man," said Judith. "And I have never before had reason to tell him that he was kind and giving. But I am nearly three moons gone. What am I going to say when the baby comes early?"

"I know a midwife," said Tamar. "She'll grant me a favor." *She'll be especially interested in the fact that Tamar and Judith might have created this child together*, thought Tamar.

Judith nodded. "I trust that your advice is sound and that this is for the best."

"Friends?" Judith held out her hand.

"Friends," said Tamar clasping Judith's hand.

"And don't forget. You are not in this alone. I really do love you. And I will help you raise our ... I mean your daughter. Together, we will teach Her the old ways." In Tamar's mind, the baby was already a goddess.

Chapter Eleven

"There is a famine in the land of Canaan," said Pharez.

"Would you like a piece of goat cheese? I made it several moons ago."

"Sure, Auntie. I love your goat cheese." Pharez took a large bite from the crumbling white block.

"Mmmm." He brushed crumbs from his bushy beard. "I guess there is a famine everywhere else in the land but here. Zerah and I and my sons are taking a journey to Egypt with our father."

"Judah?"

"Mmmhhh," said Pharez, still chewing.

Tamar wondered if Tabitha had ever told the twins that the shepherd was their real father, not Judah. She probably had told them nothing. It would be better that way. If Judah ever found out that Tamar and Tabitha had tricked him, the twins would be innocent.

What did it matter who the actual father was? Judah was rarely around. But that was true with most fathers. Judah was a wealthy man. Being known as his sons would make their lives easier -- even if they had to take a journey now and then so that Judah could show off his late in life "progeny."

"We are going to meet our Uncle Joseph. Jacob, my grandfather, knew not that his lost son Joseph was the ruler over all of Egypt, second only to Pharaoh. But he knew that Egypt had grain because they had planned well for the famine years."

"Yes, I heard about the Pharaoh's dream that Joseph interpreted," said Tamar. She sliced the rest of the goat cheese. Then she went to the cupboard and pulled out a clay container of almonds. They rustled as she poured them into the clay bowl. She was only going to fill the bowl half way. But she emptied the container. Pharez could finish off the almonds easily.

She had begun thinking of him as a man, as a nephew and as a son, even though he had been born as a son and a daughter. He had started growing a beard several years ago. Now, it was thick and full. He had taken a wife -- a young beauty named Adina with gentle ways and deep set shining eyes. The two of them had twins: Hezron and Hamul. Pharez had confided in Tamar that the twins were actually born as sons and daughters, each of them, but that they were being raised as sons. Pharez was always trying to please his father.

Pharez nodded. "Yes. Mother told me about the two dreams that Joseph had -- the ears of corn eating each other and the cattle rising from the sea."

Tamar refrained from commenting.

Pharez took another fistful of almonds. After he finished chewing, he continued. "So my uncles journeyed to Egypt to buy grain from the governor. When they saw him, they bowed down. Without the grain, their families would starve. They didn't know that the governor was Joseph, their brother -- my uncle -- whom they had sold into slavery. He was wearing fine linen and a gold chain. His brothers' clothes were tattered and dirty from their long journey. Even so, Joseph recognized them. But he pretended not to know them. He accused them of being spies who had come to his land to see how blighted it was from the drought. They protested and said they were not spies -- that they were brothers who had come to buy grain. Then they said that all the brothers had come except for their youngest, who was with their father."

"Benjamin? He is about ten years younger than you," commented Tamar. She thought it ridiculous when men who were so old they were nearly dead fathered children -- but she kept her opinions to herself.

"That's right, his name is Benjamin. He is younger than me, but he is still my uncle. Joseph said that his brothers were spies. He put them all in an Egyptian jail for three days. I guess he enjoyed lording it over them for a while. They did put him in the pit after all."

"And sell him into slavery," added Tamar.

Pharez nodded. "Joseph relented and said that if they were not spies, they would leave one brother with him and the rest would return with Benjamin. So they left Simeon. He was put into an Egyptian jail for three days. When the brothers returned home and opened the sacks of corn that Joseph's steward had prepared for them, they saw that their money was returned. They were afraid."

"What were they afraid of? They got corn and their money back." Tamar stood and went to the cupboard. This time she brought out a container of fresh figs that Naomi had traded her for a block of goat cheese. Ezzie's kids, Yael and Yaffa, were at the age where they were producing milk. Naomi's trees were ripe with figs. There would be more fresh figs. Tamar wasn't bothered by the fact that she didn't have much money. She had little use for it.

Pharez shrugged and reached out for a fresh fig. He held the plump, green fruit in his hand as he spoke. "It is like the Garden of Eden in here with all of the fresh food. It's too bad that the rest of the people don't have your knack for survival. The famine is very bad in the land. My grandfather would not send his youngest until Uncle Reuben said that Jacob could slay his own two sons if he did not bring Benjamin back."

"And?" Tamar had to admit that she was getting caught up in the story. She bit into the fleshy fruit of a fig. She savored its sweetness. She reached up and removed a tiny seed from her lip. She usually didn't think that the outside world -- the men and their affairs -- had anything to do with her. But Pharez's visits were increasingly rare, so she followed his story closely.

"So they took their youngest brother, the lad Benjamin, and they also took twice the amount of money that that had taken the first time, so they could settle their debt and buy more corn for their families. Jacob also told them to take the governor some presents -- the best fruit they could find: honey, almonds and spices. When they arrived, they told the steward of the house that on their last visit their money was returned with the grain. The steward told them not to be afraid. The God of their father was with them. He brought Simeon out of jail and showed them that Simeon was well. He invited them to have lunch with Joseph. His brothers were very surprised because Egyptians consider breaking bread with Hebrews to be an abomination. At lunch, Joseph asked about their father who was his own father, of course. He must have thought he was being very clever by not telling them who he was. But then everything caught up with him and he had to excuse himself from the table to weep in his chambers."

"A man weeping?" Tamar cupped one hand and swept up the small pile of fig stems on the table in front of her.

"Of course, Auntie. Things are changing. Men weep openly all the time now, or least some times. I wept when the twins were born."

"Of course you did," said Tamar, reaching out to stroke his cheek just above the dark line where his beard started to grow. "But you are a different kind of man... I mean you are gentle and know your female nature."

Pharez nodded. "I know what you mean. I am not offended. But I am not the only gentle man. When Joseph finished crying in his chambers, he came back to the table to finish eating with his brothers. And again he had his steward return his brothers' money in their sacks. He told the steward to put his silver cup in Benjamin's sack. Benjamin was the youngest of the brothers. When they left, Joseph told his steward to follow them. The steward was just going to take Benjamin back to be a servant to Joseph -- as punishment for his false crime. But the brothers insisted on going back to try to reason with Joseph. My father offered to be a servant to Joseph in Benjamin's place. He explained that his father's favorite son was Benjamin. He said that his father had another favorite son of his old age, but he was lost in the wilderness. Judah said that if he didn't bring home Benjamin, he couldn't bear the guilt.

"When he saw how his brother felt, Joseph wept aloud. Then he told his brothers who he was. He told his brothers that he forgave them because it was God's will that he be sold into slavery so that he could rule over Egypt and prepare for the famine. He told them to go home and get their father and bring him to Joseph. So they went home and told their father. Jacob could not believe that Joseph was truly alive and ruling all of the land of Egypt. But then he changed his mind. He decided to travel to Egypt with his sons so that he could see Joseph before he died. And so that is the journey that I am going to make with my father, and uncles and with," -- he hesitated -- "Zerah, and also my sons, Hezron and Hamul."

"The twins also? They just learned how to walk. Who will watch them?" Tamar didn't want to interfere, but she was alarmed.

"Zerah offered to keep an eye on the twins," Pharez reassured her.

"How is Zerah? I haven't seen her since last growing season." Tamar locked eyes with Pharez.

A few years ago, Zerah had confided in Tamar that she identified as "she" even though Judah still thought of her as a son. She told Tamar that her breasts had started to develop and she had to bind them. Tamar had badly wanted to tell Zerah that Judah wasn't her real father and that it didn't matter what he thought. But she had taken a deep breath and said nothing. It was better that the twins didn't know. They still didn't know that Tamar was their mother's twin sister. They may have suspected since they saw Tamar's face in her tent and must have noticed that she looked almost identical to their mother. They also knew that she covered her face whenever they went out. But they never said anything. They accepted the story that their mother told them, that Tamar was her close friend and that they would call her 'Auntie.'

"I was worried about her," he said. "She didn't want to leave the tent for almost an entire growing season. But then our old nursemaid, Milcah, who lives with father now, introduced her to someone named Eila. I wasn't sure at first if Eila was a man or a woman. I don't think that Zerah knew either. Maybe that's why she was drawn to her. Zerah glows when they are together. She told me that Eila is a woman, one with no small amount of facial hair." Pharez stroked his beard. "Not as much as me, of course, but a lot for a woman. I expect that she and Zerah will get married soon. I doubt, however, that they will be able to have sons."

Tamar gave him a shrewd look. Pharez was a fine young man. She could tell that he genuinely cared about Zerah. But still there was a strong current of sibling rivalry between them and Pharez had already pleased his father by having "sons."

"You never know," said Tamar.

"Finally," said Judith, "She is sleeping."

Six months after Pharez's visit, Tamar looked over at the baby in the makeshift cradle that she had set up in the tent and smiled. Aziz and Azizi stayed outside when Judith and the baby were visiting. Judith had named the baby, Batshemath, after her favorite aunt who had died young. Their nickname for the baby was She.

Judith sat down at the table.

"I saw Obodas today in the market."

"Who?" Tamar said as she set out a bowl of black olives stuffed with goat cheese. The olives were from her tree. She had picked the ripe ones and soaked them in salt water for several moons. Then she added goat cheese that she had made from the milk of Yael and Yaffa. She was going to put slivered almonds on the top, but she didn't have any almonds. Naomi had several almond trees that rained down pale pink blossoms in the spring. She usually had plenty of almonds, enough to give to her family and to Tamar when she came to make the camel cheese. But the trees bore less fruit in the drought. The trees produced fewer almonds. Naomi gave them to her sons.

"Obodas is the Nabataean perfume seller who I buy my Egyptian water lily scented cream from."

"Oh? I see you're on a first name basis now." Tamar smiled at Judith. She was pleased to see that Judith had no guilt about allowing herself this luxury that her husband forbade.

"Obodas told me what he had heard about the journey of Joseph's brothers and their sons and grandsons to Egypt. Obodas told me more than Bram did. Bram was happy briefly after I gave him wine and told him that he had lay with me. Then when I told him that I was with child, I could tell that he was proud. But when I gave birth to a daughter, I could tell he wasn't that proud. He didn't say anything, but he didn't have the big parties with the fresh killed goats, that he had thrown for the birth of our sons. Of course, there is a famine in all of the land," said Judith, looking down. Color rose in her cheeks.

Tamar thought that Judith must have just remembered that she didn't eat meat. Since the famine had begun, Tamar had become a little self-righteous. She couldn't stop herself.

"If people kept their goats, instead of eating them, if they ate goat cheese instead, we wouldn't have a famine," said Tamar.

Judith rolled her eyes.

Tamar could see that Judith had made the right decision in going back to Bram. Judith and Tamar had remained friends. They saw each other frequently. But Tamar had decided not to lay with Judith any more. She didn't want to risk Judith becoming with child again and showing up on her camel with her baskets of belongings. Apparently, Judith felt the same way. Her place was with her husband and her six sons and now her daughter, She.

Judith's silver necklaces glinted in the light from the oil lamp.

"So let me tell you about the journey," said Judith. "But first let me try one of these olives."

She popped a gleaming black orb into her mouth.

"Mmmmm."

She chewed intently and finished before she spoke.

"The goat cheese center is delightful. If you took these to the market, you could make a bundle."

Tamar closed her eyes momentarily. Some things weren't worth talking about with Judith.

"You were about to tell me about the journey," Tamar said.

"Well Obodas told me that he heard from the sandal maker that Joseph was so glad to reveal himself to his brothers that he gave each of them a set of new clothes, very expensive clothes. But to his youngest brother, Benjamin, he gave five sets of new clothes and three hundred silver pieces."

"I guess Joseph was grateful to have met Benjamin since he was too young to be with his other brothers to betray him at the pit," said Tamar. "Or was Benjamin born after Joseph was sold into slavery?"

"Beats me." Judith shrugged her shoulders. "Obodas didn't say. But he did tell me that Jacob was overjoyed to learn that Joseph was not only alive and well but that he was the celebrated governor over all the land of Egypt."

"Why was he celebrated?" asked Tamar.

"Because he interpreted Pharaoh's dream and prepared for the famine." Judith's voice rose. "You really need to get out more."

"I do get out. I go to Naomi's tent and make camel cheese one day a week. If more people learned how to make cheese, we wouldn't have a famine."

Judith pointedly ignored her.

"And Israel embarked on his journey to Egypt," said Judith. "He rode in a camel train with his sons and their sons. They took their goods and also their cattle and sheep with them, just as Joseph had instructed. There were close to forty men and boys in the caravan. Zerah and Pharez went with him and Pharez brought his sons Hezron and Hamul. But I guess you know that."

Tamar nodded.

"How is Zerah doing, by the way?" asked Judith.

"Zerah is fine since he met Eila. They are betrothed."

There was an awkward silence. In public, Tamar referred to Zerah as "he" -- since that is what everyone assumed. But Judith knew everything. But she hadn't mentioned anything since the time that she had threatened to go to Judah with the information so that her sons could go to Egypt instead of the twins. Especially since soon after that Judith was preoccupied with being a mother to She.

"Zerah is such a nice person," said Judith. "I've met Eila a few times in the market. At first I wasn't sure if Eila was a man or a woman. I guess it doesn't matter. As long as Zerah is happy. I'm sorry that I threatened to go to Judah. I was just desperate. All I really wanted was a daughter," said Judith. She looked over at the sleeping baby in the cradle and then back at Tamar. "And thanks to you, there She is."

Judith looked at Tamar with shining eyes.

Tamar realized that Judith's eyes were brimming with tears. Being a new mother had changed her. Tamar realized that she had longed for Judith to be humble. But, at the same time, she felt uncomfortable seeing Judith like this. It was as if she had dropped her robe and was naked again in front of Tamar.

"What else did Obodas say?" asked Tamar.

Judith touched her silver necklaces and told Tamar what she knew.

"Jacob stopped in Beersheba, at the sacred shrine where Abraham planted the tamarisk tree."

Tamar looked at her quizzically.

Judith answered before Tamar could ask the question.

"Abraham, our ancestor. The one God's chosen one. He was the father of Isaac, who he sired with his wife Sarah. Remember? Abraham also had an older son with his maidservant Hagar. But his wife Sarah became jealous. So Abraham sent Hagar and their son, Ishmael, off into the desert. The one God became their protector and Ishmael was fruitful and multiplied and now we have the Ishmaelites. Abraham was left with only one son, Isaac. God came down and commanded Abraham to sacrifice his only son. Abraham was willing to do this -- thereby proving his loyalty to God. But in the end, God let Abraham's son live. Isaac was the great great great grandfather of Jacob. Jacob is also known as Israel. Abraham planted the tamarisk tree to mark the spot where he called on the name of the Everlasting God, Yahweh."

Tamar nodded. Now she remembered. Judith was going back a few centuries at least. Tamar was unsure if Abraham actually existed, but managed to hold her tongue. Everyone was entitled to their own beliefs. Judith was no exception.

"And then?"

"Jacob offered sacrifices to the one God and--"

Tamar's mind wandered as Judith continued talking. *Poor goats*, she thought. She was tired of hearing about the sacrifices made to the one God.

Judith continued: "And God spoke to him and told him not to be afraid to go to Egypt and then God promised Jacob 'for I will there make of thee a great nation' and then God told Joseph that He would be with him. And so Jacob and his train travelled to the Land of Goshen, the region where the Hebrews dwell in East Egypt."

"The Hebrews have their own region in Egypt?" This was news to Tamar.

Judith raised an eyebrow.

"Pharaoh established a region in Egypt, some time ago, for the Hebrews to live. It is far enough away from the other towns so that the Egyptians won't have to run into them. Plus it is fertile land so the Hebrews can tend to their flocks," explained Judith.

"You know that the Egyptians consider that is an abomination to be a shepherd," commented Tamar. "All the men in Jacob's family are shepherds. That's why they were in the wilderness when they put Joseph into the pit. Pharez and Zerah are also shepherds. That is all they know. They take after Judah. But Judah is wealthy enough to employ other shepherds."

"That's why Pharaoh gave them their own region, so they can tend to their flocks without bothering the Egyptians," said Judith. She rose and walked over to the other side of the tent, and looked down at She.

"She is still sleeping -- like a little angel," Judith whispered as she tiptoed back.

Tamar smiled.

"I, too, have heard that the Egyptians aren't big on the Hebrews. I hope the twins and Pharez's sons are going to be alright," said Tamar.

"I hope all of Jacob's family is going to be safe," said Judith. She reached for a black olive filled with goat cheese.

"Yes, of course," said Tamar contritely. It was natural though that she think of the twins first and their children.

She thought of the new babies as her grandchildren. Tabitha may have given birth to the twins, but they were of Tamar's line, too.

Judith finished chewing her olive.

"All of the Hebrews who come to Egypt will be safe as long as Joseph is the ruler of all the land," stated Judith. "Still, I am happy that my sons are home safe and I do not have to worry about them. And, of course, now I have She. It is much better to have a daughter than sons."

Tamar looked at her. She noticed that Judith still only had six silver necklaces -- one for each son. Her husband had not bothered to give her one for having a daughter. But Tamar did not point this out. She took a deep breath. She let the feeling pass.

"Then what happened?"

"Jacob sent Judah to go and tell Joseph that they had arrived in the land of Goshen. Then Joseph came back with Judah. He hugged his father for a long time and wept. Jacob said he could die because he had seen Joseph and because he was alive," answered Judith.

"How old is Jacob, now?" asked Tamar.

"He must be about one hundred and thirty years old by now," said Judith. "Perhaps he lived so long because he was waiting to see his son again."

Tamar wondered if Joseph had been telling tales about his age to make it look like he was well-preserved for his years. She had never heard of anyone else living so long, at least not in their time.

"Joseph told them that he was taking them to meet Pharaoh and that he would ask them what they did for a living," continued Judith. "Since they had their flocks with them they would have to be honest and reveal that they were shepherds. But Joseph told them that even though the Egyptians considered shepherds to be an abomination, that Pharaoh would make an exception for them. Joseph was right. His brethren met Pharaoh and he made them rulers over all the cattle. He gave them a parcel in the land of Rameses which is in Goshen. The Rameses is very fertile since it is near the Delta East tributary of the Nile. They lived there for almost a year. Joseph made sure that his brethren had all the bread they needed. But then the famine worsened -- even in Egypt. There was no bread in the land. Joseph gathered up all the money he had gained from the sale of his stock piles of bread and brought it to Pharaoh. Then the money failed in Egypt. What good is money when there is no food to buy?"

Tamar nodded. "It is better to barter."

"Maybe you are right," acceded Judith. "Although, there are many nice things to buy. Obodas told me that soon he will have face creams from far away exotic lands."

"Hmmm," said Tamar.

"Obodas told me that he heard that after the money failed in Egypt, Joseph was trading bread for cattle," commented Judith.

"I thought that Joseph was out of bread," said Tamar.

"I guess he still had some in reserve." Judith shrugged her shoulders. "You know how rulers are."

"Yes," said Tamar. "They are gracious only as long as they can afford to be."

"That is true," replied Judith.

"I am concerned for our people," said Tamar.

Just then a wail came forth from the cradle.

Chapter Twelve

Tamar looked down on herself. Her body lay on her bed.

Tabitha was at Tamar's side. Her eyes were wet. Tamar knew why her sister was crying. They were almost the same person, from the same womb, from the same egg split into two. They were identical in looks, if not in spirit. They shared the same secret -- that of tricking Judah.

Zerah and Pharez were still living in Egypt with Judah. Tamar saw a well-built man, younger but no longer young, dusting sand from his hands. He must have been digging the hole outside. Tamar somehow knew that the hole was where her body would be buried.

Shaggy salt and pepper hair brushed his shoulders. Light circled his head. She remembered that he was the young shepherd who had lain with Tabitha. Tamar had met him several times when he was a boy and his mother had brought him to her tent.

Tamar came back to herself, opened her eyes, and stared at her sister.

Tabitha looked down at her and said, "I am past my bleeding time now, so there won't be a scandal."

"Good," Tamar said. That was her final word.

Tamar took her last breath -- or so she thought. But in death, she found that she was breath. She was the gentle breeze sweeping from her mouth as her lifeless body was put in the ground. From the sky above their heads, she looked down and saw a small group of mourners. Judith was there. She was wearing her brown and white striped robe. It did not look like she was wearing her silver necklaces. A fat tear slid down her face, leaving a glistening trail. Judith was holding the hand of her youngest. She was now old enough to walk and to understand that the woman she had known as "Auntie" was no longer with them. But Tamar was not sad. She felt like herself -- only like more of herself. She was the silence. Then she realized that someone else was with her. Aziz. He had gone before her. He had died in the last growing season. She had made arrangements to leave Azizi to Tabitha who had matured and was more of an animal person. When she was still living, Tamar had thought of Aziz every day. Now she felt a soft furry breeze next to her. They were together again. She caressed the face of the mourners. She lingered for a moment on Judith's tear stained cheek. Then, in a gust, she took off across the desert. She had places to go.

Her first stop was the marketplace. She had told Tabitha not to tell Naomi that she was dying. She only saw Naomi when she went to her tent to make the camel cheese. But they had struck up a friendship. Naomi's daughter-in-law Ruth was left on her own when Naomi's son had died. Naomi had confided to Tamar that she loved Ruth. The famine was still bad in the land, and Naomi feared that Ruth might starve since she was on her own. Tamar had known that Ruth was fretting, and that was why she forbade Tabitha to tell Naomi that she was dying.

Tamar was a breeze blowing through the marketplace. She wanted to caress Naomi's rough face, to thank her quietly for bringing her Azizi and for teaching her to make the camel cheese. But most of all, she wanted to thank Naomi for being a friend. A friend was hard to come by in the harsh desert. But Naomi's stall in the marketplace was empty. So Tamar flew to her tent and found that she could slip inside the flap.

Naomi was still small and stooped. Tamar recognized her black and white striped robe. But it was no longer new. Time had left it in tatters. Ruth had aged too. Tamar had been right about Naomi's skin. It had become brown and crinkled like the skin of an almond.

Ruth was beseeching Naomi: "Intreat me not to leave thee, or to return from following after thee: for whither thou goest, I will go; and where thou lodgest, I will lodge: thy people shall be my people, and thy God my God."

The two women embraced.

"I will think of a plan," said Naomi, in her gravelly voice, "so that we can be together."

The younger woman looked at Naomi with shining eyes. Tamar saw that they loved each other as lovers. The two women began caressing each other so tenderly that they looked like they might create a daughter.

The gentle breeze that was Tamar caressed Naomi's weathered face and the shining hair of Ruth. Tamar gave them her blessing. Then she left the tent and blew into the village. She blew into other tents. She saw that other women loved each other tenderly and found ways to be together. She saw bearded men wearing prayer shawls and reading from scrolls. Some of these men were tender with each other. Tamar saw men and women being tender with each other. She saw women giving birth. Most of the infants were girls or boys. But more than a few were both male and female. She saw mothers wrapping their infants in swaddling and telling their fathers that they had sons -- even when the infants were daughters or sons and daughters together. The mothers wanted their children to learn to read. Tamar saw more than a few mothers themselves learning to read in secret. She saw a woman kneeling over a scroll, learning to say the word, "Om," and repeating the incantation.

Tamar blew through the seasons. In the spring, she idled in the fertile crescent. She rested in the feathery pink blossoms of the tamarisk tree. She picked up the delicate scent and blew it far into the desert. She nestled in the white blossoms of gnarled olive trees. Light and shadow fell through her. She made the leaves rustle. She flitted through the branches of a young almond tree, settling on a white flower with a pink center. The clear blue sky was behind her. She could feel it shining through her as she sat next to a honey bee and watched as it knelt and drank nectar. So mesmerized was she, that she wasn't sure how long she stayed. When she left, she flew through time.

She blew across the desert to Egypt and found the house of the governor. She looked down and saw that Joseph was ready to give up the ghost and die. She felt very sad. It was as if Joseph had been her brother. He was, in fact, her brother-in-law since she had been married to Er, the first son of Judah.

She swept down and caressed the cheek of Pharez. He knelt next to his grandfather's coffin. Since Tamar was wind, she couldn't speak. She could only caress his cheek. She longed to tell Pharez that he need not mourn so much, because he and his twin were not from the seed of Jacob. But it was too late to tell him this. Pharez and Zerah and Pharez's sons (who were really sons and daughters, both and neither) Hezron and Hamul were counted among those in the Tribe of Judah.

She blew gently at their backs, watching over them, as the sons of Jacob took him home to the land of Canaan where he had asked to be buried. Then she followed them back to the land of Goshen in Egypt where they returned to their flocks, because life was good there.

Then she saw a new king, who never knew Joseph, become installed in The House of Pharaoh.

She knew this would come to a bad end. She blew around the land of Goshen until she was moving faster, faster. She tried to warn her people, but there was little sand to kick up and sting them with. They ignored her.

The new Pharaoh saw that there were many children of Israel in his land and that they were strong. He told his people to force them into bondage, for much hard labor was needed to build the cities of Pithom and Rameses from brick and mortar.

Tamar blew by the mouth of the King and heard him speaking to the Hebrew midwives, Puah and Shiprah: "When ye do the office of a midwife to the Hebrew women, and see them upon the stools; if it be a son, then ye shall kill him: but if it be a daughter, then she shall live."

She swirled around the ears of the midwives and entered her minds, and heard their thoughts: *We are the midwives, the keepers of life. We will save the male infants.*

The warm breeze of Tamar caressed the faces of her people. The children of Israel multiplied and grew stronger in the land of Egypt.

She blew around the King as he listened to the Egyptian midwives explaining that, "the Hebrew women are not as the Egyptian women; for they are lively, and will do as they want."

The King became enraged. But he was crafty and had houses built for the Hebrew midwives first. Then after a time, he threatened to take away their houses unless every Hebrew son who was born was cast into the Nile.

Tamar knew not what to do. She was concerned for the future generations of her line -- Pharez and Zerah and their children. And she cared for all the children of Israel because they were her people. She counted herself among Judah's line since her family claimed him.

She blew gently around the villages, rather than choosing to ripple across the sands of the desert as Aziz was doing. She blew through a window and saw a Hebrew couple hiding a baby boy. When they could hide him no more, the mother built an ark of papyrus, the marsh plant that grew by the side of the Nile. The ark was small but large enough to hold an infant. Tamar watched as the young mother sealed the edges with pitch and slime.

Tamar was a gentle breeze blowing above the young mother's head as the woman hushed her infant's cries and placed the ark in the river, pushing it into the current.

Tamar watched as the mother spoke to the infant's sister. The girl hid behind the reeds as she followed her brother down the Nile. The infant-sized ark was headed toward rapid currents. Tamar blew behind him and then under the ark until it was lifted and landed near the daughter of Pharaoh who was washing herself in the river. When the Pharaoh's daughter saw the ark, she sent her maids to retrieve it. When the daughter of Pharaoh opened the ark, the baby wept. The warm breeze of Tamar blew compassion into her.

"It is one of the Hebrew babies," cried the princess.

Then the infant's sister appeared from the reeds and asked the princess if she needed a nurse for the child.

"Yes," said the princess.

The sister ran back to get her mother. Tamar stayed in the village until his mother brought him back to live with the princess for he was old enough now not to need a nurse. The princess named him Moses because she had drawn him out of the water.

Tamar watched as Moses grew up. One day he killed an Egyptian who was mistreating a Hebrew slave. Seeing Moses killing a man made her sad, but she knew that the deed was necessary for Moses to understand himself and to lead his people out of Egypt. As the wind, she could blow ahead of herself and glimpse the future. There were plagues. There were locusts. The plagues were brought down on Egypt to show Pharaoh that Moses and his one God were serious. Finally, the red sea parted in front of Moses and his people. It closed behind them on the pursuing Egyptians. Tamar was almost lost in the angry gusts of wind that ruffled the waves in the sea until they were enraged with white froth. The sight of this prompted her to think maybe the one God does exist: *I have heard of red tides and plagues before, but the parting of the sea is impressive.* Tamar was happy to see her people escape. But even as the wind, Tamar felt that any violence was wrong. The gentle rain of her tears fell on the bodies of the Egyptians who floated like logs on the frothy waves of the Red Sea.

She saw Moses ascend the mountain and come down with tablets of laws that he claimed contained the word of God. The laws were written in stone. Moses did not like what he saw when he looked out on his followers. The multitudes were worshipping a giant golden calf. When she saw the face of the calf -- its long nose, slanted eyes -- she was reminded of the small clay bull vases one of old women from the province of Arsawa had given her. The vases had spiral lines engraved into them. On the tops of each vase were four dots above the bull's eyes.

The old woman had explained that these four markings represented the phases of the moon. As Tamar swirled around the golden calf and saw the adoration in the eyes of the crowd at the base of the mountain, she reflected that, of course, they would be drawn to this ancient symbol even if it was considered to be an idol. Plus it was gold.

Moses smashed the tablets.

Tamar blew through sky. She moved clouds into formations that resembled fluffy sheep and horned goats and camels with two humps and dromedaries with one hump. She thought she would entertain the gatherers as they waited for Moses to come down again from the mount. She heard the deep voice of Moses booming as he spoke the laws out loud. This time he said that the laws were written in stone with the finger of God.

Some made sense such as the one that stated, "thou shalt not kill... or covet thy neighbor's house ... thy neighbor's wife nor his manservant, nor his ass."

Many of the laws made sense. Tamar had always thought that jealousy was a useless emotion. But other laws concerned her such as the one that said, "Thou shalt not lie with mankind, as with womankind: it is abomination." Tamar didn't think it was anybody's business. Besides, men lay with men all the time. Everyone knew that. Tamar noticed that women were not forbidden from loving with other women. But women really didn't matter. They were forbidden to write. And the inner circle that gathered around Moses was all men. That's probably why there was no response to the rule that said any man who lay with his wife during her bleeding time would be cut off from his community. Tamar saw a young, bearded man who widened his brown eyes and looked down. She swirled around his head and entered his ear to read his thoughts: Who will know? It is a private matter between myself and Miriam.

She swirled back out of his ear in time to hear Moses utter another rule: "thou shalt not suffer a witch to live." That one gave her pause. She was not sure what a witch was. But she had a nagging feeling that she may have been one. The women of the goddess cult had worshipped the moon. She hadn't only worshipped the one God. There were the goddess figures that the old women had brought to her. They taught her how to make charms and amulets. She had learned to read in secret and she had shared the scrolls and the secrets of "Om."

The wind that was Tamar blew around the village. She saw people filling earthen vessels with water at the well, tending gnarled pomegranate trees with red fruit hanging from lush green branches. She saw women and men churning butter, grinding flour. She blew into their ears and heard their thoughts. They prayed to the one God that their crops would grow and their families would be fed. She heard the prayers of believers. She also heard the prayers of those who weren't sure they believed, but promised they would if their prayers were answered. It seemed as though people just wanted to be listened to. She saw that people were kinder in times of plenty. She saw famines come and go. During a lean time, she wafted over the village in the land of Canaan, doing her best to be gentle. She hoped to give the villagers a nice distraction. But they had their own way of entertaining themselves during a famine. A plume of smoke rose above a crowd behind the market. Tamar lowered herself into a current. In the center of the crowd, a woman was tied to a wooden stake.

"She's a witch," shouted a villager.

"I knew it," said the man next to her.

Tamar recognized him as the butcher who slaughtered live goats in the stall behind Naomi's. "Camel cheese is the food of witches," he said. "Worshippers of the Lord eat goat."

Tamar looked closer. The woman was short and terrified. Tamar recognized her wide spaced eyes in her crinkled dark face, her crooked nose. Fear contorted her face. Naomi had aged, but Tamar could tell it was her.

"She's not a witch," said a woman in the back of the crowd. Tamar saw that it was Ruth, on in years. She was wearing a brown cloth on top of her hair. The folds of her tattered brown robe fell into the dust between her sandaled feet. Her faint voice lifted up on a current. Tamar heard her say:

"All she ever did was to love me back."

"It's unnatural," yelled a woman. "Two women loving each other like that."

"Yes. She must be a witch. She put a spell on her daughter in law," said the man standing next to her. "She made Ruth love her more than a husband."

"That's right, more than a husband," said the woman standing next to him. "I never loved my husband that much. The love between those women is unnatural -- disgusting!"

"It is more than the love of God," said woman standing on the other side of the circle.

"Idolator!"

"Idolator!" echoed the crowd.

Tamar was angry. Ruth probably had loved Naomi more than Tamar had loved Judith. Tamar had really only loved Judith like a lover for one night. But Ruth and Naomi had the kind of love that could last a lifetime. It was the kind of love that proved that there was a force greater than the simple fact of the two of them. Love bound them together. It was larger than both of them. Love was a good and necessary force. Who created love? It was something that couldn't be seen. Theirs was the kind of love that could prove the existence of God.

Tamar whipped herself into a frenzy. She coiled around

in the sky, like a serpent. The flames around the bottom of the stake crept toward Naomi's robe. Tamar swept down with all her fury and blew the embers and the flames away from Naomi.

"Light another fire!" a woman called from the crowd.

"Burn her!"

"BURN THE WITCH!"

The crowd roared.

Naomi stood bound and gagged in the middle of the crowd. She was standing on kindling. A hooded man stepped out of the crowd. He held a flame low to the ground and lit the dry sticks. Naomi's eyes bulged.

Tamar hovered above the crowd. When the flames caught onto the kindling, she swept down. She was so furious that she blew out the flames.

The hooded man hurried forth from the crowd and set the fire again.

Tamar swooped down again and extinguished the flames.

"The fire is no good," shouted one of the women. "Perhaps we should have another executioner -- and burn this one since he cannot defeat the wind."

The henchman lit the flames again.

Tamar hovered above the crowd in the sky. She was enjoying herself by now. But she still had enough fury in her to sweep down and put out the fire.

"It is the breath of God," said the henchman.

"The wrath of God is on us," said a woman standing next to him.

"Untie her. Let her go free," said a man.

And the crowd echoed him: "Let her go free. It is the will of God."

A few people in the crowd started to run -- as if they could flee the wrath of God. The others followed.

Tamar smiled to herself in the golden smile of the wind as she watched the henchman untie Naomi and steady her with a hand on her back as she hurried away.

Tamar watched the crowd disperse. She coiled and uncoiled. She blew above their heads. Her breath scattered clouds.

She enjoyed playing God. She blew across the blue sky.

The years fell away.

Tamar saw her people led to the promised land where they were thrown out again until they got it right (according to the one God). The one God, by His own admission, was a jealous one. As the wind, Tamar was capricious. She still doubted, even after God had led her people out of Egypt. Clearly, He had parted the Red Sea. But where did He get his power from? Where did He come from? Was the one God made up from the power of the many gods?

He had to have a maker -- a mother. And She was most likely angry that Her arrogant son was taking all the credit.

Tamar knew that a little doubt was good for faith. If she kept searching, maybe she would find something. She blew toward the heavens and then back toward the earth. She let the currents pull her along. She arrived at a house, one of the few abodes that was not a tent, and saw a woman inside kneeling at a shrine. Her long white hair shone like starlight. Tamar blew around to the front of the woman's face. She knew right away who it was. The woman had the same sea-green almond shaped eyes. The Egyptian water lily scented cream that she had always bought from the Nabataeans at the market must have had magical qualities because her face was still smooth and, except for the crow's feet around her deep set almond eyes, unlined.

Judith looked like she was praying. Tamar blew into Judith's ear so that she could hear her thoughts. Her husband had just died. FINALLY, said a loud thought in Judith's mind. She was left to fend for herself. Her sons had inherited control of all of Judah's flocks, and had turned their backs on their mother. The youngest son, Eli, who had long been her favorite said that his mother loved his younger sister more than him. Judith was aggrieved by all this. She loved all her sons, especially her youngest, who she was closest to. But what Eli said was true. She had thought she loved being the wife of an influential man and the mother of six sons. But she really knew what love was when her daughter came. Judith loved She so much that she had told her the circumstances of her birth. She realized later that this was a mistake. When she became a woman, after thirteen years, Batshemath came to her mother and told her that she was leaving. She said that she had met some young women, in her goddess cult, who were moving to the desert. She told her mother that she had to go before her father married her off. Judith had protested, saying that she would never give her consent. Batshemath told her that it didn't matter. If her father wanted to marry her off, he could. She was his property. The next day, she was gone.

At first, Judith had cursed the Goddess cult. The women had taken her daughter. But then she realized that

Batshemath was right. She belonged to Judah, because people believed he was her father. Going to live in the wilds of the desert with other women was her only escape. Judith knew it was best for her daughter, but still she missed her fiercely. She had been widowed by her husband and betrayed by her sons. It had come to pass that her deepest fears had come true. She was alone. Judith bowed her head to her altar.

Tamar longed to tell her that everything was all right -- and that she could live on goat cheese. But Judith had her own way of handling things. She was concocting a plan that involved becoming powerful in her own right. She had become a member of the Tribe of Judah through her husband and sons. Her people were at war again and she would save them by currying favors from the enemy, the Assyrian general Holofernes.

She would become a hero in her own right and never would have to rely on a rich and powerful man again. Her first step would be to turn her hair black again with the Egyptian hair cream that she had bought at the market. Then she would take off her widow's sackcloth which she wore, wash and anoint herself. She would adorn herself with her chains, bracelets, earrings and rings so that she would become a goddess in the eyes of all men who set eyes on her. The details of her plan were so specific that Tamar shuddered. She didn't want to know any more so she blew back out of Judith's ear. A woman like Judith would always get what she wanted, even if she had to chop off someone's head.

Tamar went forth from a window in Judith's house and blew through the centuries.

She saw Temples built, Temples destroyed and built anew. She saw her people fleeing from the Promised Land and driven back to Babylon. She saw them praying to the one God and, she watched as, victorious, they returned to the Promised Land.

Through it all, Tamar kept an eye on her line -- the generations that came from Pharez and Zerah. There was Pharez's offspring, the twins Hezron and Hamul, who had twins of their own. Hezron and his wife had twins, Ram and Aaron. Ram had twins also, Amminadab and Dowr. Amminidab and his wife gave birth to the twins, Nashon and Eden. Nashon's wife gave birth to Salmon and Gera. Salmon's wife died in childbirth, but the baby, Boaz, lived. Boaz and his wife gave birth to Obed who married and gave birth to Jesse. Jesse's wife gave birth to twins David and Amon. All of the twins of Tamar's line had been both sons and daughters, both and neither. She was happy to see that Amon had been raised as a girl, as the child had wanted since she was small. Jesse changed Amon's name to Anna. It took a few generations, but Anna's parents insisted that their child would be raised in the gender that she preferred. As the wind, Tamar had the gift of second site. She could foresee that the next generation would be beyond gender. Children might be born as sons and daughter, but they would not define themselves as such. They would be "they" -- a pronoun that could be singular yet stood for everything.

Tamar saw David walking on the outskirts of his village one day when he was a young man. She blew down and lit on his shoulder like a bird. She swirled in his ear to read his thoughts. But his thoughts were still. All that existed between David's sandal and the sand that he walked on was silence. He observed the rippled golden expanse of sand before him that rose to the vibrant blue sky. He looked at the grains of sand as he slowly put his foot down. He bent down to look at the purple petals of hyssop between spiky green leaves.

Tamar blew out of his ear and into the plant. She carried the minty healing aromas of the flower back to his nose. He inhaled her, and she slipped into his mind. She stayed with him as he walked into a house on the outskirts of the village. She sat on his shoulder as he kissed his wife. She sat down with him at the table. When he rose to ladle out the lentil soup, she stayed with him. He served his beloved and then sat down with her at the small table. Tamar saw that his beloved was with child. There was a slight bulge under her sky-blue robe. She was surrounded by light. Tamar was mesmerized. When the woman lifted a spoon full of lentil soup to her lips, Tamar made herself very small and blew into her body. Eventually, Tamar saw that there were twins in her womb. Both were waiting for souls to inhabit them. Tamar entered one of the translucent sacks in the woman's belly. It was warm and comfortable. Tamar decided to stay.

BOOK TWO

Chapter Thirteen

In the beginning was the Mother.

In the womb, Tamar took mental notes. The heavens trembled -- at least it felt like the heavens. Maybe it was just gas. The Mother shifted. At first, it was too dark to see. It felt like chaos. Everything seemed unconnected. But then she sensed something holding her: a curved wall. It was soft and warm. Tamar's backbone leaned into it. She was half of a circle. Was she floating? There was a chord attached to her belly. She relaxed. She wouldn't drift away. It dawned on her that the parts of her body that felt unconnected were attached.

There were appendages coming out from her shoulders. She looked down, below the chord. On the lower part of her body there was a small bump. On either side of that were two more appendages. There was liquid all around her. She felt warm and safe.

WHOOSH. She flinched. She heard a slosh. Gurgles whizzed by. There was an abbreviated bubbling. It repeated three times. She had heard the sound before. She identified the sound as a hiccup. After a few moments, there was silence. Then there was a contented hum. Sound tickled her backbone. Tamar knew the sound came from the Mother, and it calmed her. Then there was a distant clang. That evening, Tamar heard the repetition of words in a pattern that she knew was a prayer. It soothed her. The Mother worked her jaw and swallowed. Something plopped down the long tube above Tamar. When it passed behind Tamar, it pushed against her spine. It was that bulky. It was spongy too. She knew that the Mother's body would transform it into food to sustain her. A little while later, Tamar flinched when she heard a huge bubble of air pass by her. It ended far above her in a loud belch. Then she heard speech being formed: "oops."

A sound reverberated throughout the Mother's body. It bubbled up in ripples that were deep and full. It brought a smile to Tamar's face. Something told her that this was called laughter. Through this all she heard a steady and loud thumping: ba bump ba bump ba bump. Every now and then it went ba bump ba bump bumbedy bump. Then it went back to normal. At first the sound came from above. It was separate from her but connected too. Then she noticed the tiny pulse that was coming from the center of her: Bump ba bump ba bump. She had something in common with the Mother.

Darkness lifted. Light glowed through the pink barrier. She looked down and noticed tiny extremities with red lines moving through them. They were attached to the ends of two appendages, on each side of her. She found that she could move them, as if she were waving or trying to grasp something. She sensed that these movements would come in handy later. The light went out. Darkness. Tamar felt herself in her body. She felt perfect.

Tamar saw a golden light surrounding her -- around her fingers, and around what she would come to know as her toes. She was made of light. A warm, comforting glow pulsed. Then it dimmed and lulled her back to a warm dark place. Sleep.

When she woke again, she blinked for the first time. It felt good so she did it again. The pinkish yellow glow came back. She clenched and unclenched her fingers. She rubbed the short one across the tips of several of the others, and felt a roughness. She felt nourishment rushing through her from the chord that was attached to her. It was good. She went back to sleep for a long while. This time when she woke, she stretched and yawned.

She put the shorter finger into her mouth. She could feel herself making facial movements. Her cheeks went in. Her lips puckered. Somehow she knew this was called sucking. She rocked from side to side, mimicking the movements of the Mother. Except this time, Tamar was the one who was moving. She was attached to the Mother but she was separate too.

These thoughts were exhausting. She fell back to sleep.

She woke to a pinkish yellow glow. It was faint and coming from the other side. She looked toward the light. She saw that there was a sack next to her. There was someone inside who looked like her. He or she had a light glowing around its edges -- just like she did -- down the extremities and around the fingers and toes. She remembered now that she had entered one body of two. Her twin was beside her. There was a large, round dome attached to a small body like hers. The big round dome faced her. The eyes were blinking. One blinked and the other stayed open. The two corners of the lips went up. Somehow she knew that this was a smile. Her twin was welcoming her. She wanted to welcome him or her back, but something stopped her. She didn't know who her twin was. She felt separate. But was her twin part of her? She wasn't sure she wanted to be part of someone else. She definitely didn't want to share Mother.

There were appendages on both sides of her twin's body -- just like on hers. There were five fingers attached to the end of each appendage. The fingers clenched and unclench-ed. They seemed to wave at her. Tamar thought about waving back, but she didn't. She wasn't sure if her twin could see her through the translucent sack. She looked further down at her twin's body. She saw something protruding. At first she thought that she was seeing a shadow. She moved her head slightly. She could turn her head and see things differently. She did it again and again. She nearly forgot why she was doing it. But then she saw the protruding shadow in the sack of her twin again. It was still there, no matter how she looked at it. She looked until the pink glow of the distant light shifted.

The Mother moved up and down. Tamar and her twin floated in inner space. Tamar felt safe, but she was also in motion. The pink glow shifted, but it was still coming from the other side of the Mother. She looked down again at the third appendage on the bottom part of her twin. It was still there. Did one of her twin's fingers fall down? She looked over at his hands. The sacks made everything cloudy, but it looked like all of her twin's fingers were there. She had a thought. She looked down and saw that she also had a third appendage on the lower part of her own body. It was much shorter than the two other limbs. She clenched and unclenched her fingers. They were all there -- five on each side, including the shorter ones at the ends. None of them had fallen off. She looked down again. Somehow she knew that this protrusion made her male. Knowing this made her angry.

She knew her name was Tamar, but she had forgotten where it came from. She knew that Tamar was a girl's name, and that she was a girl. She had a vague memory that she had come from a single egg, fertilized by a trail of light that had come just for her. Now, she remembered that another egg, fertilized with its own stream of light, had been next to her and that the two eggs had merged. They had crossed over and into each other, exchanging some vital inform-ation. Tamar's egg knew that it was female. But it absorbed a sequence of information that told it that its genetic material would be both male and female. The secret language of the cells said that each of the eggs would be XX and XY.

Her twin had a longer protrusion than her. She took comfort in that. Perhaps this meant that she was really female after all. But she suspected that her twin would most likely be lording his superiority over her forever. She looked down at her body. On the sides of the protrusion were two lower appendages. She found that she could use her mind to make them longer. Once she stretched them, she realized that these were her legs and that her feet were attached to the ends of them. She kicked at the inside of the pink cushion.

"Ow," said a woman's voice. Instantly, Tamar knew that it was the voice of the Mother. She had to get Mother's attention first.

She kicked again.

This time she felt a gentle hand push down on the other side of the pink cushion. Her twin nudged the Mother back.

"What are you trying to tell me, my son?" asked a gentle voice in the distance. Tamar had come to identify it as belonging to the Mother.

I'm a girl -- a girl just like you Mother, Tamar tried to say. But speech eluded her. She had yet to utter her first cry. But she had to get Mother's attention to tell her that there was something wrong.

Tamar looked over and saw the imprint of a large hand pressing against the pink cushion on the side of her twin.

"There, there," said the gentle voice. The pink cushion pushed in slightly. It had the indentation of fingers on it. The hand was comforting her twin.

Tamar was speechless.

I'm over here, she wanted to say.

Tamar kicked again on her side of the fleshy pink cushion.

Again, the hand pushed against the pink cushion on her twin's side. The pink cushion moved in and out.

"There, there," said the voice of the Mother.

Tamar was furious. The Mother should be comforting her, not her twin.

She looked over at her twin. He was staring back at her. He seemed to be happy. His lips were turned up at the edges. He was smiling. His mouth opened slightly. His eyes widened. He was mocking her.

It looked to Tamar that if he could speak, he would be saying, "Mother loves me better."

Tamar had no words for her fury. She drew back on of her arms, clenched her fingers into a ball and threw a right punch as far as she could from her sack into his.

He turned the other cheek.

This just made Tamar more furious. Her knuckles were sore, but she didn't care. She curled up the fingers of her right hand and socked him on the other cheek.

He shifted his face until her was staring straight at her. The corners of his mouth were drawn up again. His mouth was open. He was definitely mocking her. Even his eyes were laughing. It was as if he thought that he was better than her, as if nothing she did could hurt him. He was acting as if he could walk on water.

She would show him. She felt her muscles tense and coil. She thrust her right leg out, curled back her toes and kicked with the ball of her foot. She aimed her toes right into his protrusion.

Ha, she thought as she watched his open mouth contort into a silent howl. He shifted around. His nubby spine faced her. This seemed like an invitation for her to kick him again. But she had showed him, and that was enough.

Instead of feeling triumphant, she was a little disappointed. It wasn't as much fun hurting him as she thought it would be. She almost missed his superior smile, his mocking eyes. But she didn't want to admit this -- even to herself. So she turned around, with the circular curve of her spine toward her twin. She faced the other direction, into the side of the Mother. And she slept.

When she woke, she had grown so large that she was uncomfortable. Her head was pressed against something. She reached up and felt extremities. There were ten of them, and they were short. They didn't belong to her. She was wedged against the toes of her twin. She was looking at the bottom of his feet. Her twin was upside down. It looked like he wasn't that bright after all. She was glad that she had decided not to hurt him. She would need his help in getting out.

It had been warm and wet and secure for a long time -- forever it seemed. But now she was cramped. The pink fleshy pillow pressed into her. The line of light that had once out-lined her body had dimmed.

In the dark wet, she was ready to exit feet first, and to take her first breath. The womb had become so cramped that she was ready for the suffering to begin.

Tamar felt the pink pillow tighten as it pressed into her. Then it stopped. Just when she thought that it was over, it tightened again.

"It's time," said the distant voice of the Mother. Considering that she was about to push them out into the world, she sounded very calm.

The tightness came again and again. The loud steady sound that she now identified as coming from the Mother, slowed down. Thump ... thump ... thump....

Tamar willed her own rhythm to match that of the Mother.

The pink cushion constricted again and again. Tamar's own heart started to beat faster:

THUMP DE THUMPTY THUMP THUMP.

The Mother breathed loudly. Tamar could feel the Mother pushing.

Something slid out from beneath Tamar. She realized it was her twin!

He had deceived her and left her in the wet dark all alone!

Tamar had to let the Mother know that she was still in here. She tensed her right leg and then sent it forth in a good solid kick into the pink cushion in front of her.

"Ouch! Something is still in there," said the distant voice of the mother. "Unless it's just a placenta pain."

Tamar cocked her right leg and kicked again. She kicked so hard that her toes stung.

"Ouch!" said the Mother.

Tamar felt a not so gentle hand come down on top of the pink pillow and push into her.

"There's still a baby in there. I can feel him."

"Him?!" Tamar kicked again.

"Hurry. Get him out of there."

Tamar felt a slender hand come up and turn her around so that she was upside down, like her twin had been.

So that was the secret of sliding out easily, she thought.

She heard a few grunts from the Mother and another woman saying, "Push. Push."

She exited quickly into the woman's hands.

The woman handed her off.

Finally, thought Tamar. *I get to meet the Mother who made me.*

But the woman who held her looked like a stranger. Tamar sensed that she was the midwife's helper. With a rag, she washed off Tamar. Then she oiled her.

As the woman held her, Tamar tilted her head back and looked behind her. The Mother was gone.

The woman oiled Tamar everywhere -- even on the short appendage that protruded from between Tamar's legs.

"Hmm," she said as she looked underneath.

Tamar could feel the woman's fingers probing. It felt like there was a small hole down there. Tamar couldn't see it, but she could feel it. She knew this meant that she really was female just like the Mother.

Tamar smiled. She hardly noticed that the midwife was cutting her umbilical cord with a sharp stone.

The woman laid her down on some swaddling and wrapped her up. Then she took her over to the Mother who was now kneeling next to a cradle. Tamar looked down at her twin. He was sleeping peacefully. There was a beatific smile on his face, and there seemed to be a yellow circular light around his head. In fact, there seemed to be a golden glow surrounding him. Tamar suspected that it emanated from the Mother.

The Mother handed the twin to the midwife and took Tamar. Now Tamar had her own glow. She could afford to be gracious. She smiled at her twin. There was still light emanating from him. It could have been the light reflecting off the straw. There was straw everywhere.

"You have another son, your Holiness," said the midwife.

A son?! Tamar opened her mouth and howled as loud as she could.

"There, there," said the Mother as she patted Tamar. Tamar had never felt so content in her life -- even if the Mother thought she was male. Tamar stopped crying. She sniffed and contorted her face. It smelled like a manger. Animal dung and damp straw.

"That will never do. The people are expecting 'A' messiah -- as in one, not two," said the Mother. "There's an empty stall in the back. Put the child in there and make sure that he's safe. That way when the wise men come, they will just see one messiah. Everything depends on this."

The Mother handed Tamar to the midwife.

"Ok, Ma'am," said the midwife as she turned around.

"Wait," said the Mother.

"Let me see him again."

Tamar felt the Mother caress her face. She closed her eyes. She couldn't tell if there was a glow around her, but it felt like there was. It felt like the Mother's touch was all that she needed.

"He, too, is a beautiful baby. Still, the people are just expecting one messiah. I will keep this one for myself, since I will have to share his brother with the world."

All Tamar heard was, "He."

I'm a she, Tamar thought, *and I have the hole to prove it.*

Tamar began to cry.

"Sshhh. Sshhh." -- The Mother reached out to sooth her brow. "For my sake and yours, please be quiet. I don't know what will happen if they find a second child. And I will need you later to stay by my side."

The Mother was touching her. The Mother was talking

to her. Tamar stopped crying. She'd tell her mother later that she really was a she and not a he.

"We'll call him Thomas," said the Mother. Then she turned away.

The midwife handed her twin back to the Mother. She took Tamar and walked the stall at the back of the manger and laid her carefully in the straw.

Tamar fell asleep, thinking of the touch of the Mother.

Chapter Fourteen

Tamar lay in the hay and cried.

"Sshhhh," said the woman who took care of her. "Your Mother has enough on her mind. King Herod has heard that the three wise men from the East are on their way to see your twin on the fortieth day after his birth which is any day now. Herod has threatened to raze the homes of anyone who is found to give the wise men lodging. So your Mother has to tell them to leave as soon as they see your brother. Is that any way to treat guests?"

Tamar continued to cry.

"Didn't you hear a word that I said?" With large brown eyes, the young woman looked at Tamar sternly. A lock of dark hair slipped out from under her white head cover. "The wise men from the East will be here soon. I have an idea. We'll play a game. Let's pretend that you're my child and that not even Mother knows you're here. You're my baby girl, and you're quiet all the time and really the holy one. No one knows because you're so saintly."

Finally, someone recognizes that I'm a girl, Tamar thought. She stopped crying.

"That's my good girl," said Hannah. She rocked Tamar from side to side.

Tamar put her thumb in her mouth and sucked.

"Go to sleep my angel and remember not a peep out of you. Mama needs her job. I'm going to stay with you until you fall asleep. And then I'm going to go to the other room and help the Mother greet the wise men. If you wake up and I'm not here, don't be afraid. Just remember that you're my good little girl, and go back to sleep."

Tamar closed her eyes and drifted off.

"Last night I had a dream," said the tall man with sandy brown hair down to his shoulders. He stood in the doorway of Tamar's room, blocking the light. "An angel of the Lord came to me and told me to take the young child and his Mother and flee to Egypt, because Herod is seeking to destroy the child."

"I was just starting to settle in," said the Mother. "But this is a manger." She paused and sniffed. "So there is no loss in moving on. And you did have a dream. The wise men left us two camels as gifts when they went away. They must have known that we would have to take a journey. The ass is already saddled up since I was going to go to the market this morning. Hannah can stay here in Bethlehem with her family and keep Thomas with her."

"But Ma'am ... Your Holiness. If I stay here the baby will be at risk," said Hannah. "I heard that Herod intends to have his soldiers kill all the male infants under the age of two in all of Bethlehem."

"That is probably just a rumor," said the Mother. "Herod is not that bad. I can't imagine that he is so threatened by an infant that he will really have all the male babies killed. We're really just fleeing to Egypt as a precaution." The Mother's emerald green eyes flashed. "Thomas can come with us, but you stay here with your family. You'll be fine."

"But Your Holiness -- if Herod's soldiers find out that I am your nursemaid they will kill me, too," exclaimed Hannah.

Tamar started crying.

"Okay, okay," answered the Mother. "You can come with us. I'll need your help taking care of the twins."

Tamar stopped crying.

There was a bit of commotion as the family and Hannah packed their belongings onto the backs of three camels. Mother rode first. She sat sidesaddle on the ass. The tall man with the shoulder length hair walked beside them. A golden glow circled the Mother's head. The ass's tail switched under her.

Tamar kept her eyes on the Mother as she rode behind her, snug in one of Hannah's arms. Her twin was in the other arm. The camel's gait moved from side to side. Tamar reached out and touched the camel's neck. The golden hair was bristly and soft. The camel twisted its neck and turned its head backwards so that he faced her. He pulled back his lips and smiled. A third camel, carrying their belongings, trailed behind them. Pots and pans rattled.

There were stops and starts. The journey seemed to take forever. Tamar slept through most of it. When she was awake, she glared at her twin nestled in Hannah's opposite arm. This was all his fault. She noticed that he only had a glow around his head when the Mother was holding him.

They stopped by the sea. The ass came to a standstill. The camels halted. They disembarked and walked toward the shining waves. Hannah picked up Tamar and held her so that the foam tickled her toes. The water was warm and frothy. It felt soothing -- like she was back in the belly of the Mother.

The desert unfolded in ripples of sand. Tamar felt the camel's step quicken. The camel drew back its head. He sighed long and contentedly. Then they went up a narrow mountain path. Tamar looked out and saw the sun shining on the sea. Then she looked up and saw an angel. The angel had a circle of light around her head -- just like the Mother. The angel's wings fluttered as she looked down upon them.

They passed a scrawny tree with a gnarled trunk. Limbs stuck out with sparse green leaves that were long and pointy. Sure-footedly, their camel followed the Mother's ass and descended down the other side of the mountain. The up and down motion lulled Tamar to sleep. She woke to a glittering city by the sea. They entered a large square filled with throngs of people. The women were wrapped in white tunics. The one closest to them had long straight black hair. Her right shoulder was bare. The air tinkled with the sounds of tambourines and bells. Behind them, people carried life-size golden statues of women and owls. Atop long poles, feathered fans curled toward sky.

A tall black man with gleaming skin and broad muscular shoulders carried a tray of fancy bottles -- some of them midnight blue, others clear glass -- with elaborate stoppers and slender chains hanging from them. Tamar sniffed. The air smelled spicy. Nearly naked children played on the stone square. One of the children, with straight black hair, looked up at them and smiled. The child was wearing a necklace and a string around the waist connected to a white cloth for modesty. She wondered if the child was a boy or a girl. Then she wondered if the child was both a boy and a girl. Did this mean that the child was more than a boy or girl? Was the child They? Maybe it really didn't matter. The thought drifted away.

She wondered if the people in the square were there to meet them. There was a procession on one side. Women stood and strummed hand held harps, rang bells, shook rattles. On the other side of the square, children played. Most of the people didn't even look their way. There were palm trees in the distance. Behind them, high stone temples the color of golden sand rose into robin's egg blue sky.

Tamar decided that she liked this place.

They kept riding on the camels until they came to a yellow stone house on the outskirts of the city. As the camels stopped and they disembarked, Tamar closed her eyes. She smelled salt air.

"Welcome," said the man who answered the door. "You are among family -- you are safe."

Inside, Tamar breathed a sigh of relief. There was no straw in sight. No manger animals. Tamar and her twin shared a room with Hannah.

One day, another maid servant came into their room and made a big deal of presenting an infant to Tamar's twin.

"This is John the Baptist," said the woman. Tamar could see fine black hairs sprouting above her upper lip. "You are going to be great men together. People will remember you both forever."

Tamar turned her head to the wall.

The days passed. Tamar saw much more of Hannah than she did of the Mother. But Tamar sensed when the Mother came into the room. The Mother seemed to glide above the floor. There was always a circle of golden light above her head.

"How's our little messiah doing today?" she would say every morning as she picked up Tamar's twin.

Tamar hated that the Mother picked up that other baby first, but she didn't cry. She knew that if she was a good little girl, the Mother would pick her up next.

"And how's my little Thomas?"

When the Mother picked her up, Tamar could feel the warmth of the glow that surrounded her. It came from the Mother. Tamar decided that this was love. Whoever the Mother loved and whoever loved the Mother would start to glow.

Tamar was so happy that she didn't mind if the Mother called her Thomas.

When the Mother picked her up, Tamar looked up at her and said, "Ma."

The Mother smiled. The golden circle around her head became brighter.

"Ma, Ma," said Tamar.

"Look," the Mother said as she held Tamar higher in the air, kissing her on the forehead.

"Little Thomas knows my name."

"Everyone knows your name, Mother," said Hannah.

Tamar looked over and saw Hannah smiling.

"But you are right. Your child knows that you are the Mother," said Hannah.

Tamar loved Hannah, too, but in a different way. Hannah was the one who knew her secret -- that she was really a girl. She was a good little girl, and the Mother loved her.

More days passed. Tamar began to sit up. Her twin was doing the same thing, but Tamar did her best not to notice. Not everything was about him.

Tamar began to crawl.

When the Mother left their room, Tamar crawled after her. But Hannah always noticed and came and picked her up.

The next day Tamar took her first step. She sat down again before her brother could see. She didn't want him to imitate her. Maybe this was something she could do better than him.

The Mother came in to their room that morning, like she usually did.

When she left, Tamar crawled after her. Then she stood to her full height and took a few steps down the hallway. Hannah must have been busy with her brother. Tamar heard him crying. *He probably went in his swaddling again,* she thought and crinkled her nose. She saw the back of the Mother's blue robe go through a doorway. But when Tamar came to the room, the Mother was nowhere to be found. So Tamar settled back on a shiny pillow that caught her eye with patterns of straight lines and spirals. She waited for the Mother to return.

"There you are," said Hannah, poking her head through the door. "Thank God I found you," she said. She picked up Tamar and carried her back down the hallway.

Tamar would have to find a different way to follow the Mother.

Many days passed, but Tamar hadn't forgotten. It was good that she waited. She could walk more quickly now.

One morning when Hannah was washing her twin, Tamar snuck out in the hall again. She heard someone coming. She ducked into another room and sat down. She sat there for a long time. In the middle of the room was a circular matt made from reeds. Tamar crawled over and sat on it.

She was almost asleep when a blue mist appeared in a column of yellow light. At first Tamar thought that the beam of light was spilling through the window and that the blue tint was dust. But then the blue robe of the Mother materialized. Her arms and feet appeared. Tamar looked up and saw the golden light around her head.

"Oh," said the Mother when she looked down and saw Tamar. "It looks like you caught me."

Tamar looked up at the Mother and nodded. She couldn't speak many words yet, but she could understand when the Mother spoke to her. The Mother looked slightly irritated.

"I have things to do," she said. "But if you must know, I found out how to travel to distant places without leaving the house. I've been to Nazareth in the Palestine which is where we are going to live next. I went to the market and ran into my Aunts Sapphira and Claudia, two old women who sell loaves and fishes. They were thrilled to see me, of course. But I pretended to be someone else. It is better that way. If Herod's soldiers find them, they will not know anything. Herod is ailing, but he is still alive -- which is why we can't go back yet. I'm telling you this so you know what's going on. When you start to talk, don't tell anyone."

Tamar nodded silently. Then she stood up and walked out of the room. There was nothing that she loved more than to be around the Mother, but it seemed like she wanted her privacy. Besides, they shared a secret now. So she felt closer to the Mother, even if she wasn't the next messiah -- whatever that was.

Days passed. One morning Tamar decided to take a walk. Hannah was nowhere to be found. Her twin was behind the house playing with the other boys. The last time she looked out of the back door, the boys were standing on each other's shoulders, grasping hands and rolling around like wheels. Tamar preferred to stay in the house and play with a Nubian doll that she had found.

Tamar left her doll in the corner. She went to the door-way and looked both ways. Seeing that the coast was clear, she wandered down the hall to an empty room. She sat on the mat again, idly gazing into space. She thought about the first word that she spoke, 'Maaaa.'

She had said it many times since the first time, of course. But she had gotten so much approval from the Mother for saying it, that she hadn't bothered to try to say anything else.

She repeated the phrase over and over again.

"Maaa. Maa. Maaa. Maa. Maa. Maa. Maaa."

Tamar was so busy repeating it, that she didn't see the pillar of light in the middle of the room, until the Mother materialized.

"You called?"

Startled, Tamar looked up.

The Mother smiled down.

"I was just kidding," said the Mother. "I was coming back anyway. But I did hear you saying my name."

Tamar stood and said, "Maaa."

"I have good news," said the Mother.

"Herod is on his deathbed. His nurse was out of the room for a minute. So I pretended that I was her and spat into the bucket that he drinks from."

Smiling, the Mother bent over and reached for Tamar's hands.

"So soon my little Thomas, my boy, we can go home to Nazareth."

Tamar looked at up at the Mother. Then she looked down at her own small sandals. The time had come for her to speak to the Mother. Her twin was already speaking, of course. It seemed like he did everything first -- coming out of the Mother's womb head first and being proclaimed messiah and rough housing with the boys outside, some-thing that Tamar definitely didn't want to do anyway.

"I'm a girl, NOT a boy," Tamar announced.

The mother looked surprised.

"But, of course, you're a boy," she answered. "I named you Thomas."

"I'm a GIRL. My name is Tamar."

"Tamar? Where did you come up with that?" The Mother bent down and peered at her. Tamar didn't know how she knew her own name. It seemed like it had always been with her.

"Well, I do remember the midwife saying something to me." The Mother looked doubtful.

"I don't get involved with the swaddling," said the Mother. "That is Hannah's job."

She knelt down in front of Tamar. They were almost eye to eye.

"Tamar is a good name. It has a familiar ring to it."

The Mother paused and then spoke: "Let's say that you are a girl. You're a bright child. Even though you haven't spoken much, I can tell that you understand me. It shouldn't matter if you are a boy or a girl. But it does matter. You will have a better life if you are a boy. Only boys are allowed to learn how to read. Do you want to learn how to read?"

Tamar nodded.

'Well, then. You are a boy."

"I'M A GIRL," said Tamar.

"Shhh..." -- The Mother looked out in the hallway. "Okay. You can be a girl. Just don't tell anyone that it was your choice. I can teach you how to read. I, too, had to learn in secret. No one talks about it, but women used to rule the world. I can teach you the old ways."

Tamar smiled and walked back to her room.

Finally, she had spoken. The Mother had listened.

Many days passed.

Tamar spoke full sentences to Hannah. She ignored her brother, but spoke to her doll. She didn't tell anyone that she was a girl. But she didn't say she was a boy either.

One day she was walking down the hall and stopped at an open door in time to hear the Mother speaking to the tall man. She stood in the hallway and peered around the doorframe.

"It is safe to travel back to Nazareth now. Herod is dead," said the Mother.

"I did have a dream last night where God told me to leave Egypt," said the man. "He said that Herod is dead. How did you know?"

"I was at the burial this morning. I watched as he was wrapped in linens and lowered into the ground. I wanted to make sure he was really dead. We have a lot riding on this." Mother tapped her foot impatiently.

The man was silent for a moment.

"I guess we will finally get married when we go back to Nazareth," he said.

"We'll see," said the Mother. She bent over, stood on one foot, and bent the other leg. She fiddled with the brown leather strap of her right sandal.

When she was done, she stood back up.

"We do have two children together," said the man. "We don't want the townspeople to talk."

"If you say so," said the Mother.

Chapter Fifteen

"I am going to read you the story of Adam and Eve and the serpent."

"You'll remember from our bedtime stories that Adam and Eve were said to be the first people. They were made by God, in His own image -- supposedly from a pile of dust. Adam was the first man. Eve was the Mother of all. One story said that she was taken from Adam's rib. Another story said that when she came to life she blew the breath of spirit into Adam and awakened him."

Tamar wiggled in her small chair. They had lived in Nazareth, now, for three years. Yeshua was off with his tutor. Last growing season, Tamar had sat on the Mother's lap to hear the old stories. But now she sat at her desk and listened. The Mother said she was a big girl, and that she would learn better this way. Tamar missed sitting in Mother's lap. When she did, she felt a warm glow all around her. Was the feeling Mother? Was it love? Was she really glowing? She missed the feeling -- whatever it was. But Mother was right. Tamar could learn better this way. Her wooden tablet was on top of her desk. A thin sheet of wax

covered it. Her metal stylus was next to it. It was one of the
new ones with the flat end. She could rub out anything that
she wanted to erase.

"I've read this story to you before, but today I want you
to think about the serpent. You know what a serpent is,
don't you?"

"Yes, Mama. I've seen them in the desert. Some are
poisonous, and some are friendly. I don't touch them unless
you say it is okay," said Tamar. She picked up her stylus.

She drew a squiggly line and looped it around in the
shape of a serpent. It had a fat body and held its head up.

"That's right," said Mother. "And that's a very good
picture. But serpents usually have a forked tongue sticking
out. This one has to stick out her tongue and hiss to get
Eve's attention."

"Okay, Mama." Tamar picked up her stylus and drew
a forked tongue in the soft wax.

"That's very good," said the Mother. "We'll pretend
that the tongue is pink like this."

The Mother stuck out her tongue. Tamar giggled.

Tamar looked forward to her lessons. She loved being
with Mother. At first she was envious of her twin. Yeshua
started his tutoring sessions last growing season. When he
had gone to his lessons, she moped around the house.
Having tired of her dolls, she followed Hannah around and
tried to help her with the chores. Mother said that she hated
to see a good mind go to waste. She told Tamar she would
teach her how to read if she promised not to tell anyone.
Tamar realized that she didn't have it so bad. She was lucky.
She had chosen to be a girl.

"Now when I read the story to you again, think about the story from the serpent's point of view. Remember the serpent is also known as the Female Principal and the Instructor."

"What is an Instructor and Female Prin--?" asked Tamar.

The Mother looked at Tamar as if suddenly realizing that she was speaking to a child.

"Oh. What I mean is that the serpent has the wisdom of the goddess and is teaching the humans in the Garden how to live. Do you understand?"

Tamar nodded and smiled. She really did understand.

"Now the serpent was more subtle than any other wild creature that the Lord God had made. What do think is meant by the phrase 'more subtle?'"

Tamar looked up and gave the Mother a blank look.

"The person who wrote this might have meant that the serpent was more intelligent than the other creatures, less likely to bow down to God," said the Mother. "Who knows maybe God didn't even make the serpent. Maybe the serpent was here first. Maybe the serpent created God."

Tamar looked at her mother and nodded. She was silent as she thought for a moment.

"Maybe, the serpent wouldn't let God tell her what to do."

"Exactly," said the Mother. She nodded her approval.

"He said to the woman, *Did God say You shall not eat of any tree of the garden?*"

The Mother stopped reading. She looked puzzled.

Then she said, "I knew that there was something wrong

with this sentence. The author refers to the serpent as He instead of She. Maybe it's a typo."

"Maybe the serpent was both," said Tamar.

"Both? What do you mean?"

"Maybe the serpent was both male and female," said Tamar.

"Oh, I see. I hadn't thought of that. Maybe you have something there."

The Mother smiled down at Tamar. The golden light around her head brightened.

"' And the woman said to the serpent' -- now remember that the woman is Eve -- the mother of all." The Mother paused.

Tamar picked up the stylus and drew a woman's face next to the serpent.

"That's a nice drawing," said the Mother. But what is that in the middle of Eve's face?"

Tamar had drawn a circle with two dots in the middle of it.

"That's her nose," Tamar said.

"Oh -- her nose. Now I see. That must be what you see when you look up at a grown up. Is that what you see when you look up at me?"

Tamar giggled and covered her mouth.

"It's okay." The Mother smiled down at her. "I understand what you see. But the drawing makes it look like Eve has a pig nose on her face. Look at my nose now and draw the lines that you see."

The Mother knelt on the floor next to Tamar so that their faces were on the same level.

Tamar turned the stylus on its end and rubbed out the pig nose that she had drawn on Eve. When she was done, she flipped the stylus back around and drew the nose that she saw on her Mother's face.

The Mother went back to her chair and picked up the scroll that she was reading from.

"*And the woman said unto the serpent, We may eat of the fruit of the trees of the garden: But of the fruit of the tree which is in the midst of the garden, God hath said, Ye shall not eat of it, neither shall ye touch it, lest ye die.* Now, God warning Eve about the fruit might seem like a good thing."

"Just like when you warned me not to play with a poisonous snake," said Tamar.

"That's right," said the Mother. "But as it turns out, God wasn't exactly being honest."

Tamar felt her eyes widen. The Mother continued to read.

"*And the serpent said unto the woman, Ye shall not surely die: For God doth know that in the day ye eat thereof, then your eyes shall be opened, and ye shall be as gods, knowing good and evil.* So you see, the serpent was guiding Eve to the self-knowledge that can lead to enlighten-ment. Some people say that it was wrong of God to tell Eve that she couldn't eat from the tree of the knowledge of good and evil and that he must have been worried that she would be as smart as him."

"Just like Yeshua," said Tamar.

"What do you mean? What did your brother say?"

"He said that boys are smarter than girls and that's why he goes to a tutor to teach him to read and I do not."

"Hmmm....boys are taught that. But thinking that they are smarter than girls just makes them arrogant. And I did tell him that he was getting special tutoring because he is going to be the next messiah. I wanted to make sure that he takes his studies seriously. But I don't want him to develop a messiah complex."

Tamar nodded. She hadn't heard that word before, *complex*. But she could imagine what it meant.

"You didn't tell him that I know how to read and am teaching you, did you?"

"No, Mama." Tamar shook her head from side to side.

"That's good. You're a good girl. You remembered what I told you. If anyone finds out, we'll have to stop."

A line of worry creased Mother's forehead.

"Even though Herod is dead, danger still may be lurking. His sons may be on the lookout for anyone who is seen as having the potential to be the next messiah. Although it does help that now the kingdom is divided up into three parcels -- Judea, Galilee and the territories east of the Jordan.

"Can you remember that?"

Tamar looked at the Mother with a blank look on her face. She picked up her stylus and drew a thought bubble next to the serpent. Inside, she made the marks of "zzzzzz."

"What does that mean?"

The mother leaned over and studied Tamar's tablet. Her robe fell forward in soft blue folds.

"It means the serpent is taking a nap," explained Tamar. "She -- or he or neither -- was just minding her own business in the Garden..."

"Yes," Mother said. "Let's get back to the serpent. I wasn't finished with the story."

She picked up the scroll.

"Where was I? Okay, here it is. *And when the woman saw that the tree was good for food, and that it was pleasant to the eyes, and a tree to be desired to make one wise, she took of the fruit thereof, and did eat, and gave also unto her husband with her; and he did eat.*"

The Mother paused and frowned. "One problem is that the author let Adam off the hook. Adam didn't have to eat whatever Eve gave him, did he?"

"No, Mama."

Tamar had a knack for knowing the answer that the Mother wanted to hear. But the Mother had taught her to be honest at all times.

"Yeshua and I have to eat what you give us. You told us that last night. The fish was already scaled. Joseph scaled it. It was Hannah's night off so it was all we had for dinner. I didn't mind eating it," said Tamar. "But Yeshua didn't want it. Remember? You said we had to eat it, so we did."

The Mother nodded. "But I am the Mother. You and your brother have to do what I say."

"Maybe Adam felt the same way. Maybe he ate the food that Eve gave him, because she was in charge," said Tamar. She looked down at the tablet and spoke softly.

"Hold your head up," said the Mother putting her index finger and thumb under Tamar's chin. "You are free to ask questions and to have your own belief about what happened. Maybe Adam did think that Eve was in charge and that is why he ate the fruit that she gave him. I haven't heard that before. It is a good idea."

Tamar could tell that the Mother didn't like this idea, though. The golden light around her head dimmed. She sat back in her chair and picked up the scroll.

"*And the eyes of them both were opened, and they knew that they were naked; and they sewed fig leaves together, and made themselves aprons.*"

Tamar's eyes grew wide. "Naked?! You told me that I shouldn't walk around naked."

"We are naturally naked. We are born naked and we are naked when we bathe. But people have learned to hide their nakedness at all other times and this story is the reason that people act the way they do."

"How can a story cause people to act a certain way?"

"This story tells people how to live their lives. Listen and you will find out."

"*And they heard the voice of the Lord God walking in the garden in the cool of the day: and Adam and his wife hid themselves from the presence of the Lord God amongst the trees of the garden. And the Lord God called unto Adam, and said unto him, Where art thou? And he said, I heard thy voice in the garden, and I was afraid, because I was naked; and I hid myself.*"

"See Adam ate from the tree of knowledge of good and evil and he knew that he was naked," concluded the Mother.

"But wouldn't Adam know that he was naked if he hadn't eat from the tree? Couldn't he look down and see that he was naked? Maybe Adam wasn't so smart." Tamar put down her stylus and looked up at the Mother.

"He didn't know he was naked until he ate from the tree of knowledge of good and evil -- supposedly," answered the Mother. "But you are right. Adam wasn't that smart. He was just God's puppet. Eve was the smart one. She was the Mother of all and she was related to the serpent."

The light around Mother's head pulsed.

"How was she related to the serpent? Were they cousins like Yeshua and I are with John the Baptist?"

"You must have noticed that the serpent only spoke to Eve in the story. Serpents usually don't talk. This one didn't speak to God or to Adam. She only spoke to Eve. This means that Eve and the serpent were able to understand each other. If the serpent was female like Eve then it would have been likely that they spoke the same language several generations before the story started."

Tamar looked at the Mother for a long moment and said, "Maybe the serpent and Eve were both male and female like me and Yeshua and they had their own special language."

"How do you know that your brother was both male and female?" The Mother's eyebrows shot up.

"Hannah was bathing me one night and she said that Yeshua and I were the same, almost, you know... down there. But that he was made male."

"I told her that I didn't want her talking about that. Who knows who else Hannah is telling. It is okay with me if you want to be a girl, but your brother has to be a boy. People are expecting the messiah to be male."

The Mother was visibly angry. The thin line of her red lips pursed. The golden glow above her head moved down closer to her head and flared.

"I was the one who asked Hannah if Yeshua was a boy

and a girl like me," said Tamar. "She wouldn't have told me, but I asked."

Tamar spent a lot of time with Hannah and didn't want her to get into trouble.

The Mother pursed her lips.

"Yeshua and I have our own special language," said Tamar. "I always know what he's doing."

"What is he doing right now?" asked Mother.

Tamar closed her eyes tightly.

"He's practicing his Hebrew letters with his tutor," said Tamar. "He learned there are twenty two letters in the Hebrew alphabet and he is going over them and writing columns on his tablet."

Her mother nodded. "I told his tutor that he should be learning how to read and write and converse in Hebrew as well as Greek. Knowing Hebrew will come in handy."

"He is daydreaming about going out in the street and playing sticks with the other boys," Tamar couldn't help adding.

"Hmmm," said the Mother, narrowing her eyes. "I have promised to pay the tutor a handsome amount when Yeshua is old enough to start working. I hope Yeshua takes his studies seriously."

Expressionless, Tamar looked at the Mother. She really wasn't sure that she always knew what her twin was doing. But she knew that he was studying the Hebrew letters. Last night, he had shown her the entire alphabet -- *Alef* through *Tav*. The letters were written from right to left on a piece of stone. And she knew that he liked to play sticks with the other boys. He told her so when she had asked him if he wanted to play jacks with her. It was good of Yeshua to share the characters of the Hebrew alphabet with her. Tamar was learning Aramaic, with its elongated consonants. It was the language that almost everyone spoke in Palestine. When Yeshua told her that he would rather play sticks with the boys than to play dolls with her, she respected his honesty. He had chosen to be a boy, just as she had chosen to be a girl.

"I guess the fact that he likes to play sticks with the boys means that he is a boy, too. I would rather stay in the house with you, Mama, than have to play sticks with the boys."

The Mother laughed.

Tamar laughed along with her.

"You are twins," said the Mother. "It makes sense that you are able to read each other's minds. Although, you may have two separate fathers. That reminds me --"

Tamar felt her eyes widen.

The Mother looked startled and guilty -- as if she had said something that she wasn't supposed to.

"I didn't know that I had a father," said Tamar. She realized then that something had been missing.

"Remember you are a secret. You are MY secret," said the mother. "If anyone asks, just tell them that you are Hannah's little girl. And if anyone asks about Yeshua, just say that he is the son of God. That should stop them in their tracks. God knows what a woman does with her body is her own business," said the Mother, her voice trailing off.

Tamar looked down at the picture of the serpent that she had drawn on her tablet.

"That reminds me. It is David's night to come, and he

will be here soon. I wonder what he's making for dinner? Let's finish the story." The Mother picked up the scroll.

"*And he said, Who told thee that thou wast naked? Hast thou eaten of the tree, whereof I commanded thee that thou shouldest not eat? And the man said, The woman whom thou gavest to be with me, she gave me of the tree, and I did eat. And the LORD God said unto the woman, What is this that thou hast done? And the woman said, The serpent beguiled me, and I did eat.*"

See how Adam blamed Eve?"

"It sounds to me like Eve blamed the serpent. She didn't have to eat from the tree. Maybe the serpent was just making a suggestion," said Tamar.

"You have a point there. But let me finish. *And the Lord God said unto the serpent, Because thou hast done this, thou art cursed above all cattle, and above every beast of the field; upon thy belly shalt thou go, and dust shalt thou eat all the days of thy life: And I will put enmity between thee and the woman, and between thy seed and her seed; it shall bruise thy head, and thou shalt bruise his heel.*"

Tamar looked at the Mother doubtfully. "The snakes in the desert don't eat dust. They eat lizards, scorpions and sometimes birds. That's what you told me."

"That is right," said the Mother. "But this story was written a long time ago. Though, I doubt that serpents ate dust -- even then. Notice though how this story divides the serpent from Eve. The phrase, *And I will put enmity bet-ween thee and the woman, and between thy seed and her seed,* means that God said there would be a deep rooted hatred between women and serpents, going forth from Eve and the serpent to all of their descendents. This separates Eve from her wisdom which is the serpent."

Tamar didn't know exactly what her mother meant but she nodded.

"And this is the worst part," said the Mother as she picked up her scroll again: "*Unto the woman he said, I will greatly multiply thy sorrow and thy conception; in sorrow thou shalt bring forth children; and thy desire shall be to thy husband, and he shall rule over thee.*

See the story of Adam and Eve and the serpent is used as an excuse for men to be in charge of women."

"But you always said that Yeshua is the next mess --," said Tamar. She didn't say what she was thinking, but she could feel it on her face: not me.

"Messiah. That means he is the promised leader of the Jewish people. At the very least, he'll be a prophet. I did have a vision that I would give birth to the next messiah. And as a single mother, the income would help. But I just picked him to be the messiah because he came out first and because he is a boy. He may not have chosen it, but he is a natural. The people expect their prophet to be a man. It all started with the story about the serpent. That is why I'm reading it to you. So you'll understand why men are valued over women, and so you'll understand that the serpent really is the wise one."

Yeshua is as much of a man as I am, thought Tamar.

But instead, she said: "It is fine with me that Yeshua was picked to be the prophet. I am proud of him because he is my brother."

The Mother beamed at her. She sat back in her chair and picked up her scroll again: "And unto Adam he said,

Because thou hast hearkened unto the voice of thy wife, and hast eaten of the tree, of which I commanded thee, saying, Thou shalt not eat of it: cursed is the ground for thy sake; in sorrow shalt thou eat of it all the days of thy life; Thorns also and thistles shall it bring forth to thee; and thou shalt eat the herb of the field; In the sweat of thy face shalt thou eat bread, till thou return unto the ground; for out of it wast thou taken: for dust thou art, and unto dust shalt thou return. And Adam called his wife's name Eve; because she was the mother of all living.

"They got that last part right. Eve was the mother of all living, including Adam. Although this story never mentions that when Eve was taken out of Adam's rib, she blew spirit into him and awakened him. I read that in another scroll that was being passed around in secret," said the Mother.

Tamar nodded and stifled a yawn.

The Mother began reading again: "*Unto Adam also and to his wife did the Lord God make coats of skins, and clothed them. And the LORD God said, Behold, the man is become as one of us, to know good and evil: and now, lest he put forth his hand, and take also of the tree of life, and eat, and live forever: Therefore the LORD God sent him forth from the garden of Eden, to till the ground from whence he was taken. So he drove out the man; and he placed at the east of the garden of Eden Cherubims, and a flaming sword which turned every way, to keep the way of the tree of life.*"

Tamar was going to ask what the tree of life was, but just then she heard the front door open. David walked in. Tamar had only meant this man a few times. The other man, Joseph, was the one who travelled with them to Egypt.

Joseph was too aloof for her to think of him as her father. She felt closer to David. She remembered what her mother said -- that her brother and she may have different fathers.

The man tousled her hair when he came into the room. Tamar smiled. She always smiled when he greeted her. But now she had a different reason. She didn't have to ask about the tree of life, because she had just figured it out. This man was her father. He was her tree of life.

Chapter Sixteen

"The Spirit of God moved on the face of the waters."

Tamar looked at the line that she had copied onto the top of her tablet from a scroll that was called "The Book."

Seven years had passed since the Mother had read her the story of Adam and Eve and the serpent. While she didn't love her Mother any less, she loved having a father. David had moved in. Joseph just came around when there was a carpentry project to work on, like the time they needed a new front door. Yeshua worked with him, learning how to measure and how to drive in nails, sometimes slanted and sometimes straight. David always had somewhere to go when Joseph stopped by. Eventually, Tamar figured out that Joseph was probably Yeshua's father. She had known for a long time that David was her father. He didn't say anything. She just knew. For one thing, she looked like him. Hannah had told her that she had the same greenish brown eyes as David. Both of their eyes changed color depending on the light or their moods. Both had dark brown hair that in a certain light glinted red. Her father's hair came to just below his ears. Tamar's hair was longer. The ends splayed out on her shoulders. Her father's hair was swept back into a blunt cut. When he stood in the sun, the same red strands that Tamar saw in her own hair, flared on his head.

The Mother had left her alone with her lessons, telling Tamar to write a story based on the questions that she had after reading the scrolls. They would go over it later. Tamar had mastered Aramaic with the Mother and Hebrew with Yeshua.

She unraveled another scroll. This was one of the secret ones that the Mother told her not to mention to anyone, even her brother. Yeshua's tutor lived on the other side of Nazareth, up the hill. His home sat on the ridge that opened up to the most majestic view in all the land, or so Yeshua had told her. He walked through the village freely, across the town square and up the far hill to the home of his tutor where, after his lessons, he played outside with the other boys. Tamar didn't want to play with the boys, but she was envious of her brother's freedom.

She took another look at the line that she had copied to the top of her tablet: "*The Spirit of God moved on the face of the waters.*"

She whispered this line to herself, over and over until she could feel the words in her mouth -- like pebbles dropped into still water, rippling into circles. There were other lines, too, that moved her. But there was so much that didn't speak to her. She unraveled one of the secret scrolls that Mother had given to her, telling her to read the story and to write down her own story that it inspired.

She began to read the scroll titled the "The Reality of the Rulers."

She traced her index finger down the left margin of the page as she read the Greek. There were smudges here and there. Some of the words were missing. She filled in the letters that looked like they belonged there:

"*Then the Female Spiritual Principle came [in] the Snake, the Instructor; and it taught [them] saying "What did he [say to] you? Was it, 'From every tree in the Garden shall you eat; yet -- from [the tree] of recognizing evil and good do not eat?'*

The carnal Woman said, Not only did he say Do not eat,' but even 'Do not touch it; for the day you eat from it, with death you are going to die.'

And the Snake, the Instructor, said, 'With death you shall not die; for it was out of jealousy that he said this to you. Rather your eyes shall open and you shall come to be like gods, recognizing evil and good. And the Female Instructing Principle, was taken away from the Snake, and she left it behind merely a thing of the earth."

Tamar sat in her chair and gazed into space. Where did God come from? Where did the serpent come from? If God created the heavens and the earth, didn't He create the serpent too? And if He created the serpent, then why did the serpent speak against God? If God created the serpent, then why did the serpent point out to Eve that God said what he did out of jealousy?

Where did God come from? Didn't He have a mother too?

Tamar held her stylus above the wax sheet on her wooden tablet and began to write from the voice of the serpent:

I was dreaming of paradise and then I was awakened by the woman Eve. It was then that I realized that I was in paradise and God had created someone who I could talk to. Eve was no dummy. I don't know why she listened to God in the first place. When she told me what God said about the tree of knowledge, I questioned his motives.

First of all, it wasn't true that if she ate from the tree, she would die. I've eaten from the tree plenty of times, and I'm alive and well. Eating from the tree made me what I am: a superior creature full of self-knowledge. I know what's good for me and I know what's bad for me. I would know if I was naked. As it is, I have scales.

The closest that I ever get to nakedness is after I shed my skin, something that I do almost once every month. My skin is different shades of brown. Since I'm long, I can turn around and look at myself. I have a thin stripe the shade of sand that travels down my spine. Most of my body is dark brown -- the color of tree bark and earth -- but I have another light stripe close to my belly. My skin gets dry easily from being out in the sun and the wind so much and also because it is my nature. But when I shed my skin -- rubbing my chin against rocks and cacti to help pull it from me -- the scales of my body glisten. When I was young, I shed each time I reached a larger size. Now that I am grown, I still shed every year or so. For a day or two I am moist and sleek and new. Each time I shed my skin, I gain new insights into myself and wisdom about the world.

If I see the gleaming cat eyes and the furry face of a mongoose coming toward me, I hide under a rock or in the shade of the leaves of a dark green or brown desert plant -- such as the vines of a bitter pumpkin. If there's no cover around, I stay still as a stick on the desert sands. But I NEVER go back into my old skin. This is the first playtoy of the mongoose -- crinkly and paper-thin as it is. Once it is off me, the skin is extra dry and scaly. Why would I even want to crawl back into it? Besides, it no longer fits me.

I know that other creatures usually don't see me -- maybe they don't want to. I've heard that many are afraid of me. They think that I might kill them with one bite (or look) or that I might eat their young. Now that I think back, it was brave of Eve to talk to me.

I was sleeping on a branch of the tree of knowledge of good and evil when I was awakened by a nearby rustling. It was Eve, parting the branches as she searched for the forbidden fruit. "Hello," I said. I had heard about Eve, the Mother of all, who dwelled in the Garden. But I had never met her.

The hand pulled back and the leaves fell together.

"Do not fear me," I said. "For I am your friend -- the serpent who God has made to keep you company in the Garden of Eden."

I made up the part about God creating me. I've been in this garden for so long that I may have been here before God. But I thought that saying this would put her at ease.

The leaves parted again. Eve's face appeared. A smile slithered across her face.

"You are a cute little serpent," she said. Then she looked down the end of the branch at my tail that curled around the tree trunk. "Oh! You're not so little after all."

"No. I'm not," I answered. "But I'm still your friend. Now tell me what it is you are looking for -- or tell me anything."

"Anything?"

"Anything," I answered.

"But I don't know if you are male or female," she responded.

"It shouldn't matter. I actually never think about it. I just assumed I was male but I laid a few eggs last year, so I guess I'm female."

"Or maybe you are both," said Eve.

"Yes, maybe I am both. I am the only serpent in the Garden and so there is no other to compare myself to. I am very self-sufficient. I take care of all of my own needs if you catch my drift."

Eve giggled. "Yes, I do. I'm pretty good with that myself. God may have created Adam -- but I have to tell him what to do. Take the example of when I told him that I was thinking of eating from this tree, all he had to say was that, 'God told us not to.' He didn't even ask whether the fruit was ripe or what it looked like."

"God told you not to eat from this tree?"

"Yes. He told me that I could eat from every tree in the Garden except this one. He actually went as far as to tell me not even to touch the tree and then he said, 'for the day you eat from it, with death you are going to die.'

"I guess it's too late. I already touched the tree. Now I am going to die -- even though I don't know what death is. Maybe you could tell me."

"Death is part of life," I answered. "To fear death is to fear life. Death happens to everyone so don't let God threaten you with it. You can think of it as a long sleep where you wake up rejuvenated, sometimes born into a new life. If you are really lucky and you have lived right, not harming anyone and not intentionally causing any suffering, then you will become part of the heavens -- part of the stars, and the dust that circles them. If you enter this realm you will become everything -- this *tree branch I am resting on, the dark green leaves that surround your face."*

Eve peered through the branches at me. "That doesn't sound so bad," she said.

"It's not," I replied. "It's all about energy -- the stuff that you and I and everything is made from. Energy is always changing -- especially when we are born and when we die."

"Wow," said Eve. "That means that when I die, I could transform into you."

"Perhaps," I answered. "I'm not sure of all the details of how it works. But that's pretty much the way it is. We are all connected and we have more in common than we think. But let me tell you something."

I shimmied forward on the branch so that I was closer to Eve. "You will not die if you eat from this tree. The fruit is quite tasty and I should know, since I have eaten from it often," I said.

"But why did God tell me not to eat from it?" asked Eve, her eyes widening.

I could tell from the bewildered look on her face that Eve was perplexed.

"God said this because He is jealous and insecure. This is why I wonder if He really is that powerful. Real power lies in accepting truth as it comes and not in being anxious about others acquiring the same type of power that you might have."

"If I acquire the same powers as God, does that mean that I could become God?"

"Exactly," I said, and gave my new friend a big smile. I stuck out my tongue in a salute to her intelligence. "When you eat from this tree you will know everything that God knows --

starting with the good and evil inside yourself. When you know this, you will know everything that you need to know -- where you come from and where you are going. You will live your life with the knowledge that if you bring happiness to people, you will be happy. You can live in each moment. And when the moment of your death arrives, you will be not afraid."

"I can live with that," said Eve and gave me a wide smile.

I let my gaze linger. Eve had dimples at the corners of her lips and dark flashing eyes. She was, even to a wise old serpent like myself, kind of cute.

"Then why don't you try the fruit," I said. I looked up. There were several pods hanging from the branch above me. "The pod hanging on the end of the branch, right above your head, looks like it is ripe."

Eve reached up and plucked it.

"Good girl," I said. "Now crack open the pod. The fruit is inside and believe me you won't regret eating it. It is heavenly."

Eve cracked open the greenish brown pod and looked inside. She hesitated. A look of guilt clouded her features.

"But what if God is right?" she asked. "What if death is something to be feared? Maybe I shouldn't eat from this tree."

"What do you have to lose?" I smiled craftily. "You already touched the tree and God told you not to touch it or you would die. Look at me, I live in the tree and I'm still here. Besides, the fruit is out of this world. You're going to love it."

"Okay," said Eve.

She took the pod with her left hand and shook into her cupped right hand. Then she took one of the small red fruits between her thumb and index finger and popped it into her mouth.

"Mmmmm."

She swallowed, and said, "It has a very distinctive flavor. It's rather tart, but I like it."

She popped the other two fruits into her mouth. It looked like she was starved for knowledge.

I smiled at her.

"Let me take some back for Adam," she said, and gathered as many pods as she could hold. I was going to tell her that the fruit makes a nice paste that tastes good with stews, but I just sighed and closed my eyes momentarily.

I shuddered and opened my eyes. "Before you leave, there is something I have to tell you."

"What?" she said, peering at me through the leaves.

"I have the gift of second sight. Just now when I closed my eyes, I saw the future. God is going to find out that you ate from this tree. He has his ways, but this time it will be very easy. He will cast you and Adam out of the Garden and forever on there will be enmity between my offspring and yours."

"But I feel a kinship to you," replied Eve. "It is like you are a friend, but more. It is like I have always known you."

"I feel the same way," I said. "Let's make the moment last."

I slithered forward on the branch so that I could reach her. She pushed her head through the branches toward me. I stared into her flashing brown eyes. They were deep set and flecked with gold.

Apparently, Eve found me just as mesmerizing. She moved her head from side to side as she stared back at me.

Something inside me melted. Maybe it was distrust of others -- especially this human who was made in God's image -- although I couldn't say that for sure, since I had never met Him.

I moved toward her. She moved toward me. And suddenly it happened. Our lips touched. I have never kissed anyone before, not even another serpent. I swear to God, I have no idea how those eggs I laid were fertilized. But they did turn into little serpents. Every now and then I see one and am filled with a mother's pride. I imagine this is how God felt when He created someone in his image.

Eve's lips were as moist and supple as if she had just shed her skin. Our lips parted.

She stood still for a moment. Then she stepped back.

"You are beautiful," she said. "And I do feel a kinship with you....but my place is with Adam."

Then she retreated.

Tamar sat back in her chair. She had filled four tablets covered in wax sheets. There was a box of stones on her desk that she used to keep the end of her stylus hot. Her hand hovered above the stones. They had grown cold.

She would heat them up again. But first she gazed off into space. She was suddenly exhausted. This was more than a writing exercise. She felt like she had visited with the serpent. She felt this so acutely that she missed the serpent. It felt like a part of her was missing.

She sat for a while and felt her feelings.

Then the door opened. Startled, Tamar jumped.

"Tamar, I can't find your brother anywhere. His tutor just sent word that he hasn't seen him for two days. I thought that Yeshua got involved with his lessons and didn't bother to come home last night. But now I'm worried about him. Can you help me?"

"Yes, Mother. *Of course* I can help you."

Tamar could feel the cold fury of adolescence rolling in. *Yeshua, Yeshua.* It is always about *Yeshua,* thought Tamar. She carefully placed her tablets on the floor -- so the wax would dry evenly without distorting any of her letters.

Then she went to her room and sat down cross-legged in her special place in the corner, near the back window.

"Maaa," she began. "Maa, maaa."

She breathed deep into her abdomen until there were no thoughts in her mind. There was only breathe and the vibration of Maaa.

She continued to chant until she saw a picture in her mind. Yeshua was in a grand temple. Tamar knew immediately that he was in the Temple -- the place that her brother went with Mother and Joseph where they presented themselves as a family on the holidays. Tamar's own father, David, boasted on more than one occasion that he never went to the Temple. It could be that he was not a believer. Maybe he stayed away out of allegiance to his daughter, Tamar, who was hidden away and never was asked to go. But Tamar suspected that it was more likely that her father didn't want to be around Joseph.

But when Tamar saw her twin in her mind questioning the elders at the Temple and answering their questions intelligently, she saw Yeshua through new eyes. With his shoulder-length hair and angelic face, he looked more like a girl than she did. The bearded elders never would have discussed such weighty matters with women. But she was impressed to see that they looked at Yeshua with awe in their eyes. She had new respect for her brother.

Through her sight she saw a wizened man with a skull

cap and a beard. He leaned on the crook of a cane. "How does a boy your age possess such wisdom?" he asked.

"I am only conducting my father's business," answered Yeshua.

"By father, do you mean Joseph, the carpenter?" asked the old man.

"No. I mean my father in heaven, God." The golden light around Yeshua's head beamed a little brighter.

It was an old trick. Tamar knew how to do it to. Even when she was away from the Mother, she always had a slight glow around her head. Hannah had noticed it. If Tamar thought bright thoughts, the glow around her became brighter.

But the old men in the Temple believed him. Their eyes widened. Two of the men looked at each other. One of the men whispered in another man's ear: "Herod's sons are correct."

Tamar could hear the man even though Yeshua couldn't.

She had seen enough.

"Maa, maa," chanted Tamar, coming back to herself.

She breathed deeply, putting her hands together and thanking her sight, her ability to travel places with her mind. She gave thanks to the Mother for instilling her with such power.

"Mother," said Tamar as she walked out to the hallway. "Yeshua is at the Temple. He's telling people that he's the son of God. Herod's sons are on to him. He may be in danger."

"Oh, Jesus," said the Mother.

Tamar studied the long crack in the clay wall of the hallway.

"I don't know what I'm going to do with him," said the Mother. She sat on the low stool in front of the crack. Tamar looked at her Mother. For the first time, Tamar noticed that the Mother looked defeated. The vertical lines between her eyebrows deepened as she frowned.

"I'm really not going to be able to pull off this Blessed Mother act if I'm fraught with anxiety about Yeshua's safety," she said. She threw back her white head covering that she wore around the house. The yellow glow around her head was dim. Usually shiny, her hair was stringy. It looked dirty. She wore a blue robe on top of her white house dress. She had three sky-blue robes. She was always wore one of them when she was in public -- when she went to the Temple, or to the market, of just outside to water the garden. She had told Tamar that wearing blue would help to distinguish her as the mother of the messiah.

"We have a lot riding on this messiah idea, everything in fact. Joseph is only letting us stay in this house because he thinks that he is the father of Yeshua and I do not know that he is not. They do have the same nose -- long and straight -- and the same wide spaced brown eyes." The Mother stared at the floor in front of Tamar. She looked like she was lost in her thoughts. "And Joseph is teaching Yeshua carpentry. That is a good skill to have. But if Yeshua becomes the messiah, we will be set. I will not have to depend on Joseph."

The Mother looked up at Tamar as if suddenly realizing that she was standing there. "I'm sorry. I shouldn't go on about such things in front of you. You're wise beyond your years -- so I always think of you as older. But you're really still a child."

Tamar nodded. Most of these things had already occurred to her. She had also thought about the fact that most women didn't work outside the home. If something happened to Yeshua, they would always be poor. They couldn't afford to lose his future income -- whether he became a carpenter or a messiah.

"At least Yeshua will be safe in the Temple. Joseph and I must have left him behind when we attended services for Passover. I had a feeling that we forgot something. I neglected to look for Yeshua in the caravan."

Tamar nodded. She didn't point out that she was never invited to the Temple, so she didn't know what it felt like to be left behind.

"He'll be safe in the Temple. I'll leave him there for another day before I send for him. Maybe that will teach him a lesson. He shouldn't be going around saying that he's the son of God. People will talk. That is why Herod's sons are on to him."

"But Mother, you told Yeshua that he is the son of God."

"It's not like you to side with your brother," said the Mother.

"But you told me that I should always be honest," said Tamar.

"That I did. You are right," the Mother conceded. "I should not have told Yeshua that he is the son of God. It appears it went to his head. He is really the son of a

Goddess. If he told people that, they would really talk. And I'd be stoned to death."

Tamar felt her eyes widen. She looked at the Mother. The golden light around the Mother's head shone brighter. Tamar sensed that She was telling the truth. If she was, then that meant that Tamar, too, was born from a Goddess. She was female, too. This meant she was more likely than her brother to inherit the special powers.

"Let's take a look at your lessons."

Tamar followed her Mother into the small study and sat with her while she read her tablets.

The Mother was silent for a long while as she read. Finally, she looked up.

"You wrote these by yourself? You didn't copy anything?" she asked.

"Of course, Mother. I just read the serpent story on the scroll that you gave me and then I wrote my own story. Though I have to admit, I don't remember most of what I wrote. It felt like I fell into a trance."

"Your story is very good," said the Mother. The circle of golden light around her head pulsed.

"But I need you to promise to me that you will not show it to anyone. People won't understand. I'll get some India ink from your brother's room. We'll copy these pages onto a blank scroll. When we're done we'll let it dry, roll it up and store it in an empty clay jar. We'll wait until the next perfume caravan leaves for Egypt. Then we'll send the scrolls with the other goods from the market. The woman who stores the goods can keep the jars in her kitchen. Your story is too good to destroy, but we can't leave it here. There is an old widow who lives in Chenoboskion on the west bank of the Nile in Upper Egypt and collects scrolls. Maybe the scroll will end up with her. Someday your story will be found and read widely. By then everything will have changed, and they'll be no more need for secrecy.

The Mother was a goddess -- not a prophet.

Chapter Seventeen

The Mother took a spoonful of David's famous chili.

"Mmmm," she said with her mouth full.

Yeshua had left early for his usual day-long tutoring session. Tamar was eating lunch with Mother and David. Mother hated to cook. The three of them were eating leftover chili that David had made the day before. The hot chili peppers mixed in it burnt Tamar's mouth. She still loved it. It tasted better on the second day. David called it his "Wheels of Fire Chili."

"I need to speak to David privately," said the Mother. Tamar was scraping the last bit of chili from the bottom of her terracotta bowl.

Tamar excused herself and left the room. But she only went as far as the hallway. She pressed herself against the opposite side of the bumpy clay wall.

She heard clatter. David must be clearing away the clay dishes from their wooden table.

"We have to send Yeshua away," said the Mother.

"What do you mean?" said David. "He is doing fine here."

"He's in danger. Herod's sons have it in for the next

messiah," said the Mother. "You know that Herod and his sons are just puppets -- appointed by the Romans."

David was silent. *He probably doesn't agree with Mother,* thought Tamar, *but doesn't want to say so.*

Tamar wasn't surprised when he changed the topic.

"So who says he's the next messiah?"

"He does," answered the Mother.

Tamar heard a clay plate breaking against the floor.

"Shit," said David. "How do you know?"

"Someone told me that when he was at the Temple, he started calling himself the son of God."

Tamar was glad that Mother honored their pact. It was their secret that she could always know what her brother was doing. But at the same time, she wanted to take credit for her special powers. She knew her father loved her, but she wanted him to be proud of her, too.

"I see," said David. "I thought he was my son. That should be enough."

His voice sounded compressed, like he was bending over, picking up the shards of plate from the floor. David kept a clean kitchen. Tamar speculated that was why Mother let David live with them. Joseph was pleasant enough and he could fix things. But he left his dirty dishes on the table and expected Mother to serve his meals.

Tamar could feel her eyes widen as she pressed herself to the wall a little tighter. She hadn't known that David thought that Yeshua was his son. *Now, I have to share my father, too?* But Mother probably had her reasons for not telling him that Joseph was probably the father of Yeshua.

"Well..." said Mother. She sounded hesitant which was rare. "I may have put it in his head that he was related somehow to God when I was talking to him about being the next messiah. I just wanted him to take his studies seriously. I see now that I was wrong to tell him this. He is in danger. That's why we need to send him away."

"I see," responded David.

"Elizabeth and Zechariah sent John the Baptist to live at Qumran with a secret sect called the Essenes. They told me that they are grooming him to be a prophet," said Mother.

"Essenes? I've never heard of them," answered David.

"They keep a low-profile, but they are well regarded," said the Mother. "They have the philosophy that they must live separately from other Jews who have been influenced by the Romans and have become too much like them. The Essenes have strict rules, especially about keeping kosher and observing the Sabbath."

"It figures that Zechariah would know about them. Just because he is a priest, he thinks his son is going on to great things," grumbled David. "Perhaps he is right. But Yeshua could be just as great, and he is from far more humble beginnings."

"It would be hard to be from a humbler place," laughed the Mother. "Born in a manger and raised in a hovel by a single mother."

"I've been telling you that we can get married anytime," said David.

"Perhaps," said the Mother.

This wasn't the first time that David had suggested marriage. But Mother always had the same answer. Perhaps.

"Let's decide what to do about Yeshua," continued the

Mother. "I don't want him in harm's way. Qumran is very protected because the community lives in caves atop the mountains that overlook the Salt Sea. Maybe Yeshua will learn to fish. Besides, Herod's sons are stupid and lazy. They will only think of looking for him among the Pharisees and will not want to travel as far as Qumran."

"Come to think of it, I have heard about the Qumran caves from a fellow at the market who sells salted fish. The sect you're talking about must be the same society," said David.

David was the one who usually went shopping at the market. He stopped there on the way home from visiting his rental properties that he had bought after he sold the flocks that were passed down to him from his father and grandfather.

"The caves are to the North of the Salt Sea in the direction of Jericho. Some of them overlook the sea," he added.

"En Gedi is on the western shore just below the mountain caves. There are fresh springs and tall palms. Remember? It's an oasis next to the Salt Sea. We always wanted to take a trip there," said the Mother.

"I do remember," said David. "We were going to get away together but then you realized that you were pregnant with the twins and you had the morning sickness all day. En Gedi always sounded like the perfect place with its vineyards and clusters of henna blossoms."

"Plus it is an historic area -- famous in the time of Solomon and allotted to the tribe of Judah. I'll bet there are some quaint inns there," said the Mother.

Tamar heard a rustling, then her father's low growl and Mother's giggling.

"Not here," chided the Mother. "We don't want to risk Tamar walking in and finding out how she was made."

Tamar felt a wide smile spread envelope her. So David was her father.

The Mother was still talking, but in hushed tones.

Tamar moved toward the doorway of the kitchen so she could hear better.

"We could take Yeshua to live at Qumran and stop at En Gedi on the way back. But I am not sure that I want to leave him with that bunch of bearded men who dwell in the caves. They say they are nonviolent and that they do not eat animal flesh, but who knows what they are into."

"Joab says that the Qumran community is sincere. They are peaceful people and they take their spiritual practices seriously. In fact, they have written rules for living in their community. Most of the men are celibate. But some of the men are married. They live separately in nearby towns where they live daily lives but devote themselves to God."

"Joab? I have never heard the name before," commented the Mother.

"Joab is the seller of salted fish at the market," answered David.

"I see. So this makes him an expert on where we should send our son?"

Still pressed into the wall in the hallway, Tamar nodded silently. Mother had told her how it irritated her when men valued the advice of other men rather than listening to her.

"Just because Joab is a seller of salted fish doesn't mean

he is any less knowledgeable about worldly matters than other men. Remember, I used to tend flocks before becoming a landlord," said David.

"And you are an excellent cook as well," said the Mother. Her voice rose a notch. Tamar smiled.

"Forgive me, darling. You are correct."

"It makes sense that Elizabeth and Zechariah are sending John the Baptist to live there," said David. It will keep Herod's sons from harming him and also will give the young man some training in the mysteries. You know that they've been predicting a messiah for years."

"Yes," said Mother. "Someone who will be able to heal the sick and raise the dead."

"Oh? I hadn't heard the details," said David.

"I go to the market myself every now and then," replied the Mother.

"Oh. That's right," said David. "Joab told me that the order advocates the equality of all people and that they are against slavery. They take a vow of poverty and many live to a ripe old age, past the age of one hundred."

"That doesn't sound so bad," said the Mother.

"And Joab told me that they live apart from society -- from the hustle and bustle and the pursuit of riches -- so that they may pray and work for a better world. And they only serve water with their meals -- never wine. The feasts are followed by singing and skits about the old stories."

"The old stories?"

"You know the stories that everyone tells. Joab told me that some of the sect's skits are about Moses and his sister Miriam at the Red Sea."

"Oh, THOSE stories," said the Mother. "I don't really

take much stock in them. But the skits sound harmless enough. But I wonder if they will take Yeshua? We do not have much to offer," she added.

"That's true," replied David gravely. "Elizabeth and Zechariah have more to offer. Zechariah's priesthood is going well. He is attracting followers."

"Maybe the Essenes would take an interest in Yeshua because he is the cousin of John the Baptist. Neither of them would be able to join the sect for a few years anyway. Elizabeth told me that the initiate lives outside for a year, but they place him under their way of life," said the Mother.

"Hmmm," said Joseph. "Now that I reflect on all that Joab told me, I think this sect would be a good place for Yeshua to live."

"I guess you are right," said the Mother. "I will talk to Elizabeth."

Tamar heard footsteps coming toward the kitchen door. She quickly walked down the hallway to her room. She picked up her stylus and started writing on a new scroll and ended with, "So this is how the Mother convinced David that it was his idea to send Yeshua to Qumran to live with the Essenes."

A day later, Yeshua left with Mother and David. Tamar was left with only Hannah for company. At first Tamar didn't mind. Hannah took her to the market for the first time.

"If anyone asks, just say that you're my cousin from Galilee."

"I thought that I was your daughter," said Tamar. She

had to walk fast to keep up with Hannah's longer strides. She tripped over a stone, caught herself, and kept walking.

"You're getting too big for us to pretend you're my daughter," said Hannah. "You're twelve now. Soon you'll be able to have children of your own. That would make me a grandmother. We can't have that. So we'll pretend that you are my cousin. Besides, I'm not married yet. It would look strange if you were my daughter. That's just a game we used to play among ourselves."

"Ok," said Tamar, "I'm your cousin from Galilee."

The fact was that Tamar didn't much care if she was pretending to be Hannah's daughter or her cousin. She was thrilled to be going to the market. She rarely went out of the house when Mother was home. She had begged to go to the market, but the Mother told her that the town of Nazareth was no place for a young girl.

They walked up a hill. In the distance were small flat roofed houses and short trees with what looked like wide green arms that brushed the ground.

"What are those?" Tamar pointed to the trees below them.

"Those are dwarf palm trees," said Hannah. "Doesn't the Mother ever take you out?"

Tamar was quiet. She didn't want to say anything bad about the Mother. The Mother had taught her how to read Coptic. She had learned Hebrew from Yeshua. But the Mother had forbid her from telling anyone. She hadn't told Yeshua, even when he was surprised at how fast she had caught on to learning Hebrew. Yeshua had forbid her from telling Mother that he was teaching her Hebrew.

But it was true that her Mother never took her out any further than the walled garden next to their tiny house. Tamar remembered looking up at the patch of clear blue sky and asking the Mother if they could go beyond the wall.

The Mother had changed the subject by showing her a white flower with a crimson center growing on an okra plant alongside some small green pods. The flower was beautiful. It was a world in itself, just like the Mother had said. But Tamar remembered wistfully looking up at that patch of sky before she went back into the house.

If she had Yeshua's freedom, she'd know what a dwarf palm tree was. She kicked a clod of dirt.

"God damn Yeshua," she muttered. She watched the clod scatter into pieces.

"What does your brother have to do with anything?" Hannah stopped walking and turned around to face Tamar. The wind rippled her white head scarf. "You know that you shouldn't be taking the Lord's name in vain."

Tamar looked down at the dry earth. She felt her face burning. She had good reason to be angry. She looked up at Hannah and explained herself:

"Boys get to do everything. He's been going across the village to his tutor's house for years. One time he even was by himself at the Temple for a few days. Now he's ..."

Tamar sucked in her breath. Just in the nick of time, she remembered that the Mother swore her to secrecy about Yeshua going to live with the sect at Qumran. Mother had specifically said that she should tell no one -- including Hannah. When Tamar asked the Mother why, she said that Herod's sons had spies everywhere. That, while they loved

Hannah like a family member, she was leaving them soon to get married and live with her husband. They could not tell her anything, because she might mistakenly tell the wrong person.

"I don't know where he went. But he is somewhere with Mother and David. And they left me behind...again."

"But you are with me," said Hannah, stooping down slightly so that she was eye-level with Tamar. "And you should be thankful that you are a girl."

"And why is that?"

"For one thing, you chose to be a girl. Since you were small, you insisted that you were a girl. I remember that Mother had the midwife come with the priest to perform a circumcision on your brother eight days after his birth. The midwife told me that Yeshua was made male that day. But when the midwife offered to do your surgery at the same time, the Mother told her 'No.'"

Tamar hadn't known the details. She stood still and stared at Hannah. They were standing higher on the hill that overlooked the town. Small, square houses sat in a circular basin. Tamar's house was somewhere in the middle of the village. She could see the wooden doors of some of the houses that must have been owned by more well-off people. There were so many little houses huddled together that she didn't know which one was hers. She tightened her grip on Hannah's hand.

Past the houses was the rise of another hill, beyond that another rise. Far in the distance, Tamar spotted a mountain range. The dry brown earth was dotted with green trees that thinned out into the horizon. Yellow earth met blue sky. The Mother and David and Yeshua were out there somewhere. Tamar knew that the Qumran caves were in the direction of Jericho, but she didn't know which way that was.

As Tamar looked out into the horizon, she felt uneasy. There was nothing holding her in place. The Mother, her brother and her father were gone. She couldn't even hold onto her usual resentment of Yeshua, because she sensed that he was in danger. She was worried about him. She was also concerned about the Mother and David. She hoped they would be safe on their journey. But she couldn't admit any of this to Hannah. She stubbornly clung to the one thing that she knew to be true.

"I'm a girl," she said, looking up at Hannah. With the sun behind her head, Hannah looked like she was surrounded with light -- like the Mother.

"Of course you are," said Hannah. "It's just that you had a choice when you were born. You could have been a boy or a girl. You chose to be a girl."

"But I didn't choose to be a girl. I just am one," insisted Tamar. But it occurred to her that she was different than most girls. Other girls were more like Hannah. They didn't know how to read. They took care of children. Tamar hated children -- especially Yeshua.

"I'm female, just like the Mother," she said. She thrust out her chin.

"Is that what this is all about?" Hannah smiled at her.

Tamar nodded. She loved the Mother and wanted to be just like her. She had even asked the Mother to find her a sky blue robe.

Hannah laughed. "We all want to be like the Mother,"

she said. "And wise boys want to be like Her also. I bet Yeshua feels the same."

Tamar shrugged. This was the first time she thought about it.

"But he gets to go out and have adventures," said Tamar.

"The Mother is just protecting you by not letting you go out," said Hannah. She spoke resolutely.

"From what?"

"From war, for one thing. We are lucky that Nazareth is such a small town -- not to mention that it is poor -- and overlooked by the Romans. But my cousin in Galilee told me that the Romans come through towns every so often and rape and plunder. And the men who live in the towns have to fight them."

"Wait a minute," said Tamar. "I thought I was your cousin from Galilee."

"You are my pretend cousin," answered Hannah. "I have a real cousin who lives there."

Tamar considered the fact that she wasn't the only little girl in Hannah's life. But I'm not a little girl any more, she chided herself. She was twelve years old now.

"What does rape and plunder mean?"

"Trust me. You don't want to know," said Hannah. They turned and started walking down the hill toward the market. Tamar looked down to the bottom of the hill where she saw people huddled together and yelling at each other across tall tables.

"Is that war?"

Hannah's laughter was swept away by the breeze. "No, the people are just buying food for their dinners."

At the bottom of the hill, Tamar saw a man in a tattered robe smiling at her. He had a scruffy dark brown beard.
His hair was long and matted.

Hannah was looking down at a patch of stars of
Bethlehem wildflowers on the ground. She dropped Tamar's
hand.

Tamar smiled at the bearded man and walked toward
him.

When she came closer, she saw that the man's hand was
inside his robe, moving up and down.

"Hannah," Tamar cried out.

The man reached out to grab her. Tamar jumped back.

"Quick. Run," Hannah grabbed Tamar's hand.

The man opened his robe. Something that looked like a
pale snake fell from his abdomen. He was pulling at it.
Suddenly it grew. It looked like it had an eye on the end of
it. It was looking right at her.

Tamar knew what he was pointing at her. She had a
much smaller version of it between her own legs. But she
peed through the opening behind it and only touched the
small appendage that hung there when she washed.

Hannah yanked her hand. Tamar stumbled but caught
her footing, as the two of them ran down the hill. When
they reached the bottom of the hill, Hannah let go of
Tamar's hand.

Tamar's hand tingled. Her fingers were red. Her hand,
where Hannah had gripped it, was white.

"He won't come after us down here. There are too
many people around," said Hannah. "I heard that there was
a man around who likes to hurt children, but I thought that
was just a story."

"Who was that man?" Tamar followed Hannah as they walked toward the throng.

"Remember what I told you about rape and plunder? The Romans aren't the only ones who do that. The man doesn't look like a Roman -- he doesn't wear a uniform and Romans would never let themselves go like that. But I've heard it whispered that he shows himself to young girls. Who knows what else he'd do if he had the chance."

"Why is he allowed to do this?"

"He hasn't yet been caught," answered Hannah. "One of these days, we'll see his head on a pole."

Chapter Eighteen

The hairs on the end of the golden camel hair blanket tickled her nose. The blanket felt soft and warm -- if a little scratchy -- over her nakedness. She had come to bed early to explore her body. The seasons had passed quickly. Tamar was now twenty-one. She learned as much Greek as the Mother could teach her. She was also re-reading the Hebrew scrolls that Yeshua had left for her. It wasn't enough to keep from feeling restless and bored.

Tamar spread fingers on her on her small firm breasts. She didn't like to draw attention to her breasts. Around the house, she was sure to wear oversize robes. But here, under the blanket, it felt good when she touched them.

She let her fingers linger on the nipples. It felt like a lightning rod moved down her body. Between her legs, the small appendage throbbed. She kept her hands on her breasts, moving them in wide circles. She liked making herself wait. She wasn't sure she wanted to touch the appendage. She remembered her day on the hill with Hannah when the man with the scruffy beard parted his robe and exposed himself. She remembered feeling revolted but, truth be told, also fascinated. His appendage, with the eye on the end, was disgusting. But thinking about this wouldn't make the sensation between her own legs go away.

Her left hand stayed on her breast and her right hand drifted down her naked body. She felt the flat plain of her stomach and abdomen. Her appendage throbbed. She pressed down on it with her index finger and her middle finger. She made circles on top, then pressed harder. Under her fingers, her flesh felt hot, engorged, slippery. She moved her fingers around and around. And it was good.

Underneath, the opening demanded her attention. She stroked the surface. Then she plunged several fingers inside of herself. She slid them in as far as they could go. Wetness enveloped her fingers. Her body felt like an underground spring. She pulled her fingers out and plunged them back in. She did it again. She moaned quietly. Her body called to her fingers to come back inside. She slipped her fingers in again. Pulled them out. Plunged them back in. She pulled her fingers back out and listened to the slurp of her slippery cave. She smelled the musk and the salt of her body. She pressed down on her appendage. It felt small and squishy, not like something that got in the way when she was walking or going to the bathroom. She flattened it with her two fingers and moved them around in a circle. Faster. Faster. She shuddered. Liquid shot out of the opening. She could feel the wet spreading under her as she lay in the stillness. Her heart pulsed between her legs.

She closed her eyes to go to sleep, but she was wide awake.

Several years had passed since Yeshua had gone to live with the Essenes. Tamar couldn't go -- even if she wanted to. It was all boys. No one knew that Yeshua had a twin.

Mother said it would ruin their plan if people knew, because a Messiah stood alone. But she used her special powers to visit -- unseen and unheard. A few months after the Mother and David had returned from Qumran, Mother had asked Tamar to check in on her brother to make sure that he was okay. He was living in a special cave for initiates and he was with several other boys his age. They wore white robes. They spent most of their time praying and singing. Sometimes, it seemed like they were doing both. They moved their lips in unison as they read the Hebrew letters written on the scrolls. It sounded like bees in a hive.

Yeshua was accepted into the sect a year or so after he first went to live there. Tamar found out from Mother after she had visit Aunt Elizabeth and Uncle Zechariah the parents of John the Baptist. They had sent her cousin to live at Qumran six months before Yeshua -- so John was in an earlier group of initiates accepted into the Essenes. Her aunt and uncle had been to visit John who had told them that Yeshua was well regarded by his peers and was doing well in the sect. Mother had told Tamar not to bother checking in on her brother, to think about her own studies instead.

Tamar wondered if the Mother knew that she had always envied the fact that Yeshua had so many adventures. But Tamar knew that it wasn't envy that prompted her to think of Yeshua all these years later. She was bored. She had read and re-read all of her scrolls. Mother didn't have any new ones. Tamar had learned all of the Hebrew letters and words that were in the scrolls that Yeshua had left for her. Her body was an adventure, but it wasn't enough. She wondered what Yeshua was learning.

She closed her eyes tight. If she concentrated, she could imagine being back in the womb of Mother's belly where she and her twin had floated in the same salt water. She felt a buzzing in her mind. Then she felt detached from her body, as if she were riding on a current of air. She lit onto the wide wing of a soaring bird, and together they flew through sky. Eventually, they circled ivory colored mountaintops of sandstone and salt. Tamar looked closer. She saw the black openings of caves. The bird hovered. For a moment, it looked still -- suspended in sky. To the right, below the cliffs, lay the vast blue Salt Sea. The bird flew down and alighted at the doorway of one of the caves. Invisible as the wind, Tamar slipped in.

Inside the doorway to the right was a set of stone steps that led down to a square pool of water. It must be a purification bath. She had heard Mother and David talking about the ritual baths. She looked to the right of the descending stairs and saw ridges that would direct rain water down into the bath. She had heard that there were ritual baths everywhere -- even in the Temple in Nazareth. The bath was for purification, but the water looked dirty.

Tamar had never seen a ritual bath before. She stared at it in wonderment. She remembered that she was invisible and had the power of wind. She could not enter the water, but she could skim across the surface of it and make it ripple. Then she swept across the bath in the opposite direction. She watched the ripples converge. Then she remembered why she had come: to find Yeshua. She wafted up to the top of the stairs where she surveyed a cavernous room.

Shaped like a bell, the cave had a high ceiling. Young men in white robes sat in a semi-circle on the floor. Most were too young to have beards. They wore white shawls covering their heads. It was hard to tell them apart. But Tamar spotted her twin sitting in the middle, shoulder to shoulder with the other boys. He stared raptly at the teacher. There was a slight glow around his head, emanating through his white shawl. The teacher was standing in front of the semi-circle, talking to the group.

"Beelzebub, also known as Satan, was once an angel. A messenger of light can also be a messenger of darkness. When Beelzebub was an angel, he was a heavenly spirit connected to Hesperus, the evening star. He fell to Earth because he was tempted by lust. Because he was knowledge-able about lust, he caused destruction by igniting lust in the loins of priests and causing men to worship demons who took the form of tyrants. By awakening lust, he also caused envy and war."

Even as the wind, Tamar remembered that she had recently explored her own body and committed what the old man would probably describe as the sin of lust. Would the lust she felt for herself inspire envy and war? She shook with terror. Then she looked at the faces of the young men who were listening to their teacher. Some were still boys. With their beardless, smooth faces under their head coverings, they could be girls. But girls were forbidden to be here. Her terror gave way to anger. Maybe exploring her body was natural -- even if lust were involved. What did this old man know?

The anger that she felt caused her to whip around in a

frenzy. As wind, she gusted in the direction of the teacher. She blew his shawl off his head. One of the boys sitting next to Yeshua tried to hide a snicker behind his hand. She spun in the opposite direction and saw the teacher's balding head surrounded by dirty, matted hair. It looked as though he hadn't had a ritual bath in a while. He picked up his shawl, put it back on his head and continued talking.

"What I'm talking about is very important -- and no laughing matter." He stopped and glared at a snickering young man. "Evil comes from the serpent in the Garden of Eden who tempted Eve to eat from the tree of knowledge of good and evil. Eve corrupted Adam and all of mankind. It can't be said often enough that Eve was evil.

"Isaiah told us that 'the Lord is coming to punish the inhabitants of the earth; and the earth will disclose the bloodshed upon her, and will no more cover the slain.' And the Lord will take his great hand and slay the Leviathan, the twisting serpent that is the dragon in the sea," continued the old man.

"This is why we must guard against Beelzebub. For if the Lord must be vigilant -- then we must take extra heed to keep ourselves pure. Only by being pure, can we learn to be healers. Healing the sick starts in your minds, not your hands. People become sick because something bothers them. They can't forget about it. It plagues them. You must learn to fill yourself with light. Pray when you wake in the morning. Think good thoughts and only say good things to people -- especially to the sick. They have heard enough bad things from others and from their own minds. This is how they become diseased."

"But master," said a young man with an oval face and dark skin sitting next to Yeshua. "How do we prevent ourselves from being infected if we spend time with the sick? Won't we become sick if we touch them?"

"Good question my son. When we fill ourselves with light and truth, we lessen the chance that we will become sick. Instead of infecting us, the sick become like us. They take on our pureness. That is why it is important to pray every morning. At first you will be tempted to keep to your old ways and to think bad thoughts. When you enter the cleansing bath each day, think of the water as washing away any bad intentions that may still be with you. When you pray in the morning, inhale the sunlight into every fiber of your body. Listen to your breath as it moves in and out. Remember that you have the power to change your thoughts. There may be people who tell you otherwise when you are out in the world. Women may try to distract you and tell you not to believe. The scrolls are full of stories where women try to distract men from God. That is why you should not listen to women. Do you understand?"

Several of the boys had quizzical looks on their faces. Tamar as the wind was sexless, but she remembered that she was female. She understood the Mother's frustration at men not listening to her. Now she understood the source. The old man made her angry, but she was too bored to whip herself into a frenzy.

"But, sir."

Tamar couldn't be certain which boy had spoken, but it sounded like Yeshua.

"Are there any questions?" The master's voice boomed in the cavern.

"It's just that if you knew my mother, you'd believe what she said." Tamar saw that the boy who spoke was her brother.

The master was silent.

One of the boys snickered.

"Boys, it was natural for you to listen to your mothers when you were young. But now you are living here. That is why we keep the married men separate from the celibate men and boys. So you can be among your own kind -- unpolluted by women. Are there any other questions?"

Yeshua's head shawl drooped over his forehead as he looked down.

"Back to our lesson on healing -- when you keep yourselves pure and pray to God every day, you enter the light. When the sick come to you, they realize that they can enter the light, too. It is said that our next messiah will have such incredible powers of healing that people will become whole again just by touching the hem of his garment."

A young boy smirked. He had a red pimply forehead and sat on the left end of the semi-circle. Most of the boys sat politely with their hands folded. One was sleeping with his mouth open. Yeshua looked back up and smiled. He glowed as he listened to the teacher.

The master continued to speak. Tamar ignored him and continued to stare at her brother. A subtle glow emanated through his white hood. His face was filled with light. He did not look sleepy or bored. He looked as if all things mattered. He had defended the Mother. Tamar wondered if he really was the next messiah. She doubted that he was the son of God. He looked too much like Joseph with his brown hair and his deep set eyes.

The master finished his lesson and the boys scampered off.

"Do you want to go swimming in the Salt Sea?" asked a young man who appeared at Yeshua's side as they left the cave.

"I'm going," said another, standing next to the first young man. "We have enough time to be back for dinner."

"I hear the salt is so thick that you can practically walk on the water."

"Yes," responded Yeshua. "I will go."

As the wind, Tamar swept through sky and followed the young men down a path that led from the cave around the mountain towards the Salt Sea. She paused outside the cave. She admired the sand-colored striations -- brown, tan, pink -- of the mountain under the dark mouth of the caves.

She swept down just in time to hear what the young men were saying.

"I know a trick that will allow us to change the water into wine," said one of them.

"Why would you want to do that?" asked Yeshua, turning to him.

"I heard some of the elders talking about the end of days when we Jews are scattered to the ends of the earth and do not keep the laws of Moses," replied the boy.

"But I heard the elders talking about the end of days as the time when the messiah will lead the Jews back from the ends of earth to the land of Israel where we will again find ourselves in prayer," said the second young man.

"That's not what I heard," said the first. The elders

were talking about a time when we cease to exist -- as a people. We will probably die off eventually. For all we know, this desert could be gone tomorrow. Why should we drink water instead of wine?"

"Because," said Yeshua. "We are to keep ourselves pure so that we can heal others."

"Don't tell me that you believe old Jacob," said the first boy. He kicked a stone. It rolled down the path before him. "He's almost as old as Moses. I hear that he's senile."

Yeshua arrived at the stone before his friend did. He gave it a kick with the toe of his sandal.

"I'm sure he is," he said, smiling. "But even the old and the addled have their share of wisdom, if not more, than the average person. Jacob is right. We should keep ourselves pure so that we can become healers. The sick need us."

"Aw Yeshua, you're no fun," said the taller boy.

"Wait," said the other. "Yeshua is right. We are here to learn. And we are learning how to be healers. We should not drink wine -- for one thing, it is written into the laws of the community. How can we root out sickness in others when we are tainted with it ourselves?"

"We don't have to drink the wine," said the first. "But we can still show you how to turn the water into wine. It is a good trick."

"It does sound like a good trick," said Yeshua. "Okay, you convinced me. I would like to learn."

They reached the water's edge. The Salt Sea was large and inviting. Other members of the sect had the same idea. They were spending the afternoon bobbing in the water. Since Tamar was wind, she could only ruffle the surface. She could not dive in as the boys could. In that moment, she wanted to be one of the boys, swimming in the sea, mindless of her nakedness. But just then she heard her name. Someone was calling to her through a long tunnel.

"Tamar, Tamar, come help me with dinner."

Hannah's voice entered her mind slowly.

Tamar tossed to and fro. She blinked her eyes open. She remembered being wind -- flying into the cave, finding Yeshua, listening to the teacher, and following the young men down the sandstone trail to the Salt Sea. In the beginning, when she went to visit her brother this way, she doubted herself. Was she really there, or was it a dream? Now, there was a certainty to her thoughts. She knew that she had really been to Qumran. She could still see the bell shaped cave, the bearded teacher, the boys in their white hoods.

She threw back the blanket. She picked up her robe from the floor where it was lying in a heap and put it on.

"Tamar, I need your help with dinner." Hannah rapped on the bedroom door. "David is away and Mother needs us to cook for her."

'I'm coming," said Tamar.

"Hurry! The fish is sitting out on the table. I need your help to scale it."

"I said I was coming." Tamar felt anger rising in her voice. She jammed her sandals onto her feet.

Hot tears stung her eyes. She willed them back. She couldn't help feeling sorry for herself. Yeshua was learning how to turn water into wine, and she was stuck here, scaling fish.

Chapter Nineteen

"Jump. Jump."

Tamar was the wind on the mountain top that had settled on a bush. Rather, she thought she was the wind. Yeshua had come back from his years at Qumran, was baptized, and was currently in the wilderness for forty days and forty nights. Eighteen years had passed since Yeshua had left for Qumran. Tamar was thirty. She was still living at home with the Mother and David. She was an old maid. Like the Mother, she didn't believe in marriage. Unlike the Mother, she wasn't romantically adventurous. She preferred being alone. However, she was restless. She wished that she could use her ability to read and write to make a living. The scribes were all male. But an idea had come to Tamar.

She had watched her brother at Qumran often enough. She, too, had learned the mysteries. They were twins. They looked alike. It would be easy to put on a robe and be thought of as male. She could be the next messiah. If only there was an opening.

"Jump. Jump."

There was a rustle. A hand parted the bush. Yeshua peered through.

"Tamar, I can see you."

Tamar looked down. She saw a sandaled foot under her light blue robe. The foot was hers. So was the robe. The incantation that the Mother had given her had worked. The Mother was concerned about Yeshua staying in the wilderness so long, so she had sent some loaves of bread and dried figs with Tamar. Then she asked Tamar to stay for a few days in case Yeshua was lonely and scared. Tamar never thought she would be able to teleport like Mother. She was so proud that she felt herself glowing.

"Tamar, I could see you glowing through the bush. I had a feeling that it was you. How did you get here?"

"It's a long story," said Tamar.

Yeshua didn't know that the Mother could teleport. It was a secret between Tamar and the Mother.

"It does not matter how you got here. It is good to see you," said Yeshua as he stepped around the bush and gave her a hug. The problem with Yeshua was that he was too good. Tamar tried to hate him, but she couldn't.

Tamar started to smile, but began coughing when she caught a whiff of her brother's robe.

"Yes, I have been out here for a while – twenty days already and there is no place to bathe. I'm sorry about the smell," said Yeshua.

"I'm sorry that I was telling you to jump," said Tamar. "But I didn't think that you could hear me. You couldn't see or hear me when I came to visit when you were with the Essenes."

Yeshua gave her a quizzical look and then spoke: "I sensed that you were with me at Qumran."

Tamar nodded.

"At first I thought Satan had come back," said Yeshua. "But then I recognized your voice."

"Satan was here? What did he look like?" Tamar envied the fact that her brother was so important that Satan would reveal himself to him. She didn't like being envious. But that was how she felt.

"He had the body of a Roman soldier in uniform -- with a short sleeved metal tunic atop a flouncy skirt. He had human arms and hands, and he was pulling his hair out. He had the wings of a giant bat," replied Yeshua. "And a long tail."

Tamar snickered. This sounded like something her brother would say.

"He told me to jump, too. He promised that a band of angels would break my fall. I told him that I wasn't born yesterday. Then he promised me all the kingdoms in the world if I would worship him instead of our Lord. I told him that being in the wilderness for forty days and forty nights without food and water didn't make me covet all the kingdoms in the world. Then he cocked his head and asked me if I would like him to make loaves of bread from stones to break my fast. I replied to him that: *Man does not live by bread alone, but by every word that proceeds from the mouth of God.*

"That reminds me, I'm famished. Did you bring anything to eat?"

Tamar bristled. Of course, Yeshua would expect that the Mother would have given her food to take to him.

"You must have read my mind," said Tamar, reaching into the roomy pockets of her robe.

"I have already eaten," she said, "take these loaves and figs."

Yeshua shoved the crumbling loaves into his mouth. They were almost devoured before Tamar could blink. He shoved the dried figs into the pocket of his robe.

"I'm thirsty," he said.

"I could only carry so much," said Tamar. She wasn't telling the truth. She told herself that she was just fibbing. She had another pocket in her robe, but she hadn't felt like bringing any else. When the Mother suggested that she bring a clay jar of water, Tamar told her that there probably would be a spring somewhere near Yeshua.

"Pray with me," said Yeshua. "Pray for a spring to bubble out of the desert mountaintop in front of us."

"I doubt it will help."

Yeshua laughed. "From now on I am going to call you Doubting Thomas -- my skeptical twin."

Tamar laughed and said, "It actually doesn't seem likely that a spring would come up from the desert."

"I know," replied Yeshua. "Believe me. I've already tried. There's not much to do out here -- except to count the stars at night. I've been praying for a spring for some time now. Maybe our prayers will be stronger together."

"Okay," said Tamar. "I'll pray with you."

"Dear Heavenly Father," began Yeshua.

Tamar repeated after him.

"Let there be a spring in the desert so that we can drink from it and know you better."

She repeated this and then they said the prayer together three times. In between the prayers, she said "Ma, Ma, Ma" to herself.

To Tamar's surprise, a gurgling came from behind the bush.

Yeshua was the first to rush over to the spring. He dropped to all fours, put his mouth to it and drank. When he stood up, he brushed the sand from the wide arms of his dirty white robe.

"It is your turn," he said to Tamar. "Drink quickly, before it is too late."

Tamar rushed over, dropped to her knees and felt cold water wet her lips.

"The spring of water is from my mouth and whosoever drinks from it, drinks from my lips and knows the ways of the Lord," said Yeshua.

Tamar coughed and nearly choked. She spun around and faced her twin.

"What are you talking about?"

"The spring. I created it. You drank from it. It was like drinking from my mouth. Therefore you are as wise as I am," said Yeshua.

Tamar glared at him. He looked sincere. She was so angry that she could have pushed him off the cliff. She took a deep breath and exhaled slowly.

"We prayed for that spring together. You told me yourself that you prayed earlier by yourself and it didn't work. Not to mention that I don't want to drink from your mouth. That's disgusting!!!!" Tamar's voice rose to the heavens.

"Look the spring has vanished. I told you that you should drink from it before it was too late." Yeshua sounded like he was chiding his younger sibling.

But I'm not his younger sister, thought Tamar. *I'm his twin!*

"I'm not thirsty anyway!"

"Suit yourself," said Yeshua. "I was just saying that you are as wise as I am now that you have drunk from the spring. So what if I needed your help to pray for it. It was my idea."

Tamar turned around.

The sand was bone dry. There was no sign that the spring had ever been there.

The anger that had surged through Tamar passed. She felt weak. She was consumed with guilt for envying her brother to the point of hatred. She looked past the ledge where she had whispered for Yeshua to jump. The ledge looked over a desert with endless striations of red, brown and white amid the shadows of clouds. She imagined a band of angels hovering in the sky.

Maybe I should be the one to jump, thought Tamar.

"No. Your life is too precious to waste," said Yeshua softly.

Tamar stared at her twin.

"You have read my mind," she said.

"Of course," said Yeshua. "You are my twin. Do you not know that I can see into your mind just as you see into mine? Besides, I always say, 'Love your brother like your soul, guard him like the pupil of your eye.'"

"But I am not your brother. I am your sister."

"You are my TWIN," said Yeshua. "And, in my mind, there is no difference between brother and sister."

"In my mind there is a difference," said Tamar. "I am a girl. Because of that I have had to live my life in the house while you go off and have adventures."

"I never thought of that," said Yeshua. "I knew that you were angry at me. I just thought the Lord sent you so that I would learn to turn the other cheek."

"IT'S NOT ALWAYS ABOUT YOU!" Tamar was standing on the overlook several feet from Yeshua. She was so upset that she was shaking. Hot tears stung her eyes.

"Do you have any idea of what my life has been like? Thanks to you and Mother, I can read and write. But I can't tell anyone, and I can't go anywhere or do anything. The scribes are all men. The priests are all men. The tax collectors are all men. And most of the people selling their wares at the market are men. All women can be are wives and mothers, and I don't want to be either."

"Okay. I get it. Your life has been frustrating. But that's not my fault. You are the one who chose to be female."

Tamar stared at him.

"There's no way you could have known that -- unless Mother told you." Her legs trembled. She was getting angry.

"Mother said nothing to me," said Yeshua. "But I remember from the womb that we were both male. You were my brother and then you changed."

"From the womb?!" Tamar was incredulous. "I have no memory of being in the womb with you."

But then it all came back. Memories washed over her like amniotic fluid. She remembered striking him in the face and then when he turned, striking him again on the other cheek.

"I do remember," replied Tamar. "I was awful. I was envious, because I didn't want to share Mother. Can you ever forgive me?"

Tamar shook. She was close to tears. She wasn't usually this emotional. She might be premenstrual. Great. Stuck out here in the wilderness with no sea sponges. She hoped the wild animals left her alone.

"You are shivering. Take my cloak." Yeshua took off the cloak that he wore over his robe and handed it to her.

She put it over her blue robe.

"Of course, I forgive you," stated Yeshua. "But what matters is that you forgive yourself."

"What do you mean? I wanted you to jump so that I could pretend that I was you. I was plotting on becoming the next messiah. I am as bad as Beelzebub."

Yeshua laughed. "Beelzebub never existed. That was just an old tale. Satan doesn't exist, either."

"But you told me that you spoke to Satan!"

"Oh, I was just practicing. That is what people expect a messiah to say. But if Satan took the form of a person, he would look like a Roman soldier with a flouncy skirt and giant bat wings."

Tamar laughed. "And a tail. You forgot the tail."

"Yes," replied Yeshua, "A tail." Then, with a faraway look on his face, he said, "Mother told me that I would become the next messiah, and I've been practicing all these years. But the fact is that what some call Satan is just an evil energy that is in all of us. Sometimes it comes from having had bad experiences -- or it can come from having a tendency to have strong emotions, such as jealousy. But it is up to us to act from love and to do the right thing."

"But what about the temptations?" Tamar pulled Yeshua's cloak closer to her. It stank, but she was cold.

"What temptations?"

"Jumping, turning the rocks into loaves of bread and what was the third one? Oh, and ruling over all the kingdoms in the world," said Tamar.

"I've almost forgot about that, now that I've eaten," replied Yeshua. "I was so ravenous that I was having delusions. The temptations were my own emotions, taking the form of evil energy. The fact is that I was so hungry that I could've eaten rocks. Of course, I would rather jump to my death than endure forty days alone in the wilderness without food and water -- anyone would. I've always wondered what it would be like to be offered to rule over all the kingdoms in the world. Now that I've given it some thought, it sounds like a big headache."

Tamar looked over Yeshua's shoulder. Far in the distance, magenta light spilled across the desert sky. Soon stars would be shining down. Tamar shivered.

Yeshua turned toward the view and said, *"If those who lead you say, 'See, the kingdom is in the sky,' then the birds of the sky will precede you. If they say to you, 'It is in the sea,' then the fish will precede you. Rather, the kingdom is inside of you, and it is outside of you. When you come to know yourselves, then you will become known, and you will realize that it is you who are the sons of the living father. But if you will not know yourselves, you dwell in poverty and it is you who are that poverty."*

"I am beginning to understand," replied Tamar. "In all the years that I have stayed in the house with Mother, I have had time to reflect and to know myself. So something good has come of not having had an adventurous life where one is always looking outward. It is understandable that I would be envious of you. Even in the womb, I must have sensed that you would have a more interesting life than me. I understand now. So I forgive myself."

"I have an idea," said Yeshua. "I am stronger with you. After all, you are my twin. To be cut off from you is to be cut off from myself. I will make you male by calling you by the name of the twin, Thomas. That way we will both have adventures together in this world and enter the kingdom of heaven together."

"You cannot make me male. I am female. But I will allow you to call me Thomas since Mother told me that it was the first name that she wanted to give me. I did not know that it was Greek for 'twin.' But I know that I am female. It is not my concern if others think that I am male," said Tamar.

"And is none of my concern if anyone chooses to view me as female," said Yeshua. "I remember from the womb that I was both male and female. I know that I did not have a choice, like you did. But it does not matter. I dwell in gentleness and strength and so do you. We are beyond gender."

Tamar nodded and said, "That is right." She had wondered if Yeshua knew that he had been born male and female also.

"Then it is decided. You will be my companion. I already decided that I will have twelve apostles to help me spread the word. What is one more? No one is counting. Besides I may be disappointed by one and need another."

"When I first arrived here," said Tamar, "I wanted to take your place as the next messiah. But that was envy speaking. Now that I have forgiven myself, I want to help you. I did learn a lot when I came to visit you, unseen, at Qumran."

"Yes," replied Yeshua. "You are already knowledgeable about the mysteries. I will teach you everything that I know. And then we will be stronger than ever. But first let me tell you about my baptism and once I tell you, from the spring of my lips, it will be as if you were baptized, too."

"Not really," said Tamar. She was still smarting from Yeshua taking credit for bringing forth the spring that they had both prayed for. But he was right. It was his idea.

"What do you mean?" asked Yeshua.

"If you tell me about the baptism, it isn't the same thing as me having been there," she answered.

"But you are my TWIN," said Yeshua. "We once shared the same womb. We were made from the flesh of the Mother. We are part of each other."

Tamar considered this. There was nothing that Yeshua said that wasn't true. They were part of each other. But she remembered the Mother telling her that she and Yeshua probably had different fathers -- Joseph and David. But that was her secret with the Mother.

Tamar smiled at Yeshua.

"You are right," she said. "Now, tell me about the baptism."

"First let's pray for a bonfire to keep us warm through the night," said Yeshua.

"There are sticks here and there. We could break off some of the dry branches of that bush," said Tamar pointing. "We could take two sticks, rub them together and create fire."

"Why bother rubbing sticks together, when we can pray and make a fire?" Yeshua sat down on the cooling sand and patted a place opposite him.

Yeshua folded his hands and said, *"Our Father who art in heaven, Hallowed be thy Name."*

Yeshua paused to allow Tamar to repeat each line after him:

"Thy kingdom come. Thy will be done, On earth as it is in heaven."

"Thy kingdom come. Thy will be done, On earth as it is in heaven."

"Give us this day our daily bread. And forgive us our trespasses, As we forgive those who trespass against us."

"Give us this day our daily bread. And forgive us our trespasses, As we forgive those who trespass against us."

Tamar didn't know how she knew the words, but she found herself saying them along with Yeshua as they both said:

"And lead us not into temptation, but deliver us from evil."

"For thine is the kingdom, and the power, and the glory, forever and ever."

"Amen," said Yeshua.

"Amen," said Tamar.

Tamar was oddly moved. She brushed a tear from her eye. Then she followed Yeshua's gaze and looked up at the sky. Bright stars shone down.

It was a beautiful prayer, but they were still sitting in the dark. There was no bonfire.

"Repeat after me," she said. "Ma, ma, ma. Your children are cold. Send us a bonfire. Ma, ma, ma."

Yeshua repeated what she had said.

She folded her hands and looked up at the stars. Yeshua did the same.

A star fell to earth. The flames of a bonfire leapt up several yards away.

Tamar smiled at Yeshua. He smiled back and shrugged. "Whatever works is okay with me. I was just wondering why we were staring up at the stars. When I pray to the Father, I always cast my eyes down."

"I knew that if we looked up at the stars, they would transmit our prayer to Mother and she would send us a bonfire."

"Mother? We were praying to the Mother?" Yeshua sounded incredulous.

"Yes," said Tamar. "We were praying to the Mother, whose womb we shared."

Yeshua was silent.

"You were going to tell me about your baptism," said Tamar.

"That's right," said Yeshua. "Excuse me, I got distracted. You know I was thrown out of the Essenes for healing the sick on the Sabbath."

Tamar felt her eyes widen as she shook her head.

"I didn't know that. I thought you had just come home on your own," she said.

"When I found out that I had the gift of healing, I felt so blessed that I could help people that I forgot it was the Sabbath," said Yeshua. A man came to me and said he needed healing. His legs were withered. He could not walk. Now, he had been this way for many years and there was no rush. But I did not want to wait. I touched his legs and he threw down his crutches and walked. I told a group of my friends and word got round to one of the Essene elders. Instead of being proud of me, he accused me of working on the Sabbath. I replied that 'I was doing the Lord's work.' It was all downhill from there."

"It sounds like he was envious of your powers," replied Tamar.

Yeshua shrugged.

"It is just as well that they kicked me out. There are so many rules -- what is kosher and what is not and so on -- that it's hard to remember them all."

Tamar nodded. "I have problems remembering all the rules also."

"So then I came home. Mother told me that it wasn't fitting for the next messiah to live at home and that I would have to go out in the world and find my way."

Tamar frowned. "Mother didn't tell me any of this." *But it's okay for an old maid to live with her mother*, she thought. Living at home with the Mother had felt like a privilege. Suddenly she didn't feel so special.

"So I went to visit Aunt Elizabeth and Uncle Zechariah and they told me that their son John the Baptist would be visiting them any day. So I waited. John was surprised to see me. He had left Qumran about a year before me and thought I was still there. He agreed with me that there were too many rules, but that the principles of worship were sound. He said that he had decided to invent his own religion and baptize people's sins away. This new religion didn't sound very original to me. Baptism sounds a lot like taking the ritual daily cleansing bath at the Temple. But I liked his idea of inventing a new religion, so I volunteered to be baptized. Then he said that I was already pure and that I should baptize him. You know what a saint John is -- he'd give his head away if someone asked for it.

Tamar nodded. She felt the features of her face deepen with concern. Their uncle was the one who had ambitions for his son John to become the next messiah. John the Baptist himself was an open and trusting person. She had a feeling that others would take advantage, and that he would come to an untimely end.

"So we went to the Jordan river. I stood in the muddy water and John stood behind me. We both prayed for purity. Then he swept me backwards into the water and held me there for a moment. When I emerged, I saw the heavens open. A white dove flew down to greet me. It was a sign from our Father that I was ready to do his work."

Or our Mother, Tamar couldn't help thinking.

As she sat in the dark listening to her twin, watching the light from the flames illuminate her face, she felt held by the stars above. Yeshua had been right. She had listened to him with all her heart. It felt like she had been baptized, too.

Chapter Twenty

Since Tamar had become Thomas, ze carried a small scroll. Since Yeshua made hir male, ze could write in public. It felt liberating. Inside the Temple, Thomas unraveled hir scroll and wrote: "So this is how the one known as Tamar became known as Thomas and joined forces with hir twin to heal the sick, give sight to the blind, and raise the dead."

First Yeshua had gathered his apostles. It wasn't difficult to transition from Tamar to Thomas, one of the twelve. The other apostles were more concerned about themselves -- that they get good placements (Jerusalem was a popular destination) and with sitting closest to her brother, Yeshua. Thomas didn't care. Ze was quiet -- even meek. But ze was okay with this. Ze had heard somewhere that "the meek will inherit the earth."

Ze was sitting next to Yeshua, but the others jostled hir to the outer edges of the activity room. Thomas rubbed hir arm. Ze didn't appreciate being jostled by the other apostles. Thomas questioned their motives in wanting to be close to Yeshua. Ze pushed the thoughts from hir mind. Now that ze was helping Yeshua, ze tried to follow his example of turning the other cheek.

In the Temple, Thomas grew tired of waiting for Yeshua. He would be flanked by apostles when he was leaving anyway. Peter and James and John were always vying to walk next to him. Thomas yawned. Ze wondered what the sun dial said. It seemed like days had passed. But it was probably only a few hours. Ze slipped out the back door.

Ze wasn't waiting for a placement anyway. Ze would be travelling with Yeshua. And ze could sit next to Yeshua at any time. They were both staying with their Mother. Tamar had told the Mother that she could now call hir Thomas and that ze would be helping Yeshua. The Mother just smiled.

"Thomas?"

Startled, Thomas jumped.

It was Mary Magdalene. Thomas had met her once before. Ze recognized the angular planes of Mary's dark face. Mary's large hand smoothed a plait of her long dark hair that hung below her shoulder.

"I recognize you. You're Thomas, the twin," said Mary.

Thomas nodded, pleased that Mary recognized hir.

The transformation from Tamar to Thomas felt natural. Ze had wrapped a piece of cloth tightly around hir small breasts. Ze wore a tunic and a linen robe that ze borrowed from Yeshua. The robe was the color of toasted almonds. Hir bound breasts didn't show. The tightness of the fabric pressing into hir breasts reminded hir to lower her voice. Ze wore a shawl around hir head, loose woven linen, draped over hir shoulders just like Yeshua's. The shawl fell over hir tunic. As Tamar, ze had often worn a blue robe like Mother's. When Yeshua first saw hir dressed as Thomas, he had said that he had always known that she would make a righteous brother. Tamar took it as a compliment. Ze didn't feel like ze was impersonating a man. Ze felt more like hirself. Yeshua had told Thomas to smile less, because it would make hir appear more masculine. It was true. Ze trained hirself not to smile. The Mother smiled all the time. Sometimes it was a distant smile. A tired smile. A mysterious smile. At times an inquisitive smile. David, on the other hand, rarely smiled. It wasn't that he wasn't pleasant. He usually hummed and had a twinkle in his eye. On the rare occasions that he did smile, he lit up like the burning bush that had spoken to Moses. It was a sight that might only be seen once in a thousand years, but it was memorable. Tamar had to remember to drop hir voice when ze was dressed as Thomas -- even though the Mother had named hir Thomas when ze was born. Thomas was Greek for twin.

"I wasn't allowed in the Temple, so I took off my head scarf," Mary explained apologetically.

"What do you mean, you weren't allowed in?" asked Thomas, making sure to keep hir voice at a low register.

"When I came to the Temple to attend the meeting, Peter met me outside and told me that the meeting -- because it was being held in the Temple -- was closed to females.

"That is not true. The Mother comes to the Temple all the time. Yeshua invited you, so you are welcome," replied Thomas.

"If only all the men were like you," replied Mary. "I had a feeling that Peter was up to no good when he sent me away. He had evil in his eyes."

"Yes. Peter is jealous of you and Yeshua," confirmed Thomas.

Mary looked dejected. Thomas wanted to cheer her up.

"It does not matter," Thomas said. "You and I are Yeshua's favorites. We're the only one he trusts, really. He told me himself that there is no way to know that the apostles won't abandon him in a crisis."

"That's true," replied Mary.

"Besides, we'll be travelling with Yeshua when he performs his miracles. There's nothing that Peter can say that will change that."

Mary nodded and then spoke: "Peter treats me like an adversary. But I am trying not to respond with anger. For one thing it would tarnish the feeling that I hold for Yeshua. I do feel that he can truly save us. Also, I know that the angry person's wisdom is the seventh power of wrath."

"What are the first six powers?" asked Thomas.

"The first form is darkness; the second, desire; the third, ignorance; the fourth, death wish; the fifth, fleshly kingdom, the sixth, foolish fleshly wisdom; and the seventh, as I told you, the angry person's wisdom." Mary picked up her basket and glanced back toward the Temple. "I should go before the meeting is over and the men come out."

Thomas looked at Mary with respect bordering on awe. Mary was wise, to be sure. She had much to offer.

"I'll walk with you to your destination," said Thomas. "Yeshua would want that."

Thomas wanted to tell Mary that she was born as Yeshua's female twin. But then ze had remembered the pact with Yeshua in the desert -- when he had declared that they were beyond gender.

The next day Tamar and Mary travelled with Yeshua and Mother to a marriage in the town of Cana in the tribal region of Galilee. It was a hot day and a half a day's journey. Mother had borrowed some camels so that they could make the trip. When they arrived at the dusty grounds outside the tabernacle, Yeshua poured himself a cup of water from one of the stone jugs sitting in the shade.

"It's a shame that the wedding party has no wine," said a man standing nearby.

Yeshua drained his cup, wiped the arm of his robe across his lips, and spoke. "But the water is cool and refreshing. It is infinitely better for a body than wine -- especially on a hot day like this."

Thomas was helping Mary Magdalene with her bags and turned around and looked at the man to whom Yeshua was speaking. The man was dressed in a white linen robe woven through with widely spaced strands of gold.

He narrowed his eyes and looked at Yeshua. "I don't recognize you. You must be a traveler. Allow me to introduce myself. I am John, the son of the governor of Cana."

"Then, your father is a Roman?" asked Yeshua.

"No," replied the man. "He's a Jew -- a well-respected Pharisee."

"I see," said Yeshua. "I'll tell you what. I can change this water into wine."

The man cocked his right eyebrow. He looked amused.

"And you are?"

"Yeshua, the son of God."

Thomas had a sinking feeling in hir stomach. Yeshua was acting sincere, but ze knew that he had something to prove. It occurred to hir that Yeshua might be going around saying that he was the son of God because he wasn't sure that Joseph was his real father -- especially since David had moved in with the Mother after Yeshua went to Qumran. Thomas had a moment of feeling sadness for hir twin. The bad feeling that ze had felt when ze heard Yeshua saying that he was the son of God, didn't go away. It got worse.

"The son of God?" The man looked at him skeptically.

"Yes. I will prove it to you by changing this water into wine," answered Yeshua.

Yeshua came over and spoke to Thomas in a low voice as he took the baggage.

"I've got this. Take Mother and Mary into the tabernacle. The marriage ceremony is about to begin."

Thomas was there to help hir brother, so ze did as he said. As the only other man in the caravan -- David had stayed home -- it was hir job to escort the women. Ze offered an arm to each of them and they went inside. After the ceremony was over, Thomas came outside with Mary and the Mother. Lo and behold, the guests were drinking wine.

"People will talk. I hope he knows what he is doing," said Mary.

Wearing an orange robe, the bride stepped out of the tabernacle.

"It is a good trick," said the Mother as she threw a handful of barley at the happy couple. "But Mary is right. People will talk."

"I think that is the point," said Thomas. Ze had dates and figs in hir hand (to "sweeten the marriage," said the woman who handed them to hir. Thomas was going to throw them at the bride and groom, but then ze slid them into the pockets of hir robe. Ze would save them for the journey.

At the reception, Yeshua was surrounded by believers. Many had drunk the wine.

"For he IS the son of God," said a man waving his clay goblet in the air.

"Make more wine," yelled one of the guests.

"My brothers, my brothers," said Yeshua, as he waved his arms to his sides. "Let's not make frivolity from the Lord's work. Now that you are believers, let's spread the word."

"Let's go to Capernaum. It will take a few hours to travel there, but it is a good place to stop on the way to Jerusalem," shouted a man toward the back of the crowd.

"Let's go," said Yeshua. "We are doing the Lord's work!"

Several of the men hoisted him on their shoulders.

"Follow me," he shouted.

He got down and came over to where Thomas and Mary stood next to the camels.

"Not so fast," said Thomas. "We'll come down after the reception. Mother wants to spend some time with the bride."

"So do I," said Mary. She leaned down, moved her robe and scratched her right leg. "We didn't travel all this way to leave so soon."

"It is understandable. Women can't resist a wedding," said Yeshua. "Thomas can you stay with them and ride down on the camels later? I will have no problem getting a ride."

After the reception, Thomas got directions to Capernaum. One of the local fellows knew a short cut to the town on the edge of the Sea of Galilee.

"It is two towns over from where I grew up," said Mary. "I know the route."

Thomas nodded. Ze was relieved that ze didn't have to remember the way. Being the one in the caravan who was perceived as male, ze had to ride in the front.

They trudged over the desert on three camels strung together with a long rope that each of them held so that they would stay together. Thomas had only drunk water at the wedding, but ze felt queasy. Ze rose and fell with the camel's gait. Thomas felt like ze was floating up and down on the waves of the ocean. The desert unfurled in endless ridges.

"Turn left here," shouted Mary. She was riding the camel behind Thomas.

Thomas didn't see any landmarks. After they had ridden for a time, straggly palm trees on the outskirts of a town came into view. Then a stone wall. They followed a path along the wall until they came to an opening wide enough to enter.

Finally, Thomas saw someone. An old man in a dark brown robe leaned on a cane.

"We are looking for a large caravan that came to town several hours ago," said Thomas.

"Oh, you must mean the prophet and his entourage," replied the old man.

"Yes, the prophet," replied Thomas. "That is who we are seeking."

The old man gave them directions to the center of town.

Thomas thought about the fact that her twin was already known as "the prophet." Ze was sure that Yeshua would be happy to learn that. But Thomas had a sinking feeling that things would turn out badly.

They found his followers, but not Yeshua.

"Yeshua is preaching in the town synagogue," said one of his followers lounging on the ground near a camel trough. "We are looking for some more wine. Do you have any?"

Two other stragglers were reclining on the ground next to him. The rest of Yeshua's followers must have already gone into the synagogue.

Thomas shook hir head, and rode hir camel to the other side of the square.

"I just hope Yeshua knows what he is doing," Thomas said, disembarking.

The Mother got down from her camel. She put her bags on the ground next to her.

"He must be doing something right. He is already known as a prophet," said the Mother. She pushed back her blue hood, leaned over and rustled in her bags.

"Yes, I agree," said Mary. "Before long, Yeshua will be known as the messiah."

"Just as planned," said Mother. "Come, let's sit under the palm tree and have some food while we are waiting."

When they were done eating, there was a commotion on the steps of the synagogue. Yeshua had come out with his followers behind him. A man in crutches leaned on the wall at the bottom of the steps.

"I want to take the ritual bath," he said. "But I can't get down the steps."

"Uh oh," said Mary. She sidled up to Thomas and whispered, "This is when Yeshua needs our help. I almost forgot to tell you that when he's healing someone, he needs us both to send light to the infirm one."

Thomas bowed hir head along with Mary.

Yeshua spoke in a booming voice. "Now you may throw down your crutches and walk down the stairs to the bath, for the son of God has proclaimed you healed."

The man threw down his crutches and teetered for a moment. He regained his balance and took several steps to the side of the synagogue where the stairs descended to the mikvah.

"That looked easy," said Thomas.

Mary smiled. She put her hand over her mouth, stifling a yawn.

"It's been a big day," she said.

"Figs anyone?" Mother passed a bag. "I almost forgot that I had these."

Thomas took one and bit into the juicy flesh.

"Mmmm."

Thomas passed the bag to Mary.

"They are very plump and succulent," said Mary. The bag rustled as she pulled a fig out and bit into it. Midway into chewing, her eyes bulged. She gestured toward Yeshua.

He was still on the steps and was waving his hand over the withered hand of man who was kneeling at his feet.

"But it is the Sabbath," yelled someone on the edge of the crowd. "Is it lawful to heal on the Sabbath?"

"If any of you has a sheep and it falls into a pit on the Sabbath, will you not take hold of it and lift it out? How much more valuable is a man than a sheep! Therefore it is lawful to

do good on the Sabbath," said Yeshua. Then turning toward the man with the withered hand, he said, "Stretch out your hand."

The man flexed his fingers back and forth. His hand was supple.

"He did that without our help," said Mary.

Thomas nodded.

"He just needs to believe that he has our help," said Mother. "I told him that he could do this by himself."

That night they stayed with a cousin of one of Yeshua's followers. There were many disciples staying at the house, in addition to Thomas, Mary, and the Mother. When they woke there was no food to eat.

"No worries. We'll go down to the sea and catch some fish," proclaimed Yeshua.

"Good luck," said the cousin. "The fish are never running -- unless it is away from us."

Yeshua smiled.

The crowd laughed.

"It doesn't matter. We will go to the sea and catch more fish than we can eat."

Yeshua and his followers, quite a big crowd by now, went down to the sea.

"Catch," he called to Thomas.

Thomas caught the net and followed Yeshua onto a nearby fishing boat. Ze climbed aboard. A fisherman rose from his pallet.

"We have a hungry crowd here," said Yeshua. "Let's go out to the deep water and cast our net."

"It won't matter," said the fisherman. He stood unsteadily and grasped the side of the boat.

"I was out there with my nets for half the night and didn't catch a thing," he said.

"I'll show you how to have faith," said Yeshua. "Let's set sail. We'll share our catch with you."

The man shrugged. He handed an oar to Yeshua. He handed another one to Thomas.

More than a few other men climbed aboard the boat. It dipped under their weight.

"Damn, I knew I should've worn my other robe," said the last one in. "This is my good one. The bottom is sopping, and my sandals are full of wet sand. "

The men that Thomas met disproved the popular notion that women were the ones who were vain.

Thomas joined the others in rowing. Ze was surprised at hir own strength, or maybe it was that these things that ze had never done before -- because they were usually done by men -- really didn't require that much strength. With the others, Thomas cast the net into the deep water. Before long, the net bulged. The fish glinted in the sunlight. It was beautiful for a moment. Then the full net landed on the wooden planks of the boat bottom with a dull thud. There were so many fish that there was barely room for the passengers who sat precariously along the outside rim of the boat.

They reached the shore. The stench of dead fish hung in the air. Tamar scanned the beach and breathed a sigh of relief when ze saw the Mother and Mary. They had the skillets ready for frying over the blackened fire pits. Miraculously, loaves of bread were piled next to the skillets.

Yeshua had more followers when they left later that morning for Jerusalem.

"I have some business to take care of at the Temple," he proclaimed. "Let's make haste."

"The Temple?" Thomas mounted hir camel.

"Yes, the Temple," said Yeshua. "The Pharisees and the scholars have taken the keys of knowledge and have hidden them. They have not entered, nor have they allowed those who want to enter to go inside. You should be *as shrewd as snakes and innocent as doves.*"

"But the Temple is in Jerusalem," yelled Thomas. "We do not know our way."

It was too late. Yeshua's camel was already trotting along, kicking up clouds of sand.

"*Seek and do not stop seeking until you find,*" yelled Yeshua.

His camel picked up speed, and his words were carried by the wind.

Thomas, the Mother, and Mary followed on his heels.

Chapter Twenty-One

After they left Galilee, they stayed in Jerusalem for a few days over the holiday. Thomas sat in the square and wrote: "This is how the Pharisees and the Romans came to collude in the plot to crucify Yeshua. But there were a few surprises."

"The Seder was wonderful," said Mary when she came back that evening. "There was a long table in a large room laden with more food than we could eat. We all sat on the same side of the table. Come to think of it, I don't know why we did that. The food was plentiful. Yeshua was full of wisdom. Although he did say some disturbing words about one of the apostles betraying him and another one who will deny knowing him."

"That is disturbing," replied Thomas. Ze placed a hand on hir abdomen. At first ze just said that ze had a stomachache so that ze could stay home. Ze encouraged Mary to go in hir place. But now ze really did feel sick. Mary didn't think she should go, because she would be the only woman there. So in order to convince Mary to go, Thomas had told her that ze was female when ze was born.

"That explains why we are like sisters," Mary had replied.

Thomas had come to have a deepened appreciation for Yeshua because of Mary. Since Yeshua had made hir male, ze no longer envied him. As Thomas, ze could pretty much come and go as ze pleased. Ze could see that life as the messiah had its drawbacks. Still, sometimes ze thought of Yeshua as arrogant. He always seemed sure of himself. But now ze realized that it was natural for Yeshua to be arrogant. He was raised since he was a boy thinking that he would be the next messiah. Ze could see that his upbringing would have caused anyone to have delusions. Ze had to admit that ze envied his self-assurance, because ze lacked that in hirself. But, still ze could see that Yeshua's adoration of and caring for Mary was real.

It was more than the fact that Yeshua always made sure that Mary was okay when she was getting on or off her camel. It was that he really honored and cared for her, as if she were a goddess. There was something otherworldly about Mary. She reminded Thomas of the Mother. Thomas couldn't help loving Mary like a sister.

"As we were eating, Yeshua took the bread and blessed it. Then he broke the loaf into pieces and passed them to us, saying, "*Take, eat; this is my body.*"

Mary had tears in her eyes.

"Yeshua is very wise," said Thomas. "But he is not the first to say this."

"I'm sure you are mistaken," replied Mary.

"No. Mother told me about it. The ancients tradition-ally shared a meal in which they pretended to eat the flesh of their god and drink his blood," said Thomas. "Pagans have a tradition of leaving a place at the table for their gods. Sometimes they put a statue at the table."

Thomas knew that ze was upsetting Mary, but ze couldn't stop hirself from speaking.

"As long as they know they aren't really eating the body of their Lord, it's okay," continued Thomas.

Mary's eyes widened.

"Where is Yeshua?" she asked. "I thought he was right behind me."

Thomas shrugged. Ze could see that the sisterly affection between them only went so far. Mary was not going to take hir side against Yeshua.

"Maybe his premonitions were correct," lamented Mary.

They were staying at the home of cousins in Jerusalem who were away for the holiday.

Yeshua came bursting through the front door: "You must hide me. The Roman guards grabbed me as I was leaving the Seder. They meant to put me in prison but one of the guards was a follower and he said to the others that he would put me in chains and bring me along and that way they could go home early."

"It is the beginning of the holiday," interjected Mary.

"*This is true,*" said Yeshua. "*So as they left I yelled after them and gave them something to think about: Blessings on you who came into being before coming into being. If you become my students and hear my saying, these stones will serve you. For there are five trees in paradise for you. Summer or winter they do not change and their leaves do not fall. Whoever knows them will not taste death. Whoever discovers what these sayings mean will not taste death.*"

No wonder the Romans want to crucify him, thought Thomas. No one likes someone who speaks in riddles. But ze held hir tongue. Ze couldn't deny that Yeshua was wise. Ze had started to write his sayings down.

"When the others had left, the guard told me that he had someone to put in my place -- a vagrant in Jerusalem who was last seen in Nazareth. It was said that he had a taste for children. Several of them went missing," said Yeshua.

Thomas thought of the man on the hill in Nazareth who had exposed himself to hir when ze was a child, but there was no time to speak of that now.

The Mother appeared in the room. The day before, she had told Thomas that she was going away to a distant land to visit a new friend.

"I have an idea," said the Mother. "Let's shave off your beard," she said to Yeshua. "Then we can dress you in one of my robes. We can't leave tonight because they may be looking for you. But we can leave tomorrow after nightfall. I have a place for us to go that is safe."

"Okay," said Yeshua. "I trust you Mother -- with my life."

"You should," retorted the Mother. "I gave it to you."

"What? You gave me what?"

"Never mind," replied the Mother. "There is no time for repartee."

"But wait a minute," said Yeshua. "There is one thing I must do while I still have my beard."

He went to Mary and kissed her on the mouth.

Then he drew back and said, "Remember this when I am clean shaven and dressed in women's clothing so that I can escape. My name is Yeshua, and I love you."

The Mother beamed. "So the other apostles were right to be jealous. You do love her more. I can see why."

And, in this way, the Mother gave the couple her blessing.

Thomas felt a smile take away her stomachache. Ze may be losing a homeland, but ze was gaining a sister.

"But, be careful," said the Mother. "*By a kiss the perfect conceive and give birth. That is why we kiss. From the grace in others we conceive.*"

Thomas looked at the Mother. She was always herself, but sometimes she seemed like someone else.

Thomas slept fitfully that night. Ze was waiting for the knock of the Roman soldier that never came. Yeshua's follower who was the guard who freed him must have been convincing. The next evening, they departed in a caravan of camels. David was at the rear. Yeshua was in the middle -- dressed as a woman -- flanked by Thomas and Mary. Thomas was Thomas -- and Tamar, too. Mary was dressed as herself. The Mother was riding a camel at the front of the caravan.

The Mother had told Thomas that she could always disappear if someone stopped them and that, in itself, would be a distraction. She had spoken cryptically about their destination. They were taking the Incense Route to Northern India -- where her new friend Devi lived. She would only say that she had met Devi through her Mothers group and that Devi was the Mother of All and was very beautiful. Rumor had it that she had sprung up from a lotus flower and that her feet barely touched the ground as she walked. The Mother was radiant when she talked about her new friend. In fact, Thomas had never seen her so bright. David was glum. Thomas suspected that he was devoted to the Mother no matter what. And they were all protective of Yeshua. He would be an important person in India. Thomas would also be an important person in India. The Mother told Thomas that India was a kinder place, with waterfalls and grottoes and lush vegetation.

As Thomas travelled with the others through the night and into the sunrise, ze let the camel's gait pull hir into a rhythm of rising and falling, of remembering and going forward. Ze remembered a piece of writing from a scroll that Yeshua had given hir to learn Hebrew from. Ze had memorized the words and recited them now, silently:

The Lord is my Shepherd; I shall not want.
He maketh me to lie down in green pastures:
He leadeth me beside the still waters.
He restoreth my soul:
He leadeth me in the paths of righteousness for His name's sake.
Yea, though I walk through the valley of the shadow of death,
I will fear no evil:
For thou art with me;
Thy rod and thy staff, they comfort me.
Thou preparest a table before me in the presence of mine
enemies;
Thou annointest my head with oil;
My cup runneth over. Surely goodness and mercy shall follow
me all the days of my life,
and I will dwell in the House of the Lord forever.

Thomas took some mental notes. Ze would write them down later. Sentences started forming in hir mind: "So this is the story of how Tamar became Thomas and lived for the rest of hir years in India with hir twin Yeshua and the Mother."

David looked depressed, but Thomas knew that he loved the Mother so much that he would become happy because she was happy.

David would be happy, too, because he was going to live with two goddesses.

Thomas took some more mental notes: "This is the story of how Thomas, Yeshua, Mary, the Mother, and David walked through the valley of the shadow of death, yet feared no evil.

And this is the story of how Thomas's cup runneth over."

About the Author

Janet Mason is an award-winning creative writer, teacher, radio commentator, and blogger for *The Huffington Post*. She records commentary for This Way Out, the internationally-aired LGBTQ radio syndicate based in Los Angeles. Her book, *Tea Leaves*, a memoir of mothers and daughters, published by Bella Books in 2012, was chosen by the American Library Association for its 2013 Over the Rainbow List. *Tea Leaves* also received a Goldie Award. She is the author of three poetry books.

Excerpts from the novel THEY have been previously published in:

BlazeVox 15 Spring 2015

"A Perfect Mind"

Sinister Wisdom 100, The 40th Anniversary issue, 2016

"Conception"

aaduna

Summer/Fall 2015 (Volume 2/Issue 2)

"The Mother"

In memory of my father Albert Mason,
who was born in 1919 and died in 2017.
This book is also dedicated to my partner Barbara
and to my faith community at the
Unitarian Universalist Church of the Restoration.

Made in the USA
San Bernardino, CA
22 March 2018